An Alumni
of
Words

Published by Scout Media
Copyright 2023
ISBN: 978-1-960855-02-2

Cover and Story Title Designs by Amy Hunter
Formatted by Kari Holloway

Visit: www.ScoutMediaBooksMusic.com
For more information on all the *Of Words* anthologies

TABLE OF CONTENTS

Constellations in Reverse

JM Ames

Mot's ashen, bony fingers trembled. The old daguerreotype in his claw-like grasp threatened to tumble out of it and into the fire that blazed before him. It had been decades, over a century—almost two. And yet he still thought of her incessantly. Her raven-black hair, her full, red lips, her ivory skin peppered in moles.

"Like constellations in reverse," he had whispered to her that night, after removing the last of her undergarments, before kissing each of those dark stars one by one, savoring their feel on his lips, their taste.

She stole every thought from him, made him feel and do things he never had in all the millennia he was on this forsaken rock. For hundreds of thousands of years, he was sent out to reap the life of humanity when the time came. There was never any emotion or thought to it, just a fulfillment of duty.

Until her.

She had taken not only his thoughts but his coldness, his objectivity, and his drive. This obsession he had with her clouded his mind. Human population had skyrocketed as he neglected his duties. Death was never supposed to fall in love—especially not with a human. It had never been done.

Now the planet was overrun with these two-legged vermin. All because of her.

Mot stared into the glory that was her face in the daguerreotype. One long, yellow fingernail traced the outline of her lips. These old photographs never got the color right, just shades of brown, like a child's fingerpainting made of their own shit. A modern photograph would do her so much more justice. He wished he could be granted the same release he had offered others countless times, wished he could end the pain that tormented him for all these years, would torment him for all of eternity, but he knew it would never come. He was the only reaper, and he couldn't exactly harvest himself.

A thunderous boom shook the ground. Smoke from the fire swirled, then formed into the shape of a hooded figure. Realization of what was happening calmed his agonized mind for the first time since her harvesting. His arms spread wide as he closed his eyes and smiled, finally at peace. The scythe of his replacement sliced through his neck without a sound. Mot's body and head fell separately to the ground before they disappeared.

The old daguerreotype fluttered into the flames before it caught alight, and disappeared as well.

Come Back Next Tuesday

Dawn Taylor

Vivian tilted her head, swallowing the last of her lemonade. The ice cubes clinked against her teeth as she sucked to get the final drop. Beads of sweat cooled for a moment as she wiped her forehead with the chilled smoothness of the glass. She resisted the urge to drop an ice cube into her cleavage, knowing the nosey neighbors spied on her every movement. The blistering Arizona heat evaporated the remaining dampness from the towel draped on her neck.

The shade under the canvas canopy offered no respite from the desert sun. Some new life this was becoming for her. She regretted her friends' advice to move across the country. *Find somewhere warm, somewhere you can make a new start.* The well-intended guidance had sounded helpful six months ago when she had vacated her apartment and sold most of her belongings to head west. She had no qualms about leaving behind Roger and their messy divorce in Chicago; it was her tormented thoughts of a wasted life that were harder to escape. She might as well have packed the regrets beside her underwear and toothbrush in her suitcase; her depression accompanied her with the move.

Yesterday Vivian had explored the business district of the city, mainly to escape the prying eyes of the elderly busybodies who lived in the trailer court. Their constant peeking from behind the curtains of their air-conditioned trailers offended her while she baked in a tin can. Vivian directed her irritation at the property manager who had not repaired the air conditioning since her request a week ago.

As she explored the streets, a faded pink stucco building on the corner attracted her attention. Certainly, pink was an odd color for a building, but what did she know? Maybe it was the style in the West.

A large marquee, with most of its bulbs broken or missing, dominated the front entrance of The Roxy. A small rusty tin sign barely clinging to the right of the double entrance doors stated, TUESDAY MATINEE, 2 P.M.

Vivian had experienced few things in life that brought her pleasure. Escaping into a dark theater and enjoying a movie was one of them. She had sought the coolness of the building to soothe her irritation with the heat and life in general.

She returned to the building today and parked her car across the street. She approached the dust-covered glass doors. During her short time in Arizona, she had discovered the desert wind blew constantly, covering everything with a layer of grit.

The chilled air welcomed her as she entered the lobby. She followed the carpet's worn path to an ornate mahogany counter. She glanced at her watch—almost two o'clock. She raised her head and saw a man standing behind the counter.

"May I help you?" He cleared his throat, barely disguising the annoyance in his voice.

"Why, yes. Thank you. I would like a ticket to the matinee, please."

He tore a green ticket from a paper roll. "One ticket, one dollar." He slid the ticket toward her as she removed a one-dollar bill from her purse. The man reached with his bony fingers and placed the dollar in a cigar box. He closed the fastened-together-with-masking-tape lid and returned the tattered box to a shelf behind the counter.

"That's a cheap price compared to where I come from." Vivian's smile disappeared when she noticed the man—Walter, according to his nametag—refused to engage in small talk.

"This way, ma'am."

She followed him down the corridor.

He pulled back a heavy brocade curtain and motioned her into the theater.

Vivian selected a seat in the back row. Being the only person in attendance did not alarm her. Matinee audiences were always sparse, especially weekday presentations. She preferred enjoying her afternoon in solitude.

She wedged her ample hips into the narrow wooden seat. From observing the vintage fixtures, she concluded the theater had been built years ago. Red velvet drapes hung from baroque iron rods framing the small screen. A pair of masks, representing comedy and tragedy, cast their eerie expressions toward the audience from the dimness of a single wall sconce. The damp air emitted a musty odor as the ancient cooling system struggled to maintain an even temperature.

Vivian heard footsteps above her. From the slow shuffle, she guessed Walter was preparing the projector. A small theater like The Roxy likely employed one person to sell tickets, to usher, and to operate the projection room. The load of responsibility perhaps explained Walter's ornery disposition; he was an old man with limited energy to tackle the duties alone.

She leaned into the hard seat and waited for the movie to begin. She realized she had not asked Walter for the film's name. The title did not matter, as she attended solely to escape the heat and snooping of her neighbors.

The theater lights dimmed into the darkness as a beam illuminated the screen. Vivian was amused to see black and white numerals, enclosed in circles, count down to the start to the main feature. The preview was short, using only numerals from five to one. She had seen this introduction in many classic noir films. She smiled, anticipating the presentation of a brooding mystery.

The scene opened with a frazzled young woman holding an infant and preparing breakfast. The newborn wailed as the mother's attempts to soothe her failed. She bounced the baby in the crook of her arm while she fried eggs and bacon. The daughter's incessant howling forced the mother to surrender to her hungry demand. Ignoring the food cooking on the stove, the mother sat and offered her breast to the baby.

A man entered the kitchen. He glared at the woman nursing the infant while his breakfast sizzled and burned. Without a word, he backhanded her.

She collapsed to the floor while protecting the infant tightly in her grip.

What kind of movie is this? Vivian thought. The movie was silent, except for the baby's wails and the hard slap across the woman's face.

The man threw the pan into the sink and stormed from the room.

As the woman stood clutching her infant, Vivian noticed the wallpaper was the same floral pattern as the kitchen in her childhood home. She looked closer and saw plants displayed on little shelves lining both sides of the window above the sink. She remembered fondly how her mother had loved her houseplants and had taken expert care of them.

The film continued with the mother repositioning the chair into an upright position to resume nursing her baby. The camera zoomed in for a closeup of the woman rubbing her face.

Vivian gasped. That profile, that nose—

The movie ended.

Vivian remained seated in the dark theater, puzzled at what she had just viewed. The woman resembled her mother; the jawline and deep-set eyes were unmistakable. If the woman was her mother, then the man must have been her father.

She shook her head to eliminate the thought. None of the situation made sense. She had never known her father to be violent, nor would her mother have ever tolerated a slap from a man. Vivian's mind raced to solve the troubling scene, until a disturbing thought popped into her head. If those people were her parents, she realized, she was the infant.

"It doesn't make sense," she said aloud in the empty theater. She pushed her excessive weight from the small seat to find Walter polishing the chandelier in the lobby. "What's the name of that film?"

He polished the brass with a white cloth without acknowledging her.

She stood closer to his ladder. "Excuse me! I want to know the name of that film."

"It's *Tuesday Matinee*. It's the only title I am aware of, miss."

"It ended. It just stopped after one scene. I want to see the rest of it."

"Come back next Tuesday." He stepped down from the ladder, folded it, and dragged it down the hallway.

Vivian shook her fist at his back. His indifference infuriated her. *What the hell just happened?* She fished her sunglasses from her purse as she exited the theater. She replayed the scene during the ride home. Was the heat causing her mind to play tricks on her? Too many similarities existed between the film and her family. She concluded the film was a hoax of some kind.

She reached her trailer and rushed to the bedroom to retrieve the cardboard box labeled PHOTOS. Vivian had promised herself she would preserve them in a nice book, but she never found time to sort them. She scooped up a handful to search for the few images of her mother holding her as an infant.

She studied the face of her mother, Lily, as if she were seeing her for the first time. Lily's coal-black hair contrasted against her flawless milk-like complexion. She gazed lovingly upon the infant on her lap as her strong jaw brushed against the baby's hairline.

Vivian had no doubt the woman in the film was her mother. *But how could that be? It was crazy thinking. You just don't see your life portrayed in a film.*

Her thoughts returned to Walter. She wondered if he was The Roxy's owner. He was a man of few words, which frustrated her. She wanted answers, yet he provided none. She decided to rid the theater from her mind until the following Tuesday, when she would attend the matinee.

The technician had repaired the air conditioning compressor on Monday, which lowered Vivian's irritability only slightly. Doris, an elderly woman who lived next door, begged Vivian to join her for coffee. Vivian declined the invitation, as it was *Tuesday Matinee* day. She drove downtown and parked in the same spot she had the previous week.

Vivian studied The Roxy as she crossed the street. The lifeless marquee contained shattered bulbs and empty sockets where colorful lights should have mesmerized patrons. Obviously, Walter was in no rush to replace them. The constant breeze made it difficult to distinguish if the grit clinging to the doors remained from last week or if the desert winds blew fresh sand upon the panes. Vivian removed a hanky from her purse to cover the handle and opened the door.

The refreshingly cool but musty air greeted Vivian as she entered, and she noticed the absence of a concession stand. With such few patrons, she reasoned, snacks were not a priority. Walter's icy demeanor prevented her from asking about the lack of refreshments. However, Vivian missed the appetizing scent of fresh popcorn that would greet visitors at lively venues.

Walter approached the counter wearing the same matching black vest and dress slacks from last week. She assumed it was his uniform since his nametag was pinned to his vest. "How may I help you?" he asked, as if he had never seen her before this encounter.

"I've returned for the *Tuesday Matinee*. Don't you remember me? I was here last week."

He tore a green ticket from the roll and handed it to her. "One ticket, one dollar."

She exchanged her dollar for the ticket.

Walter placed the money in the cigar box and motioned for her to follow him to the same seat in the back row.

After a few moments, she heard the stairs creak as he shambled toward the projection room. The countdown from five to one ended as Vivian anticipated viewing the afternoon's main feature.

The movie opened with a scene of her mother hanging laundry on the clothesline. Vivian recognized her childhood home in the background. The bicycle she had received for her sixth birthday lay on the ground. She recalled how much she loved her bike and had always handled it with care. The film portrayed this part inaccurately, as she had never left it laying carelessly in the grass.

A boy she recognized as her younger brother, Bobby, approached Lily. There was no audio, so Vivian could not understand what he was saying. Her mother nodded, and Bobby pedaled away on her bike. A little girl ran toward her mother, shrieking while pointing at Bobby.

Vivian leaned forward in her seat. *That's me! I can't be more than seven years old.* She covered her mouth in a prayerlike pose and watched her mother attempt to console her as Vivian stomped her foot and stood with her arms crossed.

When Bobby rode past her, Vivian shoved him. He lost his balance and landed in the basket of freshly washed laundry. The bicycle chain smeared grease on the white sheets. Lily gently rescued Bobby from the fall. Before Vivian could retrieve her bicycle, Lily raised Vivian's dress and spanked her with three hard blows. Lily ignored her daughter's crying as she returned to the house, carrying the basket. Vivian's wailing face was the last closeup.

The film ended.

Vivian recalled the scene from her memory, noting it had occurred exactly as the film had portrayed. She remembered Bobby had always begged to play with her toys. Since he usually would break them, she'd deny his requests. Vivian would normally lock her bike so he could not ride it, but that day she had left it laying on the ground while she ran into the house to use the restroom. When she had returned, Bobby was riding it without her permission.

Anger roused within her as the unpleasant childhood memory returned to haunt her. She had spent a lot of money and time with therapists to work through her familial issues. She never denied the fact she had resented Bobby since the day he was born. Her mother had coddled him. Whatever Bobby wanted, Bobby would get. Lily had said it was because he was the baby. Vivian knew the truth; her mother loved him best.

Vivian had endured enough of *Tuesday Matinee* dredging up distressing memories. She dashed from the theater, passing Walter in the lobby as he tinkered with a porcelain drinking fountain as ancient as him. Vivian was in no mood for uttering pleasantries; she snubbed Walter as she neared the exit.

"Come back next Tuesday," he called out to her.

Vivian had moved to Arizona to leave her troubled life behind. Cutting ties with Roger had been easy, since distancing herself from others was her way of dealing with people. She had ended all contact with Lily and Bobby years ago. She refused to believe Lily's lies about her father's violent behavior behind closed doors. Vivian preserved nothing but loving memories of her father. She had never witnessed him striking Lily.

As Vivian was about to start the car's ignition, she stopped to think. She had never witnessed her father abuse Lily, except for what she had seen at The Roxy. She gasped. If every detail of the bicycle incident with Bobby had played exactly as she remembered it, did that mean the scene of her father backhanding Lily had also occurred? Had Vivian simply been unaware of the abuse because of her young age?

She started the car engine without turning on the air conditioning. She lowered the window to allow the heat to relieve the goosebumps erupting from her arms. She had no idea what was happening at The Roxy, but she was determined to attend every Tuesday. The revelations of the secrets of her life awaited her.

Each Tuesday, the routine at The Roxy continued with little variance during the six months of Vivian's attendance. Walter, wearing his uniform, would greet her and ask if he could help her. She would exchange her dollar for the green ticket he would tear from the paper roll. Walter would tuck the dollar into the cigar box and escort her into the theater. He would disappear into the projection room as she settled into her usual seat in the back row. After a few moments, the five-to-one countdown would fill the screen before the feature presentation played.

Frame by frame, Vivian would relive her childhood, adolescence, and college years. She had watched with happiness as the film presented her wedding to Roger. Sorrow had filled her heart as she saw herself cry in the hospital after the loss of their baby. Her temper flared as the film forced her to relive the moment when she had caught Roger and his mistress in bed, an unforgivable act that had spurred Vivian to file for their divorce.

Each Tuesday, Vivian viewed the film version of her life. Her past behavior, as she viewed objectively for the first time, mortified her. She realized she had allowed her ill-perceived beliefs to forge a wedge between herself and Lily.

Vivian had stopped speaking to her mother because of Lily's favoritism toward Bobby. The Roxy brought awareness to Vivian that Bobby had nearly succumbed to pneumonia at age two. Fearful of losing him, Lily had hovered over him long after he had recovered. After burying a child of her own, Vivian now understood Lily's fanatical concern.

Another Tuesday presentation revealed the truth of her father leaving Lily. Her father's explanation of Lily's excessive nagging proved false when the film exposed the sheriff arresting him after the last beating her mother refused to bear.

Each week, The Roxy forced Vivian to review her true family history—not the events she had misinterpreted throughout the years. Vivian attended the Tuesday matinees in a religious manner, not wanting to miss a single episode to unlock the mysteries of her past.

Doris motioned for Vivian to join her for coffee as Vivian stepped from her trailer. She declined the offer once more to head to The Roxy for *Tuesday Matinee*.

Vivian entered the pink stucco theater, eager for this week's viewing. The film had ended last week with her leaving The Roxy for the first time. If the film was replaying her life exactly as it had happened in the past, could it also predict her future? She had to know. The waiting and wondering had filled her with anxiety the entire week.

She arrived early, but Walter was nowhere in sight. She drummed her fingers on the mahogany counter as she waited for him.

Walter emerged from the storage room, holding a polishing cloth, and sighed. "How may I help you?"

Vivian wondered why he was always so annoyed when she was the only patron. She followed the unwritten script for the hundredth time. "One ticket, please."

He reached for the paper roll and tore away a green ticket. "One ticket, one dollar."

She placed the dollar on the counter.

Walter secured the dollar in the tattered cigar box. "This way, please." He ushered her from the lobby and tugged at the brocade drapes, motioning her to choose a seat, before he disappeared to the projection room.

Five, four, three, two, one and the countdown ended. Although she anticipated viewing the feature, Vivian felt uncomfortable in the hard wooden seat this week.

The opening scene revealed her and Walter in the lobby after she had watched the film. She passed him to exit as he cleaned grit from the interior side of the entrance doors.

"Thank you for your patronage," he said.

Vivian considered his odd response. Walter had always said, "Come back next Tuesday." *Why had that part changed?*

The film continued as she exited The Roxy to her car parked across the street. She was preoccupied with contemplating why Walter had changed his farewell. Her sunglasses remained in her purse as she absentmindedly stepped off the curb and into the blinding afternoon sun.

"No!" Vivian shouted in the empty theater as she watched a city bus strike her and drag her fifteen feet down the street. Blood trickled down the side of her face as a crowd gathered. A cloud of diesel fume permeated the air as the driver idled the engine and exited the bus to assist her. She lay motionless on the pavement as the cluster of people who had gathered at her side gasped at her broken body.

She jumped from her seat to find Walter. *Was this his idea of a prank? A way to get her to quit attending the matinees?* She rushed to the lobby. There was no sign of him. She ran up the stairs to the projection room, but it was … empty. No projector, no film reel, no Walter.

Vivian noticed the lobby lights were off, and the roll of tickets and the cigar box were gone. Had Walter finished his shift and left the theater unattended? He had some explaining to do, and she intended to get answers from him next Tuesday.

Her head throbbed with an impending migraine as she left the building. The image of the bus striking her reminded Vivian to stop as she approached the curb. She stood for five minutes, watching the traffic to confirm no city buses were circling the theater. Satisfied the crossing was clear, she ran to her car and drove home.

"Coffee today?" Doris asked after she had watched Vivian slam the car door.

Vivian was in no mood for company, yet she stopped as she approached her trailer. Perhaps the old woman may be a source of information about The Roxy. "Sure, that would be nice," Vivian said, clenching her jaw, and joined Doris under the shade of the veranda. Vivian did not wait for the serving of coffee before she started her barrage of questions. "You've lived here a long time, right?"

Doris smiled. "If you consider sixty-one years a long time, yes."

"Have you ever been to The Roxy?"

Doris's expression lit up. "Oh my. Many, many times as a youngster. Loved that place."

"Why did you stop going, if you loved it?"

"Stopped going when they tore that musty old building down." She closed her eyes and nodded. "She was a beauty in her day, though."

Vivian barely knew the woman and wondered if she suffered from memory loss. "No, I'm talking about The Roxy. Downtown. Pink stucco building on the corner."

Doris slapped her thigh. "Yes, that's the one. I had forgotten it was pink. It had the most beautiful fixtures— polished mahogany wood, burgundy velvet drapes. And the marquee? Oh my, it would blind you when the colored bulbs lit up at night." Doris grinned like she was reminiscing about a past lover.

"Maybe you're confused, Doris. It's still open. I go to the *Tuesday Matinee* every week. Walter runs it by himself. Nobody's ever there but me."

"Walter? Walter Higgins? That cranky old man died six months after they tore The Roxy down. That's been—what? About twenty, thirty years ago already."

"Doris!" Vivian snapped her fingers inches from her neighbor's face. "It's the pink theater, next to a bank."

Doris, talking in riddles, tested Vivian's patience more than Walter's indifferent behavior ever had. "Dear, they tore The Roxy down to make a bigger parking lot for the bank. I don't know what else I can tell you." She shrugged and folded her hands.

"Thanks for the coffee. I just remembered an errand I must run." Vivian set her cup on the table. She had guessed Doris suffered from dementia, which was the reason she had avoided her for months.

Vivian drove the short distance to downtown. She would find Walter and return with a green ticket to prove The Roxy was still open. She parked in her usual spot and looked across the street at a bank she had not noticed before—the First National Bank, not that the name mattered—and next to it was …

Vivian rubbed the blinding sunlight from her eyes and looked again. Next to the bank was a parking lot with a few cars where the pink theater should have been—where it had always been. *It can't be gone! I've been to that theater every Tuesday for months. Something's not right. It was there. It must be there!*

She removed her sunglasses from her purse for a better view against the glare. She spotted a small metal sign laying on the edge of the sidewalk near the bank parking lot. The rust covering the tin made deciphering the raised letters difficult. *Did it say Tuesday Matinee, 2 p.m.?* If she could retrieve the sign as proof to Doris, she would not need to find Walter for a green ticket.

A strong gust from the desert wind soared the metal sign high into the air and slammed it onto the curb. Before the sign had a chance to lay idle, a second gust blew it farther into the street. Vivian could not take the chance of the miniature cyclone carrying away the sign. Before the next rush of breeze, she would hold the evidence in her hand.

She tossed her sunglasses into her purse and cursed the wind threatening to eliminate her chance of recovering the sign. She dashed from the curb and zigzagged down the center of the street, pursuing the sign as it soared and landed.

The bus driver noticed the woman a half block ahead chasing something he could not see. She returned to the curb when he blasted the horn. His sigh of relief was cut short as she darted once more into the street, dropping her purse to grasp something in midair.

The screeching of the bus brakes silenced Vivian's final scream. The driver forced the bus into Neutral and ran toward her. The gathering crowd collectively whispered and gasped at the victim's crushed body. Inches from her right hand lay her open purse and two items that had flung from it: a pair of shattered sunglasses and a curious trail of green tickets.

The tantalizing scent of freshly popped popcorn wafted toward Vivian, coaxing her to open her eyes. Staring upward, she recognized a man wearing a black vest.

His bony fingers reached downward to assist Vivian to stand. Blinking green- and yellow-fluorescent lights reflected intermittent flashes in the lenses of the spectacles worn high on his nose.

Vivian glanced behind her, and the sparkle of her smile matched the brightness of the dancing bulbs on The Roxy's marquee. The lights dazzled in their repertoire of motion, beckoning patrons to enter the theater. Vivian cried out, "It's *Tuesday Matinee!*"

"Indeed," Walter answered and escorted her across the street to The Roxy.

"What if I'm a Mermaid"
Brian Paone

The clinking and clatter and chatter of the coffee shop behind Janet did not distract her as she tucked her laptop under her lanky arm's armpit. She dug into her front pocket for the small jewel-encased wallet that her mother had given her just before she had passed, just before Janet's first bestselling novel hit the bookstore shelves.

The barista bit on the inside of her cheek as she gazed up at the six-foot-six blonde woman whose face contorted, eyes widening.

Janet sighed and let her chin fall to her chest. "I … think I left my money at home."

The barista nodded and lowered her gaze to straight ahead.

"How much …?" a squeak of a voice said from behind Janet.

Janet pivoted her hips just enough to see who had spoken, and the barista leaned to the left to see around the tall customer.

"I didn't mean to eavesdrop, but I can grab that for you," the short, raven-haired woman said from behind Janet.

"That's not necessary. But I thank you for the offer," Janet said and faced the barista again, with her lips tucked into her mouth. "Sorry."

The barista stepped backward to get a better angle on the cash register to void Janet's order, but the mousy-faced woman behind Janet slid her lanky arm forward and dropped a crumpled ten-dollar bill on the counter.

"I insist, Ms. Scarlet." The woman redirected her gaze downward.

Janet shifted her weight onto one foot as she narrowed her eyes. "How did you know my name?"

The raven-haired woman wrung her hands and tapped a toe on the floor, not raising her gaze to meet Janet. "I … I might be your biggest fan."

The barista stole a glance at the line forming behind the two women and blew a pink bubble of gum until it popped onto her lips. "So, what's the verdict? The natives are getting restless."

Janet smiled at the woman. "Thanks. I owe you one."

The woman held a deep breath and rubbed the back of her neck. "Aww, shucks, Ms. Scarlet. It's my pleasure."

Janet nodded once and stepped aside toward the pickup window to allow the woman behind her to order for herself.

The woman placed her latte order and moved next to Janet. "Writing today?"

"Hmm?" Janet looked down at her armpit. "Oh, yes. I try to write here at least twice a week."

"Doesn't the noise distract you?"

"Sometimes the hubbub of people coming and going sparks creativity. Especially when I am having a block for dialogue." Janet leaned down to the woman and whispered, "Stealing juicy conversations around me for my books is a talent of mine."

The woman giggled and covered her mouth. "I'll be sure not to reveal any of my deepest, darkest secrets when you're around."

Janet straightened her treelike posture and accepted her cup of coffee from the barista. "So, which of my books is your favorite?"

"The third book in your mermaid series."

Janet took her first sip and grimaced from the liquid scorching her tongue. "The third? You're brave to admit that."

The woman chortled. "Why?"

"Of the whole mermaid series, part three was panned the most—by critics and readers alike. That's like admitting that Billy Squire's 'Rock Me Tonight' is your favorite music video."

"I don't follow."

Janet chuckled. "Look it up. You'll see what I mean. But I appreciate your honesty." She raised her cup in a cheers gesture. "Thanks for the coffee."

The woman grabbed her latte from the barista and turned to follow Janet. "Wait, Ms. Scarlet."

Janet stopped and faced the woman. "You've bought me coffee. I think you can call me *Janet*."

The woman blushed. "You said you owed me one. I assumed you meant a cup of coffee, but do you think you could repay me by letting me sit with you for a few moments? I won't interfere too much with your writing time—god knows I count down the days to your next mermaid novel— but I just want to have a friendly chat." The woman leaned her face forward so her raven-black hair fell in front of her face to hide her reaction in case bestselling author Janet Scarlet declined.

"Is a seat by the window okay?" Janet asked.

A smile crept across the woman's face. "Any seat is fine with me."

Janet headed to the empty table, placed her laptop and coffee on it, and sat.

The woman sat across from her and sipped her latte. "My name's Marianne, and I promise I'll keep it brief."

Janet opened her laptop without making eye contact. "Nice to meet you."

Marianne rested her chin on the bridge that her intertwined fingers made, elbows on the table. "Can I ask you about what inspired you to write about mermaids in modern times? I mean, you've built your whole career on them. You're the crème de le crème of mermaid experts, and your book sales show it. And none of them are cheesy *Little Mermaid* rip-offs."

Janet refocused on Marianne and paused loading the document that contained the half-written next addition to her mermaid series. "My grandfather had passed when I was young, and I helped my parents clean out his attic. My grandmother had died before I was born." She diverted her eyes to the screen when she noticed the document had loaded. "We found a chest full of handwritten letters. The pages were weathered and brittle."

"Written in cursive? Like the letters Eric finds in part five?"

Janet smirked. "That's where I got the idea from."

Marianne's eyes widened. "Super cool."

"The letters were written by someone who truly believed they—"

"Really were a mermaid," Marianne finished in a whisper.

"Good to know you weren't bullshitting me about knowing my books."

"So, do you think they *were* written by a real mermaid? The letters you found, not the ones in your book."

Janet sighed. "Whoever wrote them truly believed in their heart of hearts that they were a mermaid. I still have them in my closet. I use them as a roadmap of sorts with my series."

Marianne leaned forward across the table. "So, your series may even be nonfiction?"

Janet laughed and slapped the table with her palm. "I certainly wouldn't go that far."

"How are the letters signed? Is there a name on them?"

Janet sipped her coffee and squinted one eye. "I feel I got tricked into maybe giving you spoilers on the next book."

Marianne looked at her hands now in her lap. "I promise you, Ms. Scarlet, I'm not asking because I'm looking for info on your next book. I wouldn't want to do that to myself, spoil the experience of reading." She raised her gaze without lifting her head. "I ask because I have something I want to share with you, and I feel you are the only person on the planet who can help me."

Janet leaned back into her chair and folded her arms. "I'm starting to get the feeling that our meeting wasn't accidental."

"Don't be frightened, Ms. Scarlet. This isn't a *Misery* situation or anything. But I do follow your blog and took notes on when you would post from here. I realized there was a pattern when you came here to write, and it took me a few weeks to get the nerve to wait for you."

Janet swallowed hard. "Marianne, you seem like a nice person. You also seem harmless, and I'm flattered, but I won't lie. I'm kinda freaked out right now."

"Well …" Marianne scanned the room for any eavesdroppers. "I am a mermaid too."

Janet closed the lid of her laptop. "Marianne, thanks for the coffee. But I think I should go home."

Marianne reached across the table and rested her hand on Janet's wrist. "Please, just hear me out. Give me sixty seconds to explain." She eyed the coffee cup resting on the table to hammer her request home.

Janet scooted her chair farther back from the table to create a safer distance and rolled her opened palm toward Marianne, to give the go ahead to continue.

"I was wading in a shallow pool too close to the shoreline, as my father would reprimand me of, and this dude shot me with a tranquilizer. I woke up in—"

"Wait. Hold up." Janet waved her hand and chortled. "You can't bullshit a bullshitter. I bullshit for a living. Is this a story-idea pitch or something?"

"I wish it was, Ms. Scarlet. I woke up in his basement, and my tail had been removed."

"Removed? Didn't it change to legs when you were out of the water?"

"That is part of the manmade folklore of my kind. We only grow human legs if we lose our tails. Then they respawn in time, like how skin scabs over and creates new skin."

Janet folded her hands and placed them on the table. With a smirk, she said, "Your imagination is fascinating. Would you object to me using this respawn description on a new character I'm introducing in the next book? I'd even name her after you, for credit purposes."

"You still don't believe me. Hold on." Marianne fished her smartphone from her pocket. "Look. These are photos of all the tails I have regrown, only to have him sever them off me as soon as they have fully returned."

Janet leaned forward as Marianne faced her phone toward the author. "Do you mind?" Janet asked, reaching her pointer finger at the screen.

"Go ahead and swipe."

Janet's breath hitched in her throat as she swiped through photo after photo of severed tails hanging on meat hooks in what looked like a basement, all the same length as Marianne's legs.

"He cuts them off at my waist when they are ready and keeps them down there to dry out. Then he waits for the next cycle of tail to regrow."

Janet kept swiping, her eyes expanding with each photo of bloody carnage. "What … does he do with them?"

"So, you do believe me?"

This snapped Janet from her trance of viewing the photos and brought her back to reality. "I didn't say that. Just curious what the rest of the story is."

"He eats them."

Janet quickly looked away from the phone and shook her head. "You had me going there for just a smidgen of a moment." She wagged her finger at Marianne. "Almost had me hook, line, and sinker. These pictures look so real."

"That's because they are real!"

Janet's gaze darted around the café at the patrons who glanced in their direction.

"Sorry. I'll keep my emotions under control better. He cuts them off me to hang them to dry and saws off pieces to eat, like beef jerky. When my new tail regrows, the cycle doesn't end, and I need help. I don't know too much of you dry-lander's world, but I know in my soul that you are the only one who can help me."

"Because of my fictional fantasy series …"

"Because of how realistic your books about my kind are."

"Fictional … *stories*, Marianne. I definitely think you need help but not from me. Professional help."

Marianne closed her eyes, steadying her breathing. "Every time he cuts off my tail and human legs grow in its place, the new tail afterward has been degrading."

"I'm not following."

"Each new tail is slightly thinner, frailer, and less meaty than the previous. I'm scared that I don't have too many more tails to regrow before I won't be able to anymore, and then he will kill me. He's only keeping me alive for their meat. I'm scared what will be in their place when they won't regrow anymore."

"Can …" Janet sighed and shook her head. "Can I see the photos again?"

Marianne handed her phone to Janet.

She hit the photo app icon on the home screen so she could see an overview of all the photos instead of one at a time, swiping. She focused on rows and rows of pictures of tails hanging on meat hooks and Marianne covered in blood from the waist down. She looked up and let the phone rest on the table. "Why in God's name does he eat your … um, tail meat?"

"It gifts him immortality until his body metabolizes it. While it's in his system, he can't die. This is why he eats a little at a time throughout the day, every day."

Janet subconsciously placed a palm on her stomach. "Are you immortal?"

Marianne peered out the window at the passersby. "That's another thing you got wrong in your series about us."

"Does it hurt when he cuts it off?"

Marianne grinned. "No. Mermaids don't feel the same pain as dry-landers. He cuts me in half at the waist with a saw, then hangs my tail, and my new set of human legs grow within about five minutes, then I'm up and walking around like normal."

"How long until your …" Janet coughs. "Until your human legs turn back into a tail?"

"About two weeks."

"And does it happen immediately or slowly, like a caterpillar's chrysalis?"

"I start itching on my legs. When that happens, it takes about an hour for me to be fully mermaid again."

"And you don't die out of water?"

Marianne shook her head. "Another folktale misconception. We have noses and lungs like dry-landers."

"Then … how do you breathe under water?"

"You promise you'll name the new character after me? This is a lot of secrets I'm sharing with you."

A man and woman, trying to leave the café, bumped into the table, and some of Marianne's latte spilled.

"Excuse me. I'm sorry," the man said.

"Don't worry about it. Didn't get on me," Marianne said.

"You wanna go somewhere quieter? Less people?" Janet asked.

"That would be perfect, Ms. Scarlet."

"Please. *Janet.*" She rose from the chair, her long blond hair swinging over her shoulder, and towered over Marianne.

"You're a lot taller in person than in your author photos."

Janet chuckled. "Yeah, the photographers try to make me look shorter because they think a six-and-a-half-foot woman is intimidating."

"Well, I think you're perfect."

Janet smiled and followed Marianne around the tables and toward the door, laptop tucked securely under an armpit.

❧

They found a long wall at the beachfront to sit on. Janet's blond hair blew behind her like streamers on a bike's handlebars, but the wind didn't seem to affect Marianne's short raven-colored hair.

"The smell of salt in the air reminds me of home," Marianne said, with a sigh.

Janet beheld the violent urgency of the waves as they crashed against the rocks in the distance. "Do you think they're looking for you?"

"Who?"

"Your family. The other mermaids ... oh Christ, I can't believe I'm even entertaining this."

"The oceans are big, Janet. Larger than any dry-lander can fathom. It's not unusual for us to leave home for long stretches of time."

"How long do you live for?" Janet used a fingernail to slide a string of hair from her eyelashes.

"We don't count time like dry-landers. I don't know how to transpose that info into something you'd understand."

Janet rubbed her palms along her jeans to warm her hands. "How are you allowed to leave the house? Wouldn't he keep you prisoner? Why don't you just run right now, straight into the water and be gone?" She narrowed her gaze at Marianne, thinking maybe she had finally asked the right question to blow holes in the so-called mermaid's story that would expose her as a fraud.

Marianne inclined her chin to watch the waves from the bottom of her eyes. "As you can see, I have human legs right now. And my tails have regrown so weakly that I would sink to the bottom and die."

"So, is there any hope for you to have a strong enough new tail to live with your people again?"

Marianne glanced at Janet with tears welling in her eyes. "No clue. I just know the first step is to get away from that house and ... *him*."

"But you're away right now! Why go back? Just leave."

"And go where? To the police? You're the world-renowned author of modern mermaid tales, the equivalent of Rawling to wizards, and even you had a hard time believing me."

"I'm having a hard time believing that mermaids have the ability to read books under the sea for you to even know who me or JK is."

"We don't. I've been held captive in that house long enough, with nothing to do but read and watch TV and listen to music. When I saw an ad for your series, I hoped it would give me something I could use to help my quandary."

Janet readjusted her sitting position and crossed an ankle over the other. "Again, not saying to go to the authorities, but why not just leave, period?"

Two small children ran past on the sand below the wall. One stopped to collect a shell and pocketed it before chasing after the other child who hadn't stopped.

"Touch my legs."

Janet furrowed her brows. "What? Why?"

"I want you to feel my skin, to see it doesn't feel like your dry-lander skin."

Janet leaned back on her palms. "This just got weirder."

Marianne focused on the horizon across the ocean. "I understand. I don't want to make you do anything you don't want to." She exhaled loudly. "I'm out of options."

Janet side-eyed her and leaned forward. She touched Marianne's exposed calf and recoiled her finger. "Oh my, that's weird."

"Betch'ya never thought you'd ever touch a real mermaid's skin."

"No offense, but I've never felt something so slimy that looks so dry."

"That's how our torso skin feels too, so it matches."

Janet couldn't help scanning Marianne's body. "Everything feels like that?"

"That's bona fide mermaid skin right there."

"Again, I feel like you're skirting around answering the question. You're out of the house now. Why even go back?"

"He'll find me. I need a place where I can hide long enough to regrow a tail that will have the strength and brawn of a real mermaid tail."

"Leave town. Go far away. Live in the woods. I dunno, go somewhere far."

Marianne placed her face into her palms and sobbed. "I don't even know how to get anywhere. I'm just so … so scared!"

Janet folded her feet under her and pushed herself to a standing position on the wall. "C'mon. Let's go to my place, and we can discuss it there."

Marianne pulled her face from her palms and wiped a tear from her eye. "Thank you."

⁂

Janet opened the front door to her single-story house, and Marianne followed her inside. The mermaid stopped in the foyer and glanced left and right, inventorying her favorite human author's home.

"I never, in a million little earthquakes, would have imagined I would be in Janet Scarlet's home … and invited willingly!"

"Earthquakes?" Janet set her car keys on the wooden dining-room table.

"That's how we quantize time. There are more earthquakes under the ocean than you will ever imagine."

"But wouldn't that be an inconsistent way of keeping track of time?"

Marianne followed Janet through the dining room and into the kitchen. "I don't make the rules. The ancient scholars devised that system." She shrugged and ran a finger lightly over the glass of a hanging picture frame.

"Me and my mother during our trip to China," Janet answered before Marianne could inquire about the photograph.

The sound of a flapping rubber door rang out as the padding of paws bounded through the house.

Marianne went wide-eyed as a large ball of fur rounded the corner. "Is that Anastasia?"

"You know my dog's name?"

Marianne shrugged. "Biggest fan, and all that."

"Anastasia, no!" Janet preempted before the dog could lunge. "She needs to get used to you first. She won't bite if you sit real still."

Marianne froze and let Anastasia smell her legs.

The dog's tail wagged as she focused her nose on the weird scents emanating from the mermaid's human limbs.

"Can I pet her?"

"Lower your hand slowly."

Marianne nodded and reached down with an open palm.

Anastasia inclined her head and sniffed the mermaid's fingers. She tucked her tail between her legs, growled, and bolted back through the doggy door to the back yard.

"Well, that was odd," Janet said with a single raised eyebrow.

"Maybe she recognized that I'm not a dry-lander. Dogs have a seventh sense about those things."

Janet chortled. "You mean sixth sense?"

"No. I mean seventh. Us mermaids have already mastered the sixth sense. That's when the seventh reveals itself. It's still touch and go with that for us."

Janet pinched her lips together and nodded very subtly.

"By your expression, I feel you don't believe me."

"It's not that. Thirsty?"

"Water would be nice."

Janet wiggled a paper cup free from a stack next to the sink and filled it with filtered water. She handed it to her guest, then strolled past the mermaid and sat in one of the dining-room chairs. "I'll be honest, every time I find myself believing you, the common-sense part of my brain kicks in, and I realize how absurd all this sounds."

Marianne pulled out a chair across the table from her host and sat, resting the paper cup in front of her. "What made you want to write a mermaid series? I was under the impression they had fallen out of fashion. Aren't authors supposed to write to market?"

Janet chuckled. "How do you know those terms?"

"I'm a mermaid, not a hermit." She downed the water in her cup in one long swallow.

Janet leaned forward toward Marianne and narrowed her gaze, studying the creature.

"What?" Marianne asked, leaning backward from the woman's piercing glare.

"I would give anything to be you for a while."

"Come again?"

"I wrote the first book in the series because I have dreamed, since I was a child, that I could be a … well, a you."

Marianne dropped her gaze to her lap. "While I'm flattered, I wouldn't wish what is happening to me in that house on my worst enemy."

"That's why I wanna take a look at the tails, and if you're telling the truth, we're gonna get you outta there and back home to your people."

A smile spread across the mermaid's face as she snapped up her head to regard Janet. "Really?"

Janet nodded and folded her arms, grinning.

Marianne grabbed the empty paper cup, pressed the opening against her lips, and screamed jubilantly into it. "Do I need anything specific? I have"—she reached into the back pocket of her jeans—"twenty-five bucks." She made eye contact with Janet. "Do you think that's enough?"

Janet snickered and shook her head. "We'll gather whatever you need, then get the fuck outta dodge. We'll worry about figuring out how later."

Janet stopped her car in front of the off-white house where Marianne had pointed to.

"He's not home," Marianne said barely above a whisper.

"That's a good thing. We can get in and get out. C'mon." Janet opened the door and exited the vehicle all in the same swift motion.

Marianne took a moment longer before she eased the car door open and rose to her feet. She nodded once at Janet and headed up the small walkway to the porch. They climbed the three small steps to the screen door, and Janet glanced up and down the street for any approaching vehicles, shifting her weight and tapping her foot. Marianne pushed the door open, and Janet followed her inside.

Janet walked behind Marianne, keeping her mermaid hostess in her peripheral vision while swiveling her head side to side to glimpse anything unusual or suspect. She scanned the furnished rooms, adorned with hanging pictures of a family smiling at numerous locations during multiple points of their life.

The normality of the interior had distracted Janet enough to where she hadn't realized they had already reached the kitchen at the rear of the house, and Marianne stood while holding open a cellar door.

"Down there is where all my amputated tails are, along with my belongings."

Janet ran her tongue over her teeth behind closed lips and steeled herself to journey downward. "Lead the way. Let's get this over with."

Marianne went down the wooden steps, the walls close enough to brush against their shoulders during their descent, then stepped onto the concrete flooring.

Janet swallowed hard as hanging monstrous scaly tails came into view. She slowed her steps to take in the bluish hue of the scales and was taken aback by their girth. She spied Marianne in front of her and scrutinized her, comparing the size of Marianne's lower half to the massiveness of the hanging tails. She shook her head to clear the doubt creeping into her thoughts.

Marianne weaved around the hanging tails as if she were trying to reach the back of a stocked butcher's shop.

Janet leaned left and right, ensuring not to brush against any of the tails. She noticed they were in different states of consumption, from plump and ripe to just skeletal remains.

"These are the only clothes he's allowed me to wear." Marianne scooped up a pile of discarded pants and shirts and faced Janet. A pair of jeans fell from her arms and landed on the floor.

Janet bent to grab it. "These are men's jeans. He couldn't at least give you more form-fitting clothes?"

"Are there form-fitting clothes for mermaids?" Marianne chortled.

Janet cocked her head and read the label. "And it has some woman's name on it. Angie?"

Marianne dropped her gaze. "His ex-girlfriend. She used to tag all his clothes with her name. Power move."

Janet's shoulders slumped. "We gotta get you away from this psycho. C'mon. I'll buy you some outfits if it looks like it'll take a while to get you back to your people. There's no reason for you to be—"

"Shush!" Marianne put her finger to her lips.

Janet froze.

"I hear the car."

Janet spun her head to the dim staircase. "We need to go out the back door and straight to my car."

The sound of the front door unlatching and swinging open traveled down the stairs to them in the basement. "Angie!" a male voice screamed from above their ceiling.

Janet furrowed her brow and narrowed her eyes at Marianne.

"He calls me by his ex-girlfriend's name," she whispered.

Janet clenched her teeth and stormed through the hanging tails.

"No!" Marianne whispered with such force that a hint of a squeal resided below the words.

Janet stopped but didn't turn around.

"Angie! Where *are you*?"

"I'll go. Let me act normal, and when he goes upstairs to change, we'll make a break for it." Marianne dropped the pile of clothes from her arms.

Janet nodded and stepped aside to let the mermaid pass. She watched her clop up the wooden stairs and rubbed a stiff fingertip along her eyebrow.

"Angie! Where the fuck are you this time? Come to the kitchen. Now!"

Janet heard Marianne mumble, "He's like my personal antichrist, yellin' at me."

The door at the top of the stairs closed behind Marianne, and Janet's chin fell to her chest. She counted the seconds in her head as the pulse in her brain thumped louder than her breathing. She closed her eyes to block out the sight of Marianne's severed tails and whisked herself away to somewhere safer until she got the all-clear from above.

She snapped her face ceilingward when she heard a loud crash from above. She squinted to try to decipher what it sounded like … *chairs being toppled?*

"Stop!" Marianne's voice pierced the kitchen floorboards.

A *thwack* made Janet cover her mouth. Then another. She assumed it was the sound of a palm striking a cheek, followed by Marianne's shriek.

"You fucking stop, Angie!" his voice boomed.

Janet scanned the basement for anything viable as a weapon.

"Stop it, Benjamin!" her muffled voice reached the basement. "I didn't mean to!"

"Goddammit, Angie! Why are you doing this? I've told you to fucking stop already!" His last two words sounded like he had said them through clenched teeth, then came the sound of more chairs toppling and glass shattering.

Janet balled both hands into fists and exhaled longer than normal, summoning courage to confront the monster upstairs.

"I know what you think of me. Just a piece of meat," Marianne said, with a sob.

"I'm trying to help you, for Christ's sake! But you never shut up!"

Janet's eyes widened as she heard Marianne scream, then abrupt silence. She squinted to try to hear more clearly for any minute sounds that might tell her what was happening. She thought she heard Marianne's voice muffled behind what might be him covering her mouth either with his hand or using an object as a gag.

"Do *not* stick me with that thing again!" Marianne's voice sounded loud and clear.

"Angie, you know it's the best thing for you. Now stop fidgeting!"

Marianne released a bellow that made Janet's toes curl in her shoes. She took a few steps toward the stairs, wrestling with indecision whether interfering to help the imprisoned mermaid would result in sustaining injuries herself.

"Oh, fuck!" she heard the man say. "Garbage truck is here."

Janet raised herself onto the first wooden step and kept her eyes trained on the closed door at the top of the narrow staircase. She turned her head an iota so that her left ear faced up the staircase to hear better. She made out a distant yet familiar beeping from a garbage truck in front of the house.

"Don't do anything crazy," he said and padded out the front door.

Janet placed her feet on the next step and listened to the silence from above. The door swung open, and she startled backward and returned to the first step. She placed a hand over her chest in relief to see Marianne.

"Saved again … He forgot to put … the barrels out … Can't let evidence of what he does to me to … spoil and rot in the bags …" Marianne fell forward, eyes rolling into the back of her head.

Janet screamed and reached to catch the falling, limp mermaid's body as it tumbled down the steps. Marianne's weight and force sent them sprawling to the cement floor. Janet heard the man reenter the house through the front door and eyed the open basement door. She struggled to her feet and, three at a time, bound up the stairs to close the door.

The latch clicked, and she turned and pressed her back against the door, trying to catch her breath and slow her heartbeat. She studied Marianne's unmoving body, but she saw her chest rise and fall. Janet exhaled slowly in relief and tiptoed down the staircase.

She kneeled beside the mermaid and placed a hand on Marianne's clammy forehead. She closed her eyes and thanked whatever deity might be listening that her new friend had survived whatever he had done to her plus the fall down the stairs.

Marianne fluttered one eye open. "He drugged me. Again." Her trembling finger pointed to her forearm. "Sticks me. Here. Keeps me … sedated … so he can …" Her eye shut again, and her breathing fell shallow.

Janet raised her gaze to the door at the top of the stairs and slowly rose. She shuffled to the bottom of the steps, then climbed each one with a long pause in between. She reached the top again and pressed her ear to the door.

"It happened again," she heard him say. A long pause of silence, followed by him saying, "Okay, I'll call them. This time they really do need to take her," led her to believe he was on the phone.

"What … What's happening up … there?" Marianne mumbled from below.

Janet redirected her focus down the steps and made an on-the-phone gesture with her fingers against her ear and mouth.

Marianne's eyes widened. "He's calling the scientists! He threatened that if … if I ever tried to leave or retaliate, he would c-call for them to t-take me away to do … to do experiments on me. Cut me open!"

"Yeah, come over. I think I'll need your help this time. I don't even know where she is right now. … Yes, Ma, I gave her the sedative. She must have crawled somewhere. She can't be— … Okay, I'll see you in a minute."

Janet tiptoe-ran down the stairs toward Marianne. "He called his mother, and she's on the way over."

"She …" Marianne cleared her throat. "She lives across the street."

"So, she knows he keeps you here?" Janet stood ramrod straight with one eyebrow raised. "What aren't you telling me?"

Marianne grinned and closed her eyes.

Janet stepped backward and walked right into one of the meatier hanging tails. She felt its weight swing outward slightly before it pushed back against her. A hiccup of bile rose in her throat, and she spied the unconscious mermaid on the floor, then focused on the doorway atop the steps. She took a deep breath, held it, and bolted for the staircase.

She flung open the door to the kitchen, and her foot struck one of the overturned chairs. She went sprawling, face first, onto the tile floor, and her shoulder struck one of the kitchen table legs.

"What the fuck?" the man said, turning to face Janet. "Who the fuck are you?"

Janet grabbed onto the top of the table for support and hoisted herself to her feet, then froze as she beheld a perfectly groomed man in a black business suit—not the cannibalistic maniac she had imagined.

His eyes darted back and forth, then he lunged for the knife rack. He yanked out a meat cleaver and pointed it at Janet in more of a defensive stance than an aggressive one. "You fucking robbing me, lady? My mom is on her way over, and she doesn't like intruders."

Janet raised both hands in a show of surrender. "My name is Janet. I'm not robbing you."

"Then what the actual fuck are you—"

"*Oohh*, Benjamin!" a woman called in a singsong tune as the front door opened.

"Ma! Get in here."

A woman in a nasty floral dress that had gone out of vogue decades earlier stopped in the kitchen doorway. "Oh my. Isn't this peculiar." She looked at Benjamin. "Have you found Angie?"

Benjamin wiggled the meat cleaver at Janet. "No, but this woman came out of the basement."

"And have you called the hospital?"

"Yes, ma'am."

"Well, maybe she's in the basement." The mother strolled past Janet, who remained frozen with her hands raised, and headed downstairs. "And, Benjamin. Put the knife away."

Benjamin rolled his lips into his closed mouth and reluctantly lowered the weapon. "She was hitting herself again," he called out loudly so his mother could hear. "I couldn't figure out why, but obviously, it was a show for this woman."

Janet slowly let her hands rest by her sides. "Did you say, she was hitting herself?"

"Yes, ma'am. She was slapping her face and yelling for me to stop, as if I were doing it. She had never done that before."

Janet scratched one side of her head and surveyed the kitchen furniture in disarray.

"Oh, Lordy, Bejamin. Have you been down here since you got back?" the mother yelled from below.

Benjamin sidestepped around a toppled chair toward the open basement door and stopped next to Janet. "Not yet, Ma. I just got back. Why?"

"You need to see this. She was a busy beaver while you were gone."

Benjamin headed down the steps, his shiny polished shoes clomping on each wooden stair.

Janet decided to follow behind him, wringing her hands the entire way down.

"Oh my god …" He covered his mouth with his hand.

The mother looked up at them from kneeling beside Marianne. "How long were you gone this time?"

"About three weeks. One of my longer business trips."

"Wait. Wait a minute," Janet said, finding her confidence. "You've been gone for three weeks?"

"I'm sorry, dear, who are you again?" the mother asked. "How do you know Angie?"

"She told me her name was Marianne. Why do you keep calling her *Angie*?"

The mother rose and approached the first hanging mermaid tail. She traced a line down it with her fingertip. "She's getting better. Wish she put as much effort into her mental health as she did her craft."

"Ma'am, we'd really like to know who you are. And it's okay if you're confused. You're not the first one she's done this to."

"Okay, I'm going to make a deal with both of you," Janet said. "I'll tell you who I am and what I know, then you better fucking tell me what the hell is going on here."

The mother peeled a scale off the hanging tail to expose what looked like puffy cotton inside. "I think that's fair."

"My name is Janet Scarlet, and Marianne—"

"No …" Benjamin interrupted. "The author?"

Janet smirked. "Yeah, but this whole thing seems stranger than fiction."

"Angie has all your books in her room."

"And now all of this"—the mother waved her arm to indicate toward the mermaid tales—"makes sense. I'm sorry she dragged you into her delusional—"

The doorbell rang above.

"Medics are here," Benjamin said. "I'll let them in." He stopped when he was alongside Janet on his way to the stairs. "I'm Angie's brother. She sometimes has … episodes. I'm sorry for any stress she may have put on you."

Janet eyed Marianne's sleeping body on the floor and whispered her real name.

Soon a flurry of paramedics had invaded the basement, loaded Angie onto a stretcher, and carried her out the house to a waiting ambulance.

"Thank you for the coffee," Janet said after she had just finished recounting her interactions with Angie and raised the mug just past nose level in acknowledgment. She set the mug on the kitchen table and glanced at the two people sitting with her, all now in a righted kitchen. "Benjamin, may I ask you something?"

He nodded while taking a sip, then removed his tie and draped it over the back of his chair.

"Why didn't you just bring her to the hospital yourself? She seemed so docile and meek to me."

He arched his back so that his stomach stuck forward, then shimmied his suit shirt from his pants. He raised the bottom of the shirt to reveal a long scar that traveled from his hip and disappeared somewhere up his chest. "Don't want to have to go through something like this again. It's better to sedate her and let the professionals deal with her." He lowered his shirt but didn't tuck it into his pants. "I have a very small window before she becomes like a rabid animal."

"I can't believe she duped me this bad. I feel like I'm living in someone else's story and not my own."

"Come, dear. I want to show you something." Angie's mother rose from the table and waddled out the kitchen.

Janet shrugged at Benjamin and followed. They went up the main stairs—this one carpeted—to the second floor and into a bedroom. Janet scanned the walls and realized not a single inch of wall was visible through the pictures that had been cut from magazines and taped to the walls. She didn't realize she had been holding her breath until she was forced to inhale. Janet beheld the unmade bed, pillows on the floor, weeks-old food strewn on the carpet, papers and pens thrown about, a trashcan on its side …

Angie's mother opened the closet and stepped aside so Janet could see.

Janet shook her head and stepped over mounds of littered debris to get to the closet. The space was jam-packed with paper mâché and crafts of every color and material.

Angie's mom picked a stack of books off the floor and handed them to Janet.

She slid each book off the one below to see the covers. "These …" She made eye contact with the mother. "These are all movie special effect books."

"Theatre major," Benjamin interjected. "Angie was a theatre major. Wanted to do horror movie makeup for a living."

Janet ran her hand along the bluish material hanging in the closet. "She made the tails out of this." A bottle that looked like it had the word *Slime* written on it caught her eye. "Do you mind?" She pointed to a smorgasbord of discarded who-knows-what on the closet floor.

"Be my guest."

Janet rummaged through the pile to uncover a large tube of thick liquid. She popped the top and let some dribble into her hand. "Well, I'll be damned."

"Hrm?" Benjamin stepped forward.

"This was how she had made her legs feel slimy when she asked me to touch them."

"Do you want to go with us to the hospital?" her mother asked.

"I don't know what good that would do either of us. She obviously is having an episode, and I wouldn't want to aggravate that. Plus, I'm not sure I want to see her just yet, until I can sort this out in my head."

Benjamin nodded and left the room.

Janet saw the spine of her second novel in her mermaid series peeking out from underneath a stack of discarded playbills. She grabbed the corner and shook the book free from underneath. She ran her tongue along her teeth as she opened the front jacket and paused. She stared at her own handwriting across the title page: *Angie, Be whatever you aspire to. And keep dreaming! All the best, Janet Scarlet.*

She looked up at Angie's mom, and her fingers relaxed on the book as she felt lightheaded. "I signed this for her. I must have met her before."

As her grip loosened more on the novel, a Polaroid photo fell from the back cover and fluttered to land on her shoe. She picked it up and saw herself sitting behind a table during a signing at a popular bookstore in the mall, with a younger Angie smiling, while leaning against Janet with her arm around her shoulders for the photo. Janet flipped over the photo and gasped when she read what was written on the back in silver Sharpie.

She swallowed hard and clicked her tongue against the roof of her mouth. "Well, I think it's safe to say I might have played a part in her latest episode."

"How so, dear?" Angie's mom stepped toward Janet.

The author held the Polaroid out so Angie's mom could read what her daughter had written on the back:

I aspire to be one of your characters. And that is my dream. By all mean necessary …

The London to Portsmouth Loop

David Williams

"This is London Waterloo, our final stop on this service," a voice crackled through the train's PA system. "The time is eight twenty-seven in the a.m. on September nineteenth, two-thousand-fifteen. We hope you have a safe onward journey and enjoy your day."

Steven Anderson launched himself from the train the moment the doors opened. Unfortunately for him, he wasn't the only passenger disembarking and was soon lost in the crowd of commuters, travellers, and day trippers. His connecting train to Portsmouth was leaving in a matter of minutes, and he needed to cross to a different platform. He dashed through the crowd of people, pushchairs, and suitcases to the ticket barrier before sprinting down the concourse.

Steven arrived at platform just in time to see the train depart from the station.

"Fuck it," he shouted to no one in particular. This would be his third time late to work this month, and he knew that meant he'd be called into the office the minute he passed through the doors.

He removed his phone to call ahead and warn them he was running late when he saw a train's LED display four platforms down heading to Portsmouth too. *Looks like today is my lucky day,* he thought.

He jogged toward the waiting train and leapt through the doors just as they started to close. He wiped the sweat from his brow, straightened his tie, and began walking through the carriages in search of a vacant seat.

The train was pretty full, but Steven spotted a space at a table which would be ideal for charging his phone. Sitting at the table was a woman and her young daughter, who Steven guessed to be about six years old. Steven smiled briefly at the woman while she helped her daughter find Wally.

Steven surveyed the rest of the carriage and saw some fellow commuters checking their email, reading the newspaper, and going about their daily routine. In his rush this morning, Steven didn't buy a newspaper and forgot to bring the book from his nightstand. Instead, he stared out the window and watched the high-rise buildings flash past and morph into countryside.

Steven turned toward the table and the mother and daughter sitting opposite him. He looked at the open book on the table, full of cartoon people donning red-and-white-striped clothing. The girl caught his eye and smiled.

"Can you help me find him?" she asked in a shy, whispered voice.

Steven returned the smile and shot a look toward the girl's mother for permission. She nodded her approval.

"Of course, I can," he replied, turning the book sideward so they could look together.

"What's your name, mister?" the girl asked. Her mother held a shocked expression on her face.

"My name is Steven. What's yours?"

"I'm Sophie Isabelle O'Toole, and I'm five years old. This is my mum, and her name is Janice."

"Sophie, that's enough," Janice interrupted. "You don't need to give away our life stories to find Wally, do you?"

"Sorry, Mummy."

"Hey, Sophie. I think I've found him," Steven said. "Give me your finger, and I'll point him out to you."

Sophie extended her finger onto the book, and Steven guided her hand to the familiar face of Wally.

"Yay! Thank you, Steven," Sophie shouted as she leaned over the table to try and hug his neck.

"You're a natural," Steven heard Janice say but couldn't see her through Sophie's curly, blond locks. "Do you have children?"

"Not yet. Came close to settling down once, but it didn't take. I guess I'll find the right person eventually."

"Mummy, can I listen to music on your phone please?"

Janice pulled her earphones from her bag and set up her daughter to listen to a song by a pop singer whose name Steven couldn't remember. He leaned backward in his seat and watched Sophie colour a picture of a mermaid while humming along to the music playing in her ears. Steven studied her face intently and looked at Janice sitting next to her.

"Have we met before, Janice?"

Janice glanced up from her magazine. "No, I don't think so. I'm pretty good with faces."

"Yeah, so am I, and I'm sure I've seen you somewhere before—you and Sophie. I just can't place where we could've met."

"Maybe we've met in your dreams," Janice suggested with a teasing smile.

"Interesting thought. I guess I'll have to take a nap and see if you appear."

The train's PA system sounded a ding-dong noise, waking Steven from his light slumber.

"Good afternoon, travellers. This is the LTP-1919 Portsmouth-bound service and will call at Woking and Guildford, then nonstop to the end of the line. We'll reach Woking in about ten minutes, Guildford in twenty, and Portsmouth in around an hour and fifteen."

Did he say afternoon? Slip of the tongue, I guess.

"Once we pull out of Woking, I'll be conducting a full ticket inspection, so anyone who doesn't possess a valid ticket should disembark before I wield the only power I have. Please make sure your ticket says LTP-1919 and is for the 12:53 service, or I'll be asking you to buy a new ticket."

Steven sat up in his seat and frisked his wrist for his watch. The display told him the time was 8:32 a.m. The second hand had stopped at forty-eight seconds.

"Damn thing," he muttered as he unclasped the strap and placed the watch in his jacket. "Hey, I'm going to grab a coffee from the shop. Do you guys want anything?" he asked Janice.

She looked up from her magazine and smiled. "That'd be great, thanks. I'll take a black coffee please, no sugar." She reached over and disconnected her daughter from her pop music bubble. "Sophie, would you like a drink from the shop?"

Sophie's face contorted into a quizzical shape while she considered her options.

"Do they sell milkshakes? I'd like a strawberry milkshake please," she declared with a beautifully toothless smile.

"Two black coffees and a strawberry milkshake coming right up," Steven replied as he edged out of their table area. "Be right back."

Steven wandered through four of the train carriages before he found the onboard shop. He grabbed a strawberry milkshake from the fridge for Sophie before ordering the coffees for himself and Janice.

Another announcement welcomed new passengers from Woking and reminded everyone to have their tickets and passes ready for inspection.

I didn't even feel the train stopping. Steven thought.

"Excuse me, do you sell anything for breakfast on board?" Steven asked the attendant.

The attendant shot him a confused look and shook her head. "Sorry, sir. You're a little late for breakfast. We only have lunch time meals now."

"Lunch? What time is it?"

The attendant checked the readout on the cash register. "It's thirteen thirty-seven, sir. Is everything okay?"

"Yeah, I think. I guess I just really need that coffee."

The attendant passed him the drinks in a cardboard carry box, and he passed her a £10 note.

"Keep the change."

How can it be one-thirty when I just got up like an hour ago, and it was seven in the morning? Maybe all my clocks have stopped, like my watch. I'll have to call work and tell them I'm very late.

Steven trekked to his seat, being careful not to drop the drinks. As he passed through one carriage, he noticed an older woman reading a newspaper. The date on the newspaper caught his eye: *September 19, 2014.* The headline declared Scotland had voted *No* in their independence referendum, with a background image featuring the Union Jack flag.

How weird; that newspaper is a year old. Who'd want to read old news?

Steven continued walking through the train and spotted Janice standing outside the bathroom.

"Hey, here's Sophie's milkshake."

"Oh, thanks. How much do I owe you?"

"Nothing. It's fine. I rarely get the opportunity to buy a beautiful woman a drink these days."

A rush of colour flooded her cheeks. "Wow, smooth. What did I do to you in your dream to make you want to buy my coffee for me?"

Steven smiled and realised how close Janice was standing to him.

"Did it go a little something like this?" she asked as she leaned in and lightly kissed his lips.

"Gross!" Sophie said, giggling. "Mummy, is that my milkshake?"

The sound of Sophie's voice shot Janice backward a few feet from Steven. She fumbled the milkshake bottle and held it out for her daughter to take.

"Hey, what time is it? The shop assistant said it was like one-thirty, but when I caught this train, it was eight-something," he asked as he handed over one of the coffee cups.

Janice took the coffee with one hand and looked at her watch on the other.

"The shop assistant was right. Are you sure you caught the right train?"

"When I got off the first train it was eight twenty-seven. I missed the train I wanted to catch, but this one was going the same way, so I jumped on. None of this makes sense."

Steven looked at Sophie, who was trying to open her drink. He stared at her small face and took in the details of her eyes. He recognised her face.

"Janice, what's the date today?"

She threw him a puzzled look. "It's September nineteenth, two-thousand-fourteen. Yesterday was the eighteenth; the Scottish Referendum vote took place yesterday."

Steven's face drained of colour as he realised who Janice and her daughter were and why he recognised them. A train had crashed into a level crossing near Liss after its brakes failed, killing everyone on board. The British media had printed Sophie's face everywhere for months after the crash. They had become the faces of the disaster.

Steven stared in wide-eyed horror at Janice's face, then scanned the carriage, noticing the sides of the train start to fade. He looked at Sophie, then at Janice, and realized the same was happening to them.

They no longer looked human … or normal.

"What the hell is happening here?" Steven's voice cracked as his voice filled the vestibule.

"I was hoping you wouldn't figure it out," Janice replied in a calm and level tone. "I was hoping you were going to join us, Steven."

"Join you? Where? What's going on?"

"Well, you've worked out that you're riding the doomed LTP-1919 train from last year. You recognise Sophie and I now. Since the day the train crashed, we've been stuck in an eternal loop of the journey. Each time we crash, it resets, and we're back on the platform at Waterloo station."

So they're dead but they can still drink?

Janice took a sip of her coffee. "Occasionally, someone new boards the train and will join us in the loop. Sometimes they'll become aware, much like you, and sometimes they'll ride in ignorance to their deaths."

Steven took a long glug of his coffee. His mouth felt like the bottom of a bird cage. "There's got to be a way for me to stop this thing. Please, you have to help me, Janice."

"I'm not allowed to mess with what's meant to be. But if you die, it means we can be together forever."

"That's why you kissed me, isn't it? You hoped I wouldn't find out the truth and thought you could distract me by kissing me."

"Look, I liked you and the way you were with Sophie. I wanted to be able to get to know you more, and the only way to do that was for you to not find out. Knowing we're going to crash and you're going to die changes things for you. On the next go round, you won't remember that we had met. You'll sit somewhere else probably. But if you had died ignorant of the truth, we would have been together."

Steven walked to the corner of the vestibule and slumped to the floor. "I have to find a way to stop this train. There has to be a way for me to get the hell off."

Janice hunkered next to him. "I don't know how much you know about the crash, but it happened because the brakes failed, and we couldn't slow down for a level crossing signal. I'm sorry, but you have to accept what's happening."

Steven took another sip of his coffee, then placed it next to him. He stood up and turned to Janice. "I have to try. For my own sanity, I have to try."

Before she could reply, Steven pushed the access button to the next carriage. As he walked through, he looked at the empty faces of the other passengers. Everyone and everything around him had altered its state. The passengers seemed to know he was alive too, but none of them spoke to him.

Steven powered to the front of the train, toward the driver's cabin door. The door's sign read, NO UNAUTHORISED ACCESS. Steven slammed his clenched fist against the door repeatedly.

"Hey," he bellowed. "Hey, driver! I need to talk to you. Open the damn door."

He continued to pound his fist until he heard the latch release. The door opened inward, revealing a silver-haired man with spectacles and a moustache.

Steven pushed his way into the cabin. "Where are we right now? We have to stop this train."

The driver closed the door. "I know what you're trying to do, but it's no use. The train is on a pre-determined course and cannot be stopped."

Steven looked for the emergency brake button or lever. He was also hoping for some indication of how far they were from the site of the collision.

"Please, just tell me where we are," he pleaded. "I need to know how long I have."

Steven found the emergency brake button and pushed it over and over, hoping the train would decelerate, but nothing happened. He looked out the window and saw the train was approaching a station. The sign next to the signalling arm read, HASLEMERE. Steven studied the map on the cabin's wall, which detailed the stops along the route. Haslemere was two stations from Liss. Next to the station names was a time estimate between stations. He had approximately eight minutes before the train reached Liss and the level crossing.

"If there's no way to stop this train, then maybe there's a way for me to get off it."

Steven opened the door and marched through the carriage toward where he had been sitting with Janice and Sophie. He grabbed his belongings and walked to the next vestibule.

If I can override the door controls and open it, maybe I can jump. It'll be a rough landing, but at least I might survive.

"A window might be a better option," a voice called from behind him. "Use a hammer to break the glass and jump from the window."

Janice and Sophie stood hand-in-hand in the entrance to the carriage.

Steven smiled at them. "Thanks for the tip."

He estimated he had about three minutes left. He walked through the next carriage and found an emergency hammer in a box with a lid. Steven climbed onto the table, crouched down, and braced the hammer in his hand. With all his body weight behind him, he struck the window and watched as it splintered. He pulled back his arm and hit the window again, and the glass shattered into thousands of shards and fragments.

Steven looked through the empty space and prepared to jump. He edged closer and saw a signal sign sweep passed the window. *Liss.*

This is the signalling stop where the brakes failed. It's now or never.

Steven moved to the very edge of the table, near where the window used to be. Pieces of glass caught under his shoes and ejected through the hole.

One … two …

⚜

Lindsey Parker dragged her suitcase behind her as she rushed through the crowd of people. Lindsey saw her train on the platform and started to run.

"No!" she shouted as the train pulled away from the station.

She removed her phone and called her friend to tell him she would be late. Just as she disconnected, she noticed another train, four platforms farther down the concourse going to the station she needed.

It must be my lucky day.

Lindsey ran to the other platform and jumped onto the train as the doors sounded their impending closure. Lindsey stowed her suitcase in the luggage drop and walk through the carriage to find a seat.

She noticed a handsome gentleman sitting alone and sat next to him. Her eyes were drawn toward the book he was reading, which happened to be one of her favourites.

"Are you enjoying your book?" she asked him.

"Oh yeah, I love it," replied the gentleman.

"It's one of my favourites. I must've read it at least ten times. I'm Lindsey. What's your name?"

The gentleman turned and looked at her. "My name's Steven. Steven Anderson."

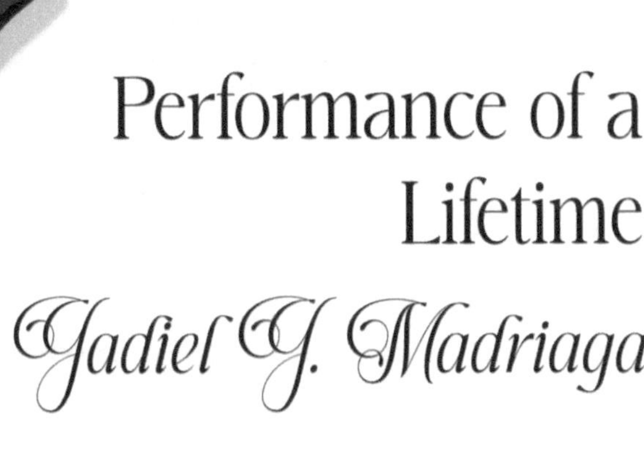

Performance of a Lifetime
Yadiel G. Madriaga

"I think it's brave to put yourself out there with your art," the lady gushes to me. "It's eccentric and thought-provoking. I can definitely feel the message you're trying to portray here through the many mediums you have on display. There is definitely a theme." The lady waves her free hand around, a cocktail in the other, not caring for the people standing nearby or walking past.

It's a diverse collection of people in a diverse neighborhood. An awkwardly placed art gallery in the center of a diverse city but nowhere near other art installations. It is plopped down between a pizzeria and a laundromat, street side, in the middle of the block, with parking in the back. Within its storefront window display case, a single, white, almost nude mannequin dons a necklace of crimson stones of varying shapes and sizes and a pair of tightly fitted leather gloves of the same color, frills embracing the wrists. It poses eloquently under a single overhead lamp that drenches it in overbearing white light. The entrance is buzzing with moving feet and moving lips. Some banter about nothing, or everything, while others whisper and listen closely to what their partner, or friend, thinks about this installment or that.

It's my debut—the opening of my very own art gallery that I've worked on for the past three years. Maybe all my life, now that I think about it. I have, in one corner, a giant phone hanging on the wall like a flatscreen television. It's displaying someone's phone usage, thumbing through apps, photos, text messages, and social media posts. It hints at the personality of a particular kind of person that is not too familiar, not too strange, and if you watch long enough, a bit dark, too.

There's a large painting on another wall in another corner. It's much taller than its width, so it touches both the ceiling and the floor but is as wide as any old doorframe. Its canvas is bronze all over, but a dozen horizontal, thick, red lines are drawn across it, all separate, from top to bottom. The giant brush was drenched, like a mop in a paint bucket, that it ran down the tall canvas in thick droplets before drying into a lower, more significant place.

No space in the venue is wasted. If it isn't a place to stand or to walk, it is a place for another installation. A ceramic statue, colored and textured like a used-up and burned-out piece of charcoal, is sprawled and hung up right in another corner. Giant ceramic chains hold the life-sized human figure in the air. Its ankles are tied to the floor and wrists to the ceiling. Its head dangles forward hopelessly.

My favorite addition to the venue runs along the walls behind the sculptures and behind the hanging canvases. A simple collection of words cover every inch, overlapping each other in contrasting shades of grey, forming such intriguing musings and sayings in one-foot-tall black letterings of various styles and fonts. Its plaque is hanging somewhere. I have a few personal favorite phrases:

"I roam aimlessly. Death is everywhere I go. I shall embrace it."

"Mosquitoes remind me that though I am at the top of the food chain, there are things out there still trying to eat me."

Some are a bit depressing: "There's no light at the end of my tunnel. In fact, I'm walking away from it with every step."

One phrase, in particular, speaks to me louder today than any other: "I want to be used up. I do not want to be loved. I'm completely used up. Easy to dispose of."

Except for the constant contrast of red, every empty space is occupied by a specific color scheme: blacks, whites, and every shade of gray perceivable.

In the center of the venue, a small stage sat just as curious as anything else there. At least in the public's eye, it was just another installation. So naturally, people smothered it and pondered its meaning.

There I stood, off to the side. I had just finished setting up the microphone when an inconsiderate, cocktail-wielding woman gave me a compliment.

"It's inspiring—truly," the lady continues. "I wish I could put myself out there like this. I don't think I could be brave enough to expose myself and let myself be so vulnerable. But I really want to do something good for the world and leave something behind that can be cherished."

"I feel the same way," I reply with enthusiasm. "That's basically the overall theme of this gallery."

"Oh, I'm confused," the lady furrows her brows, hoping desperately not to offend me. "I'm–I'm sorry, I don't mean to be rude. But I thought the theme was awareness."

I smile patiently.

"And ... you know. Suicide?"

I assure her gleefully. "If I were to die, the world would find itself to be a better place because of it."

Her jaw nearly detached from her face.

I leave her speechless to take my final circuit through the gallery, meeting and greeting and conversing with the curious crowd. They're a solemn crowd that manages to soak up the somber vibes. For the most part, they're having an enjoyable evening snacking on red velvet cupcakes and sipping on cheap wine from a box.

I eventually make my way back to the stage where a spotlight illuminates a microphone stand. I clear my throat into the microphone and compose myself for the audience. "Testing, testing," I utter softly. "Hello, everybody. I'm glad to have everyone here tonight. Ahem."

The microphone squeaks and the loud banter quiets to a murmur. Recognizing who it is behind the microphone, most stop talking, and others shush the rest.

"I'm happy to hear that everybody is enjoying themselves." I smile. "Don't forget—and to those who don't already know—that there are goodies and other refreshments in the back. Free, of course, so please help yourselves. They're all made with as much thought to the theme as anything else here on display. And if you don't already know from the flyers, I will also be performing for everybody tonight. A once-in-a-lifetime experience."

I glance at my watch. Everyone within earshot is intent on hearing what more I have to say. "In about thirty minutes or so, I will be completing my vision of this exhibit here that I created for you all to enjoy. So, until then, I will be taking questions about this presentation or any other piece on display here. And when we come to the final minutes of the Q&A, the poison I have already ingested will finally begin to take effect, allowing me to pass on painlessly and peacefully before you all to witness shortly thereafter."

The room remains silent, filled with confused thoughts clearly expressed by bewildered faces, except for mine.

"I implore everybody to take this chance for understanding." I pause to scan the room for a curious face.

Most of them stand unwavering yet confused, like a deer in headlights. Others pull their phones out to record, shining their own light back at me. A random awkward voice pierces through the thickened atmosphere: "What?" Then another, but aghast: "Excuse me? Are you serious?" The crowd bursts into a rumble of opinions, questions, and demands. "He can't do that, can he?" "He's not going to actually kill himself; it's art." "Maybe it'll be an interpretive dance." "You dummy, art mimics life. I think he's going to actually do it." "I didn't sign up for this, excuse me." "Somebody call the police!"

A panicked voice screeches, grabbing my attention. She's backing away and trying frantically to squeeze through the crowd to leave.

I urge everybody to be calm. "Don't be afraid! Don't be afraid! If you're uncomfortable, I understand. Please let them through. Please clear a way." I pause. "But you could be missing out on the chance to have a kind of closure if you're looking for it. Death is a very uncomfortable subject. Many of us have experienced our loved ones passing on—maybe even secondhand. Or sometimes it's a friend, acquaintance, or even a cherished celebrity. It comes at such a negative price to most of us that, subconsciously, we cannot reconcile with the truth and the truth is that we all will die someday. and everything in our world—our universe—will come to an end. It's just a matter of time. An essential inevitability to life and all that comes before it and after. But here I present to you a rare opportunity to look death in the eye and, hopefully, when you leave here and make it home safely, you all could begin to cherish life more—even more so than if you already do. But just like life, your chance is fleeting and you may never get this chance to ask why again. Would anyone like to know more about why I'm doing this? Raise your hand if you do."

A couple of shy hands rise at my persistence.

"You're not really going to, though, right?" another asks.

"I am, actually," I reply bluntly. I continue louder, trying my best to be stern yet informative. "And if anyone decides to call an ambulance, it will be in vain. I will be dead by the time they arrive because the poison I took cannot be remedied without knowledge of the exact poison. One that only I know of—at least until the medical examiner performing the autopsy finally discovers it many hours from now."

Murmurs sprout and genuine concern bloom across their faces at my mention of death.

I continue over them, "Also, it may be convenient for the neighboring communities that only one of you calls. There really isn't any need to jam up the emergency phone lines in case somebody else out there is in dire need of it compared to me. I am in no equal or worse position than someone having a heart attack. I have chosen this for myself knowingly, willingly, fully able of mind and body, and under the influence of no chemicals or persons but myself. I mean no harm, and I bring no malice." I step to my left and wave my arm over a classic red telephone and its receiver on a black pedestal barely hidden from the lights. "I have a single phone here for anyone who chooses to call for help. It's preset to do so by speed dial. Just hit any of the speed dial buttons." I feel I'm digressing a bit, so I try to get back on track, but someone cuts in.

"But life is so precious! Don't you appreciate all that you've been given?" cries a concerned lady up front near the stage.

"I absolutely do," I reply cheerfully, looking right into her fearful eyes. The genuine tone in her voice fills me with fervor. "So, I hope to share with you all just that. My appreciation for my life and all I've experienced in it is on display for everyone here. Not the images themselves, no—those are just the products of a certain life that I've experienced. It took certain experiences for me to be able to bring these images to fruition. It is my imagination and my craftsmanship and my insatiable need for creation. It is me, an aggregate of experiences to form this personality that I happily present to you instead of running or hiding or through anger and destruction. There are endless possibilities of experiences I'll never be a part of and that's fine with me. I am still a unique collection of experiences. The good and the bad and the worse, every single one leaves within me the memories I contemplate tirelessly much like every one of you here.

"Many people and personalities have interwoven their own lives through and around my own, creating this tapestry you all see before you. Each of you will all take home with you tonight a connecting strand—a thread to weave into your own life and do whatever it is you will with it tomorrow. This is what matters! In the end, my strand will be cut, and I will cease to exist, but I will still be connected to you all by the strands I have left behind. So, here I am, making myself available with the most authentic perspective. One you can take home with you as if you experienced it yourself. For when you kiss your loved ones to sleep and lay yourself in your bed—maybe with someone you love or maybe not— you'll close your eyes, dream a beautiful dream, then open your eyes. The morning sun will greet us all for another chance. Another day is another opportunity to get to where you need to go and do what you need to do for you to feel like doing it all over again the day after that. That's great, but all roads come to an end. There is always an end. Let's let that morning sun rise regardless of the reason for which your eyes close tonight. My end is here, so let's celebrate that! My birth has brought me here! I have celebrated that day at least once every year of my life; they're my beginnings. Let's celebrate that end every other day. None of us know when that end will come but it will come. Our deaths are worth at least as much celebration as our births, because without any beginnings, there will be no inevitable ends."

"No!" another bellows out. A man steps forward, eyes reddened by the pain of a memory. The quiver in his lip is intense. His voice trembles. "My boy. My little boy. He was only sixteen. He had—he had so … much … life ahead of him! And you're trying to—to justify suicide or something? How dare you make a mockery of his memory! And the memory of everyone who has taken their own life." He points his finger at me like a bullet. His face contorted with disgust. "Shame on you and—and … all of whatever you're doing here. I hope they—they lock you up you—you fucking heathen! You have no right to tell me what to appreciate." A woman with an equally distraught face, perhaps his spouse, grasps his arm and whispers disarming words into his ear.

I can feel their pain. The room collectively sympathizes.

Another person softly slices the air with his voice. "My son … was a soldier, a husband, a father, and my boy." The man clenches his jaw, speaking through his teeth as if it would help make it hurt less to say aloud. His eyes are strained, as if they're holding back a flood. "It's a disease of the mind. I've been to enough meetings to know enough. I've seen it all and I've heard it all, but this—this is a joke!"

"I am truly sorry for your loss," I utter away from the microphone. The noise had deadened, and my voice carried through the room for everyone to hear as clear as crystal.

"Fuck you!" the man responds, just as clear.

I pause to let that settle before responding. "I am truly sorry," I repeat, giving raspy emphasis to every word and the dead spaces in-between. "It's very powerful. It says more than anything anyone can truly express. That's why you don't hear stuff like this in everyday life. It's rare, it's raw, and it's real. And it deserves to be more apparent in our day-to-day lives than we give it. That is a part of what I'd like to talk about and what I'd like to share and celebrate. If I may," I say, softly still. "I would like to ask everybody for a moment of silence for all those we have lost. I'd like to take the time and think of this powerful moment to myself. I encourage everyone else to do the same if it is all right."

The clock is ticking, but I close my eyes, hang my head, and let darkness flood my mind. Blurry images spring before me, like a garden of white lilies. They bloom into clarity with an explosion of light, producing vivid imagery within the same place as where my emotions are felt. It's like my eyes that have been in darkness for hours are then suddenly being exposed to broad daylight. Like my ears when they hear that song for the thousandth time but relate to it for the first time. Like the goosebumps on my arms when caressed by the wind after a hard day's work. Like my nose when it catches the scent of nostalgia floating carelessly in the air on a breeze, long forgotten, and out of nowhere. Like the taste of her skin. I understand and feel what that man said. I remember the love. I remember the loss. I remember the joy. I remember the pain. My senses feel it all with no emotion to return an expression. It is sublime and macabre. It is everything in between.

On the outside, I can only smile. I have a new sense of understanding. I finally raise my head, take a deep breath, and open my eyes to see everyone else's head hanging low. I give them some more time.

A couple more minutes pass, and everyone's looking up at me with somber eyes. I clear my throat and continue softly, "I think it's safe to say that everyone that is here is here because we've been affected by a tragedy, one way or another. It is a person, whether an acquaintance or maybe it was closer to home. There is that special factor of decision-making in someone's head that just decides that it is time. As opposed to the tragedy of a life being taken, life has been given up. That, to me, is terrifying. How much pain must one endure before it is decidedly too much?"

I look around the crowd making eye contact with as many as I can, but I can feel my eyes swelling. I'm buckling and looking to the floor, trying in vain to suppress the hiccups. I can already see where I'm going with this. "To think that ... that someone who I can love so much ... who I thought loved me back ... just decides that–that there's nothing ..." I look up as if the answer may be somewhere in the ceiling. "Nothing? Worth ... living for? Is life and–and love not enough to heal the pain? Isn't that good enough? Aren't I good enough? Why am I not good enough? *Why?*"

"It's a hoax, y'all," a lame voice mutters out from the back middle of the crowd, snapping me out of my woe. "We'll be forking all our money over in due time. He's tugging at our heartstrings because he thinks it's easy pickings for him!"

I continue, forcing a smile over my grief. An all too familiar feeling. "I can only guarantee in due time," I retort. "So all I can give is my word. I don't want your money, only your time. Please, if you can, would you rather use this time to understand?"

"I understand," a voice says condescendingly, making himself visible. He's a middle-aged man, possibly alone, with a scowl on his face. "I've seen your type before, so I know where this is going. I'm only sticking around to make sure these poor folk aren't scammed in their grief!"

"That's very commendable," I say, smiling at him as well, thinking how life can be so wry. There really isn't more I could say to convince them, but I continue. "I've lived my life, and my purpose is fulfilled. So I ask myself, 'why continue?' My life can only become so much; my death will be so much more than what I can ever do living. I already know this because I know who I am. I cannot act like I will become this or that to do this or that. I'm preset. I'm only capable of what I am capable of, and this is what I am capable of. I wish I grew up being given those ingredients that can produce a person who can manage all of what life has to throw at them while chasing more. Clearly, there are many who have lived that kind of life, like the people of our pasts that we remember today. We teach about them to our youth their grandest stories of altruism or the most egregious tales of atrocities. It reminds us of all of the pitfalls to avoid and inevitably ignore. It maintains our perceptions of the ideal life to pursue but not really the conditions that allow it to flourish. There are many examples in our society of many professions and personalities that you would think we'd be able to reproduce those ideal conditions reliably, but here I am. Here we all are just fleshing ourselves out while trying to fit in. There are some lucky few here who can be proud. To all the rest of us, your purpose is to support the best of our society so that they all may transcend and hopefully bring us with them when they do. I'm saying that we're bigger than that."

"Then, it's a publicity stunt!" another voice yells in condescending excitement.

"Yeah, yeah, it's for the likes! Haha!" somebody else replies.

The crowd finally erupts into disarray: "Get out of here!" "Fuck off you crook!" "You're disgusting!" "Nobody believes you, asshole!"

I hadn't planned on this amount of dissension, but I understand it. I know just how resilient the mind can be in the face of danger, even a perceived one. There are no gun-toting terrorists here or any other kind of attack on one's physical existence.

I imagine that they must think it to be an attack on their memories. The precious memories of a little boy trouncing around the yard. Of a little girl trying on makeup for the first time. Of first loves and first heart breaks. On the last day of kindergarten to graduation, then to the last day at home. Not that one of a body bag being carted off into an ambulance. No—not that one of a lifeless statue in your arms in the middle of an art gallery. No, I've rudely interrupted happy memories. I've challenged their memories and their perceptions that receive what can only be determined to be a danger to their own instincts. They're crying aloud in panic. Maybe they're barely finding out themselves to be equally capable of such a thing as death because what does our brain know except for what we give it? Through our eyes, ears, noses, tongues, and touch. There is more to our world than what we immediately experience. There is more than one way to see a cloudy day. There is more to an odor than you think. An experience is either compared to nothing or everything. It just depends on who you ask. Ask the ears when they hear that particular jumble of sounds that makes them dance. Ask the tongue about when it remembers. To touch—to feel. I remember the feeling of floating in placid waters. Of being held by love's embrace. Oh, what a feeling.

I contemplated these ideas as the crowd jabs on. Shy folks who finally found a voice within the shadow of public outcry. They could finally express themselves within a sheath of safety. It is as automatic and instinctual as hunger and thirst. They are but flesh and bone and meat that can think and I am them. They are me. So naturally, they continued.

Many have already started for the exits, while a few waiting outside trickle inside, past the mannequin in the now dimly lit storefront display case. Cameras continue recording, while more join in as time passes. The rest move in closer to the stage as the crowd loosens. They're at least invested, but they still bicker amongst themselves even as the final minutes arrive and pass. Second by second, they let it fade away in their own heads. Their emotions drown out the unwanted. They've already made their choice. It's too late for reconciliation now. Not with their own peers. Not with themselves.

I idle, patiently trying my best to follow the chaos, but it's becoming too much. It's tiring, actually. My eyes droop, my legs waver, and my heart races. It didn't occur to me that it had begun until someone pointed out the blood trickling from my nose. I only have maybe a minute, maybe less. Who knows how long I've been exhibiting the symptoms?

"No way!" somebody yells. "This is some quality production, ha-ha!"

The others chime in, but it's all muffled and indiscernible. Tunnel vision sets in as everyone huddles around me. All I can see now are ankles and feet, but everything is getting darker and darker. I can somewhat still hear beyond the dull static, but it's fading. I search for some kind of sense to feel but all that's left is the taste of something metallic and the sound of muffled voices.

"Oh my God!" somebody whispers. "Somebody help!"

"It's just a show!" another voice murmurs. "You're embarrassing! Ha-ha! It's fine!"

Hush.

"I don't feel a pulse."

"You're probably not checking it right."

"I'm a nurse, asshole."

"You don't know what you're talking about."

Then there is nothing. The darkness engulfs me, and yet, even in that final moment, I realized something. That it is such a tragedy for people to have so much to feel—so much complexity behind their emotions—but not the means to express them all. I felt joy for still being capable of learning this and great sorrow at the idea, even at this moment in my life, that I could not show everybody how exactly it feels to have no regrets and be at peace.

Maybe now you're wondering what happens next. Do they finally see the truth? Do the paramedics finally arrive? Do those who believe cry? Oh, the look on the faces of those who doubted. Do they finally see? Do I succeed in what I was trying to do or is it all in vain? Do I make an impact or do I fizzle out? To be honest, I have no fucking clue.

The Bayou Never Speaks
Michelle Jillian Bailey

Tanya King walked down the lonely stretch of LA 22. Mosquitoes buzzed around her ears, but she couldn't be bothered enough to swat at them. More than a tiny insect was already buzzing in her head. Beads of sweat merged and darted down her flesh, pools collecting in the front of her bra. Her long dark hair stuck to her neck, its bounce gone. She walked far enough off the road that even if a car were to pass, she would remain unseen. Her mind traveled back, from the bubbles rising on the lake to the beginning of the end of this nightmare for her best friend, Sandra Fields.

Not even four short weeks ago, Tanya had received that life-changing phone call. On the other end of the line, Sandra was unable to form words, only screaming and sobbing. "I'm on my way!" Tanya had shouted into the phone. Barely taking time to put on shoes, she'd grabbed her purse and jumped in her car.

Two hours later, arriving at Sandra's house, Tanya felt as though she'd stepped on a landmine. Her brain was scrambling, trying to catch up with what her eyes were seeing. The room looked as though a Bouncing Betty had exploded. Images flashed and popped in her eyes, like a scene from a

1980's rave. Gasping for air, Tanya began to see stars on the periphery of her vision. She squelched down her panic and scanned the room for Sandra.

On the far side of the room, she was lying on the floor, cradling her trembling hands to her heart. Her hair was a wild, matted mess, and blood streaked her face. She didn't speak coherent words, only sobbed hysterically. Her body rocked and shuddered. Furniture was overturned, shattered glass wildly refracted the light from a toppled lamp.

Nearly slipping on the wet floor, Tanya said a silent prayer and bent down beside her friend. In her most soothing voice, Tanya whispered, "Come on, Sandy, we're leaving right now, forever. He'll never touch you again."

Sandra's glazed eyes searched Tanya's face. She allowed Tanya to help her stand, made more difficult by keeping her hands clutched to her chest. Once on her shaky feet, all she could manage to whisper was, "Please get my mama's pearls." Tanya nodded, and ensuring Sandra was steady, she entered the tiny bedroom to find Sandra's most precious possession. The fight must've started in there. It was too much to see the broken lamp and disheveled bed. Flashes of young innocence and dreams of love and family appeared. Tanya's heart squeezed in her chest as she thought of the dewy-eyed girl Sandra had once been. She would forever be shattered like the framed wedding picture on the floor. Tears pooling in her eyes, she found Sandra's pearls and beat a hasty retreat.

Holding the necklace in one hand, Tanya placed her other arm around her defeated friend and ushered her toward the door. Tanya's first step was to get Sandra out of the house. She could figure out what happened and what injuries Sandra had once they were a safe distance away. Sandra's gait was slightly hunched and slow; she winced with every step. Blood was everywhere. Clearly, she needed medical help. Tanya was terrified by the way Sandra was clutching her arms and knew there was damage she couldn't see. Sandra didn't say a word on the drive, just cried softly and continued to rock back and forth. Tanya pulled into the hospital parking lot. Sandra registered what was about to happen and shrieked, "No!"

Tanya paused, her left hand hovering above the door handle. She looked at her friend, and in her reassuring voice, replied, "Sweetie, you're covered in blood. We need to get you checked out."

With more force than Tanya thought she could produce, Sandra again cried, "No!" Her wild eyes communicated she wasn't going to be swayed. Her voice, tinged with horror and fear, added, "They'll take my baby from me."

Again, trying to console her, Tanya placed a loving hand on her distressed friend's knee and said, "Sweetie, they won't take the baby. They'll just check you out, and the baby. We need to make sure you're both okay."

It was then that Sandra slowly lowered her hands from her chest. Tanya had assumed Sandra was applying pressure to a wound. What she saw instead was a horror that would haunt her for the rest of her life. Cupped in Sandra's hands was her baby, tiny and blue. Fully formed, with ten fingers and ten toes, Sandra's son would never take his first breath. His skin was translucent, and Tanya could see the delicate organs that would have contributed to his life. Easily fitting in the palm of Sandra's hand, he couldn't have been more than a few ounces. Beaten out of her womb, Sandra had miscarried him only hours before. Tanya's heart shattered into a million tiny shards. Nodding, she started the car and began the long drive back to her home.

The silence hung heavy in the car; the only sound was of rubber on asphalt. Tanya agonized over not taking Sandra into the hospital. She could logically make a list of a hundred reasons she should turn back around. But in the end, she knew forcing more trauma on Sandra would be worse. If at any moment the wounds became life threatening, she would rush her back. She could hear Sandra's ragged breaths, but the sobbing had stopped. At least for now, she knew Sandra was stable.

Tanya thought back to the first time she realized Sandra was abused. Listening to her best friend had felt like a bad dream. None of the story she was hearing sounded real. However, the fuzzy dreamlike state snapped to crystal clarity when Sandra retold Ernie's haunting words.

"You can scream all you want, bitch. The only thing to hear you is the bayou, and the bayou never speaks."

Tanya wished with all her might she had taken Sandra out of the situation right then and there. Not long after, she'd turned up pregnant, and refused to leave. That all seemed like forever ago now.

The first task was to place Sandra's son somewhere. As a veterinarian, Tanya had many urns and burial boxes for when her clients lost a beloved pet. Her favorite was a heart-shaped box, inscribed with the words, *Blessed are those who mourn, for they will be comforted. Matthew 5:4.* The beautiful, polished mahogany contrasted with the murdered life she laid inside it. Sandra sobbed softly as Tanya said a final prayer for Samuel, sealing the lid over every mother's deepest fear. Outside the sky cried with them.

Late the next morning, over coffee, Sandra told Tanya the whole ugly story. Sandra had been feeling great that day, after a rough first trimester. Hoping to surprise Ernie with a dinner out, she got dressed up. She put on a nice dress, which was snug over her newly forming belly. She even took the time to do her hair and put on makeup. Ernie got home from work a little early. Walking through the door, he laid eyes on his dressed-up wife.

"Who the fuck is he?! Huh? Who is he?" Ernie rushed her. His fingers entwined in her freshly curled tresses. "Answer me, bitch!"

Caught off guard, Sandra couldn't even answer. She barely stuttered, "I–I … Wh–what?"

"Don't fucking stutter, you bitch! Answer me! Who are you meeting? Who are you fucking? Is it his baby? You nasty little whore!" The fury in his voice turned Sandra's blood to ice. The sight of the throbbing vein in his neck made her stomach wrench and shoulders pull up defensively. His spittle rained down on her face, her head yanked back by his fistful of hair. Her mind was racing to figure out what went wrong. She needed to know how to disarm him, calm him, convince him everything was okay.

Before any helpful words could form on her tongue, he slugged her in the gut. Her breath forced out in a grunt, and her knees buckled, crumpling her to the ground. Hair ripped out of the roots as she dropped, leaving a tangled mat in his fist. Brilliant pain flashed in the back of her eyes, and she cried out.

She wasn't sure where to grab. The fear for her baby and the pain in her belly was great; however, her bleeding scalp was an acute pain she had never experienced before. Vulnerable and exposed, her hands on her tender scalp, Ernie cocked his leg back and with all his force, kicked her midsection with his steel-toe boots. Immediately the pain in her womb was worse than her head. She felt a cramp and a tear from deep inside her body.

Finally finding her voice, she screeched, "Ernie, no! The baby. You're hurting the baby!"

The word *baby* from her lips enraged him further. He began kicking her in rapid succession. "Whose baby is it, you fucking slut?! Where were you going? Who are you fucking?!"

His boot repeatedly slammed into her sides, depressing slightly before the fragile bones gave way. The dry, brittle sound was as terrifying as the pain was excruciating. In gulping sobs, Sandra shouted, "I got dressed up for you, Ernie! I just wanted to go to dinner with you. It's your baby. I've never cheated on you. I love you, Ernie!"

There were a few more blows before her words sunk into his fury-soaked brain. He stopped kicking her and stared, mouth agape. The pain, fear, and trauma rolled up though her, she vomited violently on the floor. Even on the dark wood, she could see the unmistakable shade of crimson. She lay on the floor, whimpering, covered in blood and vomit. Ernie wiped saliva off his face. "What did you say?"

Sandra tried to calm her voice; she knew it enraged him when she cried. "I love you. I just thought it would be nice to go out to dinner. I got dressed up for you, Ernie."

Ernie, still shaking, fist clenched at his side, looked at the puddle of bodily fluids around his wife. "Why the fuck didn't you say so?! Look what you made me do, you stupid cunt!" With that he spun on his heels.

On his way out the front door, he picked up and smashed any item within reaching distance: last night's beer bottles, the lamp near the couch, the kitchen table. With a final primal roar, he cleared off the kitchen counter with a swing of his arms, ceramic shards and silverware pinging and ricocheting about the small cabin. He slammed the door and was gone.

Sandra lay in the silence. Fear he would come back kept her immobile, listening only to the faint tick of the clock. Once she was sure the prayer for her own death wouldn't be answered, she crawled to the phone and called Tanya. In the endless minutes waiting for Tanya to arrive, Sandra felt her insides gushing out. Warm fluids drenched her lower body. The cramps came hard and fast, crushing the breath out of her. Sorrow, deep and black, swallowed her as Sandra felt her baby's lifeless body exit hers. Holding him to her heart, she prayed for a miracle that never came.

Tanya sat in silence in her warm, inviting kitchen. The yellow walls filled the room with joy and sunshine. It was the kitchen that she shared with her kind, loving husband. She felt a fury build inside her that she didn't know was possible. Tanya knew she couldn't press charges. As the parish sheriff, Ernie had too many friends in high places. He was mean, violent, and vindictive. Those who knew him either respected him or feared him. He had also conveniently laid out a strong back story about Sandra's false mental health problems. This was his insurance in case she ever tried to accuse him of anything. He had already guaranteed nobody would believe her. And even if anyone did, they would be too scared to protect her. Divorce was out the question as well; he would never let her go. That left Tanya with only one option.

Tanya and her husband Aaron welcomed Sandra into their home, like a beloved family member. They made plans for Sandra to begin working at Tanya's veterinary clinic once her physical wounds were healed. Tanya knew that Ernie would come collect Sandra, like his lost airport baggage; she needed to be prepared for him.

Several weeks went by. Sandra's wounds nearly healed— the external ones. Ernie called Tanya at work, probably thinking it would catch her off guard. "Healthy Pets." Tanya's cadence was soft and charming.

Low and evil, his voice slithered through the line like a serpent's tongue. "Give me my wife back, bitch."

Tanya's heart slammed in her chest. Her throat tightened, but she had practiced this in her head and forced herself to remain calm. "Ah, hello to you too, Ernest. How have you been?" The mixture of her sweet-honey tone and the insincere words infuriated him.

"Listen you fucking cu—"

"No, you listen!" Tanya's sharp bite stopped him midsentence. "I'm only going to say this once, and you're going to listen to me. You fucked up, and you fucked up bad. If it were up to me, you would never see Sandra again. But for some unknown, insane reason she still loves you. She wants to come back." Tanya took a deep breath. Lying didn't come easy to her. "We've talked about it, and she's ready to come home. However, you'll need to meet with me first. I have some guidelines that must be put into place. Meet me—"

"Guidelines? You're a real piece—"

"Ernest, if you interrupt me again, I'll hang up this phone, move out of the country, and change all of our names. I have the money to do it. Do *not* question my motives to keep my best friend safe." Ernie didn't say a word, and she continued. "Meet me tomorrow night at the Park N Ride at the Highway 12 and 63 interchange. Be there at nine." She hung up without waiting for his answer. Her vision swam, her mouth watered, and she ran for the bathroom to throw up.

Tanya was a basket case for the next thirty hours. She mentally went over the plan with all the contingencies. She tried to play out all the possible things Ernie could say or do. Time crawled by at a snail's pace, and yet somehow 8 p.m. was there before she felt ready. She told her husband she needed to check on a dog at work and climbed in her truck. She drove to the office and switched vehicles, using the unmemorable clinic car kept only for deliveries and errands.

The drive felt like forever. Twice catching herself over eighty, she backed it down and set the cruise control. Her heart thundered in her chest. Involuntarily she reached out and touched her handbag; everything she needed nestled inside. She pulled into the Park N Ride at 8:45. Parking at the far end of the lot, she tried again, unsuccessfully, to calm herself down. Her palms were damp, and her breathing labored. Ernie pulled up in his patrol cruiser ten minutes later, and Tanya got out of her car.

She opened his heavy passenger side door and got in. Without preamble she demanded, "Head south on 63. We are going to Killian."

Faster than a blink, Ernie's service weapon was jammed into the soft flesh under her chin. "Shut your fucking mouth, cunt. You're not running any fucking show now, bitch. I'm in charge. You do what I say, you fucking whore."

Tanya could smell the liquid courage on his breath. She prayed it was just a little to keep him calm and not enough to make him reckless.

Internally, her bowels turned to liquid; externally, she managed to appear calm. She had planned for this and waited for him to relax. With the gun rammed hard against her jawbone, she turned her head slowly to look him in the eyes. Picturing Samuel, Sandra's unborn baby, his tiny lifeless body in a box, Tanya allowed the rage to bubble up in her. "Oh, Ernest," she said, her voice dripping with saccharine, "you really are a special kind of stupid."

He forced the barrel harder into the thin tissue, driving her head back.

The pain bloomed, but again she remained calm. "You can beat me. You can even kill me. But just know I put details in place for that. All the proof anyone needs to put you away forever will be brought to light. So, before you pull the trigger or cause more bruises on me, you might want to think about that."

Slowly he dragged his gun from her, deliberately raking the tip of her chin with the front sight. She felt the skin break and knew she was bleeding but refused to yelp or reach up to dab it. "Okay, so head south on 63." With that, she settled into the seat, looking directly out the front window.

Fuming, Ernie put the cruiser in Drive and pulled out of the lot. As they drove in silence, Tanya considered what he was thinking. After witnessing the aftermath of what he'd done to someone he 'loved,' she could graphically imagine what he would do to her given the chance. Raping, beating, and mutilating her dead body would be the nice things he would do. There would be things that would leave veteran officers in tears if they ever discovered her body. Her remains would be top-level docuseries fodder for the next millennium. She knew if anything went wrong, he would be ready, and she would die a gruesome death.

As the road hummed under them, Tanya started to second guess her choices. Her hand touched the bag, aching for a bit of reassurance. She wanted to feel fearless, but her stampeding heart said otherwise. The succinylcholine in her bag was the ticket to grace. As a veterinarian, she knew she was lucky to get her hands on a highly controlled, powerful paralytic. But with it were a few unknowns tonight. She'd had to guess on Ernie's weight, and the drug was best administered intravenously. However, knowing Ernie wasn't about to hold still for an IV, she was going to have to give it intramuscular. That left a lot of room for mistakes, and any mistakes left room for Ernie to turn the tables.

Ernie turned the car into the parking lot. Tanya's mouth went dry. She peeled her tongue off the roof of her mouth. "Park by the boat ramp."

Her fingers found the syringe in her bag, and she flicked the safety cap off. The instant Ernie's hand came off the wheel to put the car in Park, she reacted. The needle sank into the thin soft flesh of his neck, where no clothing would interfere with her jab, and she plunged the syringe down with all her force. But unlike the movies, succinylcholine is *not* instantaneous. He reacted to her movement more than the injection, his right arm flying up toward her face. His balled fist made hard contact, bringing stars to her eyes. Ernie growled and faced her; his left hand found a fistful of her sweaty hair. His fingers entwined in her locks, and she felt the deep tear begin at her scalp. But thankfully the drug was doing its job; his fingers involuntarily relaxed before he could rip her roots out.

Tanya knew she only had a scarce few minutes until the effects began to wear off. She gathered her belongings, pulled a wipe from her bag, cleaned all the surfaces she'd touched, and climbed out of the car. Quickly, around the driver's side, she ensured his foot was on the floorboard and not resting on the brake pedal. He would wake up, groggy, confused. Her research informed her that everything would be dark and his body heavy.

"Hello, Ernest," she purred like a kitten in his ear, hoping it would have the sweet and seductive feel like warm golden amber. "Wakey wakey." She was leaning in the driver's side window. She took a moment to truly wonder at the horrors that would befall her if this plan didn't work. The images of what Ernie might fantasize about were terrifying. She saw his eyelids flutter.

"Ah, there we go." She moved her head in front of his field of vision. "We've had quite a little party, Ernest. I'm glad you are coming back to us now." She raked her fingernail down his cheek. Tanya knew he could feel the pain burning down his skin but could do nothing to stop her. "Are your arms a little heavy? Oh, that's too bad." With that she slapped him hard, leaving her handprint on his slack cheek.

"Still confused? Poor Ernest. Never thought you could feel so helpless, right?" She controlled her urge to release her long-harbored rage out on him. Her desire to simply scratch his eyes out was immense. However, she wanted her plan to play out like she'd envisioned. Her back teeth ground together as she thought of Samuel and his tiny body lying in the casket.

She thought of Sandra and the sunny days at the park, pushing her son on a swing, that would never be. Tears pricked the back of her eyes, she shook them away, forcing herself to stay in the present moment.

Knowing the paralytic wouldn't last too much longer, she moved closer to him, nearly nose to nose. "So, Ernest, I know big words confuse you, so I will try to keep it all very simple." She smiled, Cheshire-wide. "You're going to die." Muscle use or not, she saw the fear sweep behind his eyes. "Unfortunately for me, it won't hurt nearly as bad as the pain Sandra felt when you beat her child out of her body."

Ernie made a faint noise. Tanya studied him closely. "Oh, I have less time than I thought." Laughing slightly, she shared, "I had to guess on your weight, and then subtract the weight of a normal man's brain and penis, since yours are so small. Did you notice where we are, Ernest? No? We're on the edge of Lake Maurepas." She fanned her hand in front of his eyes like Vanna White. "I'm going to put the car into Drive, and you're going to roll into the water. I mean, let's be honest, it would've been fun just to let the LSU football team beat the shit out of you. But, oh, Ernest, you're so vindictive. I couldn't leave you around for retaliation. So your cruiser and body will both be missing."

Ernie's shoulder twitched.

Tanya moved close enough for their noses to touch. "Tick tock. Time's up. I just want to make sure that you remember this face as you die so I can keep haunting you in Hell."

She bent down and pulled something out of her bag, keeping it just below Ernie's eye level. "Any last words?" Her loud laugh silenced the buzzing cicadas for a moment. "Oh, right. You can't talk. Well, we only have a few minutes left for this."

Slowly she moved her hand deliberately into his field of view. "I only have to take care of one more detail." In front of his eyes, she held up a rusty old pair of tin snips. "I didn't have a chance to sharpen them. But I'm not sure there's much to cut through."

As she reached inside the car with her left hand and began to unzip his fly, Tanya could see the panic truly set over him. The paralytic was moving quickly through his system. His shoulder twitched again.

"Oh, Ernest, do hold still."

She knew he could feel her warm fingers wrap around his cock. It wouldn't surprise her to know he had had this fantasy before. However, gleefully, she knew it wouldn't have included rusting tin snips.

Tanya looked down and laughed again. "No wonder you were such a bully— overcompensation. Ready?"

Forcing movement, with all his might, he made a low groan. She savored the moment, moving slowly, dragging the tin snips down his chest to his crotch.

Indeed dull, it took three attempts to cut through the flaccid flesh. Ernie moaned again and moved his left knee slightly.

Turning her head, she smacked him in the forehead with his own penis, blood speckling his cheek. "Ernest, you can scream all you want. You know why?" Then she quoted him. "'The only one to hear you is the bayou, and the bayou never speaks.'"

She waggled his decapitated member in front of his face. Tears pooled in his eyes before overflowing the lower lids. "What should I do with this?" She paused in consideration. "It would certainly feel like poetic justice to shove it up your own ass." She bounced it off his forehead again, its ragged edge still dripping blood. "I think I have a better idea."

Pinching his cheeks, she forced his mouth open and wedged it headfirst down his throat.

Ernie's right arm jerked. Tanya knew she was out of time. She reached across him and put the car into gear. The car started to roll forward. Pulling her head out of the car, Ernie's right hand reached for hers. He made contact. Tanya's heart bucked and slammed against her ribs. But he lacked the strength to hold on and his arm limply fell back into his lap. Tanya laughed one more time. "If it was me, I would've used my last-ditch effort to take my dick out of my mouth. But I guess you like it there. Good thing, since you'll be spending eternity like that—giving yourself an unsatisfactory blowjob."

She stood there and watched the car drive into the water. She stood there while it sank. She stood there as the bubbles rose to the surface. She stood there as the water returned to its smooth, reflective state. She stood there and watched the moon rise. She stood there until she felt the evil was gone.

Then she turned and walked away, never once looking back.

The Wizard of the Birds
Steven Morschauser

A very old wizard traced the edge of a small lake with his footsteps. He looked across the water and wanted to walk down into it, down to the deepest part, and simply stay there. It seemed like it would be a quiet place to be. He could sit there for a time and enjoy the silence, without the noisy traffic of the city streets to distract him. There might even be a fish he could chat with if one decided he was worth the time. The water out in the middle looked warm and inviting. It was a nice little lake in a nice little park.

Except for the garbage. The old wizard shook his head a few times over the trash bobbing up and down in the weeds at the edge of the water. It saddened him to see the beauty of the world taken for granted. Lose sight of the grandeur and it can all be taken away in the blink of an eye. He doubted whether anyone even saw the trash anymore. It simply became part of the landscape, as ubiquitous as the water and trees themselves, accepted and invisible.

The old wizard decided that it was time to sit down before he depressed himself even more. He turned away from the water and looked for a bench. His bench, the one with the comfortable seat, perfectly angled for an aging butt in search of a place to rest. It was positioned between two very old oak trees and adorned with a plaque bearing the name of the people who donated it. He didn't know who Guy and Amy Knight were, but he and his rear end would be eternally grateful to them for their generosity. They had provided the perfect bench in the perfect location, with a good view of the lake, and in the path of an almost constant gentle breeze. Even the garbage that lingered at the edge of the water was hidden by a row of well-placed boulders. There was, in his opinion, only one thing missing today: birds. It was too quiet.

He looked up at the oaks. There wasn't a bird in sight. He loved the free symphony that nature placed in the trees. It calmed him and took his mind away from the dark thoughts that intruded into his mind, thoughts of age, and a death that was never to come. He closed his eyes, cupped his hands together, and recalled the words. A gentle movement against the palms of his hands brought a smile. A small red bird poked his head up from between his fingers and looked around before wiggling free and flying off toward the trees. It began to sing, but it wasn't enough. Just as a flute by itself isn't an orchestra, so a single bird isn't enough to fill the branches with music.

Bird after bird began flying from his hands, each adding its unique voice to the performance in the trees. The old wizard had forgotten just how many types of birds there were in the history of the world, and he never made the same one twice. He giggled inside at the thought of some poor ornithologist wondering just how an extinct species of bird had appeared one day in a city park, happily singing on a tree branch. The wizard had ended up in the park, too, after thousands of years wandering the Earth and was almost extinct himself, the last of his kind, so why not?

Soon the trees were filled with all types of birds, each singing its own song. All were somehow in tune with each other, bringing to life a musical splendor that for a moment let him forget about time itself, something that rarely happened.

"What are you doing?"

The old wizard jumped. He looked up to see a little boy standing before him and blew away a feather that was gently hovering in front of his face. "What?"

"What are you doing?" The boy was pointing at a small white bird still in the wizard's hands.

"Oh!" the old wizard replied, looking down at the little creature. "This? It's quite simple." He let the bird go. "I'm making musicians." He cupped his hands together again and produced another. Its brownish head poked out from a gap between his thumbs and looked around, wondering just how and why it had gotten there. The wizard tossed the bird up from his lap. The boy backed up a step while the bird madly flapped its wings, trying to get a bite of the air, before flying off to join its newly created friends.

"You can do magic!" The little boy's eyes became really big and a smile widened across his face.

The old wizard motioned for the boy to come closer. "Watch carefully." The boy leaned in and locked his eyes on the old man's hands. He'd seen a lot of little boys over the centuries. Tall, short, handsome, ugly, smart, and stupid. Nothing about them ever seemed to change very much. The years rage on, but little boys are as permanent as the moon. This one, however, was different, exposing a level of curiosity he had seldom witnessed. It was the eyes. They had stopped blinking and fixed on every small movement made by the wizard's wrinkled old hands. They were eyes keen on knowing.

"Do it again!"

The old wizard looked up at the boy. "You can't rush such things young man," he replied, just a little bit disappointed in the boy's impatience. Oh, well, he thought, no one is perfect. He brought his hands together once again, closed his eyes, and gently opened them again. A small black bird popped out and looked around, before wiggling its way out and flying off into the sky. The child tracked it until it vanished in the branches of a tree.

"Wow!" he said. "That's even better than on TV!"

The old wizard looked up at the boy. "Real magic is far better than any of that stuff on TV or a circus. They do it for the money or to impress you. Actual magic teaches you something, makes a mark on the world."

The boy looked insulted. "They do real magic, I've seen it. One guy on YouTube made the Statue of Liberty disappear."

The old wizard rolled his eyes. "All fake, just simple tricks to get you to look the wrong way while they make a fool of you."

"I can do magic!" The boy yelled out, pointing at his chest.

"Really?" The old wizard pretended to be amazed, opened his eyes wide, and slapped his legs with both hands. "Most boys your age can't even ride a bicycle, but you do magic, huh?"

"My uncle got me a magic kit for my birthday. I can make coins appear from your ear!"

"Show me."

The boy took a step back and looked at his shoes. "I don't have a coin."

The old wizard frowned. "Oh, that is a disappointment. What coin do you need?"

"A penny. I left all my money at home."

"Check your pocket."

Something moved in the boy's left pocket. He quickly shoved a hand in there and froze. Slowly, he pulled his hand out. Wedged between this finger and thumb were two brand-new and very shiny pennies. "Wow!" Letting the coins fall into the palms of his hands, he said, "How did you do that? That's not in my magic kit at home!"

The old wizard smiled, accenting the deep wrinkles around his ancient eyes. "Lots of practice and a lot of lost coins." He leaned in on the boy. "Now, let's see that magic trick."

The boy turned away and the wizard could hear the coins clinking around. "Just a second!" After a few seconds, the boy spun around, his hands behind his back. "You gotta close your eyes for it to work."

The old wizard nodded matter-of-factly. "Yes, of course." He closed his eyes and grinned slightly. He could sense the child reaching up behind his left ear.

The boy was up on his toes as he tried to reach up to the old man. He yelled, "Presto!" and yanked his hand back. "See, I got a penny out of your ear!"

The old wizard opened his eyes and smiled. "Are you sure of that? Because I don't think so."

"Sure, I did!" The boy held out his hand and squealed a bit when he saw the brand-new quarter sitting in the palm of his hand. "How did you do that?"

"Wasn't me. This is your magic trick. Of course, if you don't want the quarter, I could always use one."

The boy quickly shoved the coin into his pocket. "Nope."

The old wizard smiled at the young boy for a few seconds before looking up into the trees. Still not enough music, he thought.

"What is your favorite color?" he asked the boy

"Purple, like my shoes."

The old wizard glanced down. The boy's shoes were indeed purple, with a few vanilla ice cream stains added for extra artistic flair. "I can work with that." He cupped his hands together, closed his eyes, and said the ancient words again. He could feel the flutter of life against his palms, a heartbeat appearing from nowhere. "Look."

The boy looked down and smiled the biggest smile his face would allow. Sitting in the wizard's hands was a handsome bird, purple from head to tail feathers, stained on the neck and left wing with splotches the perfect shade of melted vanilla ice cream. The new bird hiccupped and flew off into the waiting branches of an elm tree.

The boy returned his gaze to the old wizard, his smile morphing into curiosity. "What was that you whispered?"

"What?" The wizard tried to remember. Mumbling an incantation out loud was the mark of an amateur in his opinion. Just think and make it happen. The best never had to do that. He used to be the best.

"You said something before the bird was in your hand." The boy scowled a bit. "'Wazeria' something."

Wazeria Ses ne Puleia. An old phrase from a very old, and very dead, language. *The Young Bird Flies.* Besides himself, that boy may have been the first human being to have heard it spoken out loud in over five thousand years. The wizard looked over at the boy. "That wasn't meant for you to hear."

"Say it again," the boy begged.

"No."

"I want to see more birds! I want to make a bird!" he pleaded.

The old wizard felt hot with anger, more toward himself than the boy, and turned away on the park bench. "The show is over. Go find your mother."

The old wizard started to get up, his back screaming with the pain of having sat too long. Gravity was no longer a friend and standing up took him far longer than it used to.

"Don't go!" The boy did his best to block him from leaving. "Wazeria! Wazeria!" The boy tried to toss birds from his hands, but nothing emerged. "Wazeria!" A small black feather blew out of the boy's cupped hands and hung in the air before floating off into the bushes. They both looked as stunned as if lightning had just struck.

"Wait … what?" The old wizard sat back down, his back grateful for the change of plans. "Say that again."

"Say what again?" The boy backed up, his eyes darting in every direction but at the old man. He was still looking at his hands, just as confused as any kid who had just produced a bird feather from nothing. The wizard couldn't honestly tell if the boy was going to cry or wet himself with excitement.

"It's okay," the old wizard said with his calmest voice. "You didn't do anything wrong." He pointed at the bench. "Sit down and I'll teach you some magic, okay? I've got the feeling you'll be a great learner."

A small smile formed on the boy's face. "You'll show me?"

"It's been a long time since I've had a student, but yes, I'll teach you. But only how to make birds. We can't have you making dragons or earthquakes now, can we?"

The boy sat down on the bench and looked at the old man with an intensity that the old wizard had not seen for a very long time. He had several students over the centuries, most of which weren't any good or wanted to learn for all the wrong reasons, but this one seemed to have a genuine love for the magic itself. If it had been a different era, he would have shown the child everything, but the time for wizards and magic had passed. Mankind made their own magic these days and he was no longer necessary. But perhaps, just one more time.

"Wazeria … Ses … ne … Puleia," the old wizard said slowly. "Say it just that way, but not too fast. It won't work if you say it slowly like that. We don't want to make a bird just yet. You have to learn the words themselves first. Understand?"

The boy nodded. He closed his eyes and concentrated on the words, leaving his hands on his lap. "Wazeria … Ses … ne … um …"

"Puleia," finished the old wizard.

"Wazeria … Ses … ne … Puleia."

"Very good, well done."

The boy smiled, revealing all the front teeth that had yet to fully come in.

The old wizard smiled back. "You'll be a wiz … um, a magician in no time." He sat up straight on the bench. "Okay, now, we look at each other's eyes and say it at the same time, a little quicker this time, all right? Think about a bird when you say it."

"What kind of bird? Like a turkey?"

"No, not like a turkey. That would be like putting bagpipes in a Mozart symphony. Think of something smaller, something that makes beautiful music." The old wizard gently lifted the boy's small hands. "Something that will fit right there and can sing in the trees," he said, pointing to the row of oaks behind the bench. The old wizard could tell that the boy was disappointed, but a turkey would have been a bad idea indeed. "Tell you what, I'll think of the bird, you just concentrate on the words. Deal?"

The boy nodded and brought his hands together and they both very carefully said the words. The old wizard made eye contact with the boy and nodded. The boy looked down at his hands. A small yellow bird with blue wings wiggled its way out of his fingers and looked up.

"Be gentle, now," the old wizard said. "He's a little confused. Give him a few seconds before you open your hands up."

The boy looked at the bird, smiled, and opened his hands. The bird hopped up onto the old wizard's shoulders. They exchanged a look and the bird flew off toward the lake where it began circling the water.

"Wow! Let's do that again!" the boy exclaimed, already cupping his hands for another bird. The smile disappeared when he looked up at the old man, who now looked much older, somehow a little bit smaller, like a plant that hadn't seen the sun in too long.

The old wizard felt his body becoming very heavy, as if the weight of time, held at bay for so very long, found a way in through a crack in the wall. The feeling of weariness was almost welcome, like those moments when sleep arrived at the end of a long day. "Not now, my little friend. I'm suddenly very tired. I may have done too much today. I just need to rest."

The boy's shoulders drooped. Old people were always tired. He wanted to learn more magic. Birds were fun things to make, but if he could learn to make pizza and ice cream, everyone would want to be his best friend.

"Jason!" It was his mother. "Time to go home and have your lunch!"

The boy paused, hoping that the old man would change his mind, but he watched as the old man's eyes slowly closed and he fell asleep on the park bench. He stood up and slowly walked back to his mother, trying to make birds along the way.

After the boy left, the old wizard's body began to blow away bit by bit, like a sand sculpture eroding in the wind. The breeze caught the particles and gently carried them into the air, taking them high over the lake. The birds they had made sang beautifully, filling the park with the most magnificent sounds that nature could provide. The yellow one with the blue wings, however, remained silent, slowly circling through the veil of dust that was hovering over the warm lake water, enjoying the breeze that lifted its wings, and the freedom that came with flight. It headed for the trees, taking a moment to watch a young boy walking with his mother along the edge of the lake, and joined the other birds in the trees. The new bird began to sing, quickly forgetting the magical life that it had lived for so very long.

Deliverance Dane, the Witch
Maria Delaney

"Mom, did you see my yellow rain jacket?"

"The one that makes you look like the Gordon's fisherman?"

"Yeah."

"In the hall closet. Where are you off to?"

"Salem, to study the witch trials for Professor Screwball's class."

"Is Screwball his real name?"

I shoot an expression that validates her foolishness.

"Right, sorry. You know, I believe one of Grandma's relatives on Daddy's side was from that time period."

"Great, Mom, now ya tell me we have freaks in our bloodline."

"You want me to get a hold of Grandma and ask?"

"Gonna be late. Still hafta to pick up Jo-Jo." I throw a kiss, tuck the raincoat under my arm, and bounce out the door.

Historian Waite Winthrop, our school hired to lead the tour, is a theatrical fool. Jo-Jo makes goofball expressions as he speaks. Short spurts of laughter jump from me every time she contorts her face. The more I muffle the sound, the worse it explodes.

Waite's voice booms over, splattering rain pelting my slicker. "On top of that hill is the ancestral burial grounds where many of the witches' bodies rest."

Jo-jo mouths the word *spooky*.

I peer to where he points. Dark overcast gives the graves an eerie reveal. Overgrown with weeds, thin white wafers sit nestled on a hilltop. The vision resembles crooked teeth shifted in an old man's mouth.

"Over time, epitaphs have eroded, leaving only impressions etched against fragile stone." He acts out every word with flailing hands and almost pirouetting movements. "Our historical society has every name tucked away safe in their records."

I block him out momentarily, imagining flowers haven't graced those graves in many lifetimes nor have tears fallen from brokenhearted eyes.

He swings his arm in the opposite direction and points to the skeleton of a barn that must have burned centuries ago. Charred timbers fight to support its crumbling roof.

"July nineteenth, sixteen ninety-two, the townspeople of Salem hung a witch they believed to be possessed with evil, from those rafters within that barn." He pauses for effect. "Then they burned her body!"

Jo-Jo imitates hanging from an imaginary rope, then convulses like a slab of bacon in a frying pan. "This guy'z an idiot." She belly laughs. "What's he thinkin'? He's starring in some Stephen King movie?"

"*Shh*, Jo! He'll hear you."

Some wise guy yells, "Was the bitch guilty?"

Giggles sprinkle.

An over-animated student beside us whispers, "I've studied the trials. Waitstill Winthrop was the name of the Massachusetts Superior Court Judge during the witch trials." The excited groupie quivers both fists and prances on her tiptoes. "The tour guide must be one of his descendants."

Jo-Jo quivers her fists in mock unison, then finishes with a yawn, fanning her hand before her mouth.

Recovering from the rude ball-buster, Waite begins again. "Generations believe her angry, troubled ghost still haunts the structure's remains to this day. Her name was …"

Without warning, I'm lightheaded. Gradual and steady, Waite's exaggerated voice morphs into a sound only heard when deep underwater until it fades, and a soft feminine tone replaces it to finish his sentence. "Her name was … Deliverance Dane."

My heart races, causing my body to break into a sweat. Fear and impending doom fill my being. Scenery blooms into period time. I'm no longer with the tour group. Instead, I experience an angry mob with lit torches on a hunt. A woman fleeing for her life materializes in the darkness. I sense her panic. She races toward where the graveyard rests.

There is a heaviness in my chest, as if I've been running for some time. I observe as she tries to hurry to the top of the hill toward the wooded area in terror. She's tired, and they're gaining on her. The dress catches beneath her feet, and she stumbles.

Townspeople close in, chanting, "Witch, witch, witch …."

Trapped, she faces her accusers, pleading, "I'm innocent!"

A man of official prominence strides through the heart of the mob.

People shuffle aside, allowing him access.

He glares with contempt, curling his lip like an angry dog, and spits on the woman before addressing her. "Deliverance Dane, you are being put to death for practicing witchcraft. Your wicked soul will hang."

The crowd cheers. "Hang her, Judge Winthrop!"

Deliverance struggles but soon cedes to their grip.

Two men drag her through the dirt and into the barn. One man throws the rope over the rafters. The other fasten the opposite end around Deliverance's neck. The noose is coarse against her skin. They stiffen the knot too tight, and it constricts her breath.

The crowd goes into a frenzy. "Witch! Witch! Witch!"

Together they hoist her into the air.

Deliverance twists and contorts from her own weight. She scratches at her throat till it bleeds before surrendering. Accepting fate, life leaves her body, and the corpse swings from the rafter in an unnatural state; a vacant stare peers onto the crowd.

To the townspeople's horror, the hanging body ignites into flames, engulfing the barn. Spectators scream and struggle to flee. A handful fail to escape and perish. An evil, cackling laughter echoes.

Jo-Jo nudges me. "Hayden, you okay? You're sweating like a pig. What's wrong with you?"

"I'm fine."

Mom texts me at that moment: *Grandma says a great, great-aunt named Deliverance Dane was convicted of witchcraft. So exciting! See if you can find her grave. Take a pic!*

Better late than never, Mom.

Waite's voice comes back into play. "Over here, we have the Witch Museum."

I wipe sweat from my brow and follow the tour group to the next location.

Waite is working the counter when I arrive at the historical society that hot July afternoon. He shuffles through historical files and recovers Deliverance Dane's gravesite. "Do you need assistance in finding the location?"

"Nope. I know exactly where it is."

I climb the hill to the ancestral burial ground and place a bouquet of red roses in front of Deliverance Dane's weather-worn stone. "You were the real deal, Aunty Deliverance, weren't you? Guilty as charged."

A warm breeze carries the sweet scent of goldenrod and the maddening cackle of a tickled, old witch.

Please Don't Kill Me
Rayona Lovely Wilson

The front wheel of my skateboard seeps into a crack, jerking to a stop. I hop off to keep from falling, but as soon as my foot slams against the ground, I stumble.

"Fuck …" My arms fly widely, but I can't catch myself. My body catapults toward a wall, and the world goes black.

"Hey, hey, are you all right? Oh shit. Hey, look at me …"

I force my eyes open and struggle to focus on the blurry figure over me. As much as I want to get up, I can't. My head is pounding, and my knee and shoulder throbs.

I can't be hurt right now.

"Well, you're not dead. Want me to call an ambulance? You're bleeding … bleeding … bleeding." Her voice echoes painfully in my head.

"Uh-no." I touch my head and wince at the sting. I close my eyes and take a deep breath. "I'm 'aight."

Or I will be. I've fallen off my board several times, and I've always been okay. This is nothing new. I don't need an ambulance. I'm fine, I think.

"You hit the wall pretty hard. I seriously thought you were dead over here," she tells me.

"I'm good." I look up, and there are still two of her. Damn. "I'll be okay."

"I hope so. You been out for about a minute. I personally think you should go see a doctor since you passed out. Might have a concussion, or worse."

"Yeah, I'm good." I push myself up, and everything around me spins. I close my eyes to make the dizziness stop. I move my arm, trying to relax the muscle, and there's a pop in my shoulder. "Fuck. Fuck. Fuck." The pain is excruciating. I shouldn't have moved. I let myself fall back against the ground, holding my arm, hoping the pain stops.

"What happened? Are you all right? What's going on?"

"N–nothing. I'm good. I'm good." I push on my shoulder to stop the pain, but it only makes it worse. "Shit. I'm good. I'm—" I inhale sharply. I don't want to cry in front of her, but my body has never felt this bad.

"I live upstairs. If you want me to help you get cleaned up, I can." She touches my head, and I wince. "Oops, sorry." She lets out a small giggle, and I smile. She's cute.

I open my eyes and stare at the sky, massaging my shoulder. "Thanks."

She holds out her hand and finally comes into focus. Her eyes are painted in red eyeshadow, and her lashes are long and black, definitely bringing out the softness in her brown eyes. Her lips are full, coated in extra gloss. *Damn. She's hella pretty.* Her hair falls over her shoulders and some is pulled up into a bun.

"Come on."

It's more of an order than a suggestion, so I grab her hand, and she slowly pulls me to my feet.

She's taller than me, not by much but I have to look up at her, and she smiles.

"Don't move too fast, 'kay?"

"Uh-huh. Yeah." She still has a hold of my hand, and I lock eyes with her. I should look away, but I can't.

"You good?"

"I think so. I–I need to get my board." I take a step, but when I put weight on my right foot, pain shoots through my ankle. "Fuck!"

"I'll get it," she says, going toward the street.

"Th–thanks."

The woman places her hand on my shoulder and leads me toward the tall building I crashed into.

"Wait, you're not like a killer or something, are you?" I don't know why the words come out of my mouth, but I smack myself in the head from embarrassment and instantly regret it. "Shit. That was stupid."

My head throbs, and I stop walking and lean against my board. My hand is covered in blood. Maybe I *do* need a doctor.

"Yeah, it was. I promise I'm not a killer or anything. Just want to make sure you're good." Her voice is so soft I hardly hear her, but I nod. "So, you want to come up or …"

"Yeah. Sure," I say.

She pulls the door open, and we both step in. The warmth engulfs me, and it feels nice.

"I'm on the fourth floor. The stairwell is this way, but you might need to take the elevator." She leads the way down a long hall, and I trail behind her.

"You walk up four flights of steps every day?" I stop and stare at her.

"Yep. It's great exercise." She's matter-of-fact as she looks at me.

"'Aight. I'll try to keep up." As she turns around, I find myself watching her. She's got a nice figure; her long legs are tightly wrapped in her jeans.

"Shit. Yeah, you definitely can't take the stairs."

Suddenly everything starts spinning, and I lean against the wall in front of the elevator. I need to sit down.

"I'm fast. I'll meet you up there …" She pulls the door to the stairwell, only it doesn't budge. "Shit." She yanks it again, but it still doesn't move. "Oh, my God." She doesn't stop pulling, as if she keeps yanking, it'll magically open.

"There's a note," I tell her, pointing at the door, and she stops.

"Notice. Stairwell closed for maintenance. Please use the elevator. What the fuck? What the fuck?" Her voice goes from soft to high, and I can't help but watch as her hand falls from the door handle.

"You okay?" My stomach quivers, and my head throbs more than before. *Maybe I should go to the hospital.*

"I … How are the stairs not accessible? Normally it's the elevator. Why would the stairs be closed? This is stupid. What if there's a fire?" She runs her hand through her hair and lets her head fall against the door. "Shit."

"I'll take that as a *no*. Do you want to talk about it?" I open one eye and peek at her. "I've been told I'm a great listener." As bad as my head hurts, I'd still like to make sure she's all right, since she helped me.

"I always take the stairs, but now they want me to use the elevator." She touches her chest before letting out a long breath.

"Are you afraid or something? 'Cause it might be faster. It definitely cuts your time in half."

She glares at me, and I almost laugh, because she's cute when she's mad.

"Do I look like I want to be dangling in the air in a tiny box like that? What happens if we fall four stories? We die." She rubs her temples, and the more I watch her, the more I realize it's more serious than being scared.

"No, but if it makes you feel any better, I'll hold your hand."

"Unfortunately, that doesn't make me feel any better." She takes a deep breath in and holds it. Even through the dark brown of her skin, her cheeks turn a hint of pink.

"You should probably breathe." Now that the dizziness has subsided, I push myself off the wall and step toward her. "Hey, it's okay. You're okay."

I touch her arm, and she finally releases the breath she was holding and looks at me. Her eyes glisten with tears, and her lower lip quivers. Shit. *She's going to cry.*

I hate when people cry.

"Why don't we sit down and relax?"

I slide down to the floor and pull one knee up to my chest so I can rest my head on it.

"I'm sorry. I'm being selfish. You probably need ice or something for your head. Okay. You know what? It's probably fine. It's just an elevator. Loads of people ride elevators every day, and they're all right. I'll be fine. Come on."

I don't want to get up because my ankle hurts too bad. I close my eyes; defeat washes over me. I have a competition in two days, hoping to qualify for the X-Games. There's no way I'll be able to get in with a messed-up ankle, a hurt shoulder, and possibly a concussion. This is my chance to achieve my dreams, and I had to fall off my board.

"Hey." Her hand rests on my shoulder, and I open my eyes. "You might need to go to the hospital. What are you feeling? Lightheaded? Nauseous? Like you can't stay awake?"

"You're really pretty." I can't stop the words from escaping.

"You're funny. Come on. Let's go so I can get you some ice."

We stand in front of the elevator, but she doesn't push the button. I think about doing it for her, but she's blocking my way. She wipes her hands on her shirt, then tightens her fingers around her bag. Slowly, she reaches for the button, letting out a long breath. "Shit."

"It's okay," I whisper, and she finally pushes the button, and the light pops on.

"Yeah. Thanks." She steps back, and we wait in silence. *Why would she live on the fourth floor if she can't get in the elevator? I don't get it.*

The doors fly open, and she jumps. I don't hesitate to step inside, but she stands there, staring at the floor.

As the doors start to close, I stick my arm between them to make them reopen.

"Take a deep breath and step in. You'll be okay," I tell her.

"I can't. I can't." She wipes her forehead and shakes her head.

"You can." It is small in here, now that I think about it. "Besides, I'm right …" Everything in front of me starts to blur again, and I know I'm falling, but I can't stop myself.

"Woah. Hey, are you all right?" She's shaking me, and I force myself to nod. "Are you sure? I think you need to go to the hospital."

"Yeah. Yeah." I open my eyes to see hers wide with fear. "I'm good. My head is being weird, I guess."

The elevator doors close, and the woman spins around, fast. "Oh God. I need to get out of here."

She stands up and rushes to push the button, but the elevator moves. "No!" she screams, pushing the button over and over and over. "I need … I need to get out. I need to get out."

Ignoring the dizziness, I push myself up and hold onto the bar. "Deep breath. We'll be out of here in no time." I hold my head to try to stop the pain.

"No. No. I'm going to die in here. I can't breathe!" She clutches her chest, sucking in shaky breaths. "I can't—I can't br–breathe. I c–can't c–can't bre–bre …" Her eyes spill with tears that fall down her face.

"We're not gonna die. I promise. I promise," I assure her, grabbing her hand. "Breathe. You're okay." I need her to breathe and calm down. "Breathe." I inhale, hoping she follows, and she does, but she doesn't let it out. "Exhale," I tell her, and she finally does. "Listen, everything's okay. We're on the third floor. One more. Any second, we'll be out of here."

The lights flicker, and I'm jolted into her, and we both slam into the elevator door as the elevator comes to an abrupt stop.

"Oh my God. Oh my God." Her voice is high-pitched, and she grabs onto me so tight I think she's going to break my fingers. "We're gonna die. We're gonna die!" she screams in my ear, making my head hurt more.

"We're not gonna die. We can push the emergency button and call out." I push the button, waiting for it to ring or something, but nothing happens. Shit. I push it again and wait, but there's nothing.

"I don't want to die in here. I–I don't–don't want to die in here. The–the walls." She sinks to the floor and sobs. "The walls …"

"We're not gonna die. I'll call for help, and we'll get out of here." My stomach twists at the thought of us suspended in midair by just a few cables. I promised her nothing bad would happen, and now we're stuck.

"Call nine-one-one. Pl–please. Please. I–I need–need to get–get out."

I pull my phone from my pocket and swipe it on.

No bars.

Fuck. I don't want to tell her that and freak her out more.

I take a deep breath and sit down beside her, grabbing her hand. "Hey, listen … There's no cell service in the elevator."

"What?" she shrieks. "What? Shit! I'm going to–to die. I'm going to fuckin' die in here!"

"No. No. You're not. There's probably maintenance people on the way right now." I don't know what else to say to help her relax. "I need you to do me a favor and take a deep breath and let it out cause you gotta calm down. You're gonna hyperventilate."

She closes her eyes and tries to slow her breathing, but it's not working.

"I just realized, I don't know–I don't know your name."

"My–my name …"

"Yeah. What's your name? I'm Orion," I tell her, hoping to distract her. It always works for me when I'm nervous or scared about something.

Silence falls between us, except for her breathing, which is short and labored. I stare at my phone, hoping there's at least one bar, but nothing.

"Aaliyah. My–my n–name's Aaliyah." Her voice is a whisper, and she doesn't move, but I'm glad she said something.

"Nice to meet you, Aaliyah. Do you mind if I ask you how old you are?" My mama always said, 'Boy, don't you dare disrespect a woman by asking her age,' and I can hear her yelling at me right now.

Silence surrounds us as her chest rapidly rises and falls, and she's panting again.

"No. No. Aaliyah, why don't you tell me where your job is."

Silence.

"I'm hoping to make this qualifier for the X-Games. That's where I was coming from when I crashed. Where were you coming from?"

"Getting lunch."

"Lunch. That's awesome. What did you get?"

"I–I need to get out–out of here." Her breathing picks up again, and she still doesn't move. "My chest–it–it hurts."

"Okay, if you take deep breaths, I think you'll be okay. We'll get out of—" A sharp pain shoots through my head, and again everything disappears.

"Orion, boy, don't make me come in there and give you something to cry about," Mama yells. She's always yelling. I broke my board, and she said she's not buying me another one. "Be quiet in there."

She irritates me. She always says she's there for me, but when I need her the most, she can't help. I need a new skateboard because I want to go pro one day. I know I'm good.

"Wake up! Please … please."

I'm being shaken, so I open my eyes even though it hurts.

"I can't–I can't–you have to–to stay awake. Please stay awake," she cries.

"I'm s–sorry," I mutter, pressing against my head. I should call my mom, let her know I'm all right. It's been a while since I talked to her. "Ahh shit. Okay. I'm okay."

The elevator creaks and groans. As soon as I sit up, it gives a jolt, and we're being slammed into the wall. Aaliyah screams and wraps her arms around me.

"It's okay. It's okay." I wrap my arms around her and hold her against me. "I got you."

"I can't–I can't–I can't br–breathe. I can't." She doesn't let me go.

"Aaliyah. Aaliyah, you have to calm down. Hey …" She doesn't calm down. "Aaliyah?" I grab my phone and see one bar. "Aaliyah, I'ma try to call for help."

I need to get out of here, too.

"Nine-one-one, what's your emergency?"

"Yeah. Hi. I'm stuck in an elevator that I'm pretty sure is going to fall. It stopped, no buttons or anything work. Uh, it keeps jolting. It keeps, I think we're gonna fall."

"Sir, I can hardly hear you. Did you say you're stuck in an elevator?"

"Yes. We're stuck, and it might be broken."

"What's your address?"

"Aaliyah, what's your address?" I move her hair back to see her better, but her eyes are closed. "Shit. Aaliyah … I think she passed out. She was hyperventilating. Aaliyah?"

"Can you lay her on her back?"

"Nah, this thing's pretty small." Everything blurs, and I close my eyes. "My head is not … not okay. This girl needs to get off the … elevator. Buttons aren't working. Jolting …" I shake my head, causing more pain.

"What happened to your head? Were you injured?"

"Crashed on my board. I think I might need a doc–doctor. I fell … fell off my board, and m–my head is …"

"Sir, what side of town are you on?"

My phone beeps, and CALL FAILED pops up.

Damn. I let my head rest against Aaliyah's and close my eyes. She was right. We're gonna die.

⤔ ⟡ ⤓

"My phone's ringing," I mutter. My phone's ringing. My phone. I open my eyes and grab it, swiping to answer. "Hello?"

"Yes, this is Kelly, the nine-one-one dispatcher who answered your call. Are you still stuck in the elevator?"

"Oh shit. Yeah. Is–is somebody coming to help us?" I look at Aaliyah, still slumped against me, and shake her shoulder, hoping to wake her.

"If you can get an address, I can send help."

"Aaliyah, hey, wake up." I shake her again, and she mumbles something before looking up at me. "What's your address?"

"W—what?" She looks around, and panic rises in her eyes. "Oh God. Oh God. No. No."

"Aaliyah, hey listen, breathe. Breathe. I have nine-one-one on the line."

"Get me out. Get me out of here. Get me out!" When she moves, the elevator moves. "Help! Help! Please!"

"Aaliyah, look at me. Look. I need you to calm down, please. Breathe. They need your address so they can send help. Breathe. Breathe. Breathe." I grab her face and force her to look at me. "You have to calm down, and it'll be okay." I don't know how true it is, but if she doesn't calm down, we'll never make it out. "Take a breath in. Let it out."

She exhales, and I can't help but smile. "Okay, good. What's your address?"

My phone beeps like before, and the call drops. *Fuck. Fuck. Fuck.* I have to stay calm, for her.

"I—I'm going to—to die. I'm going to die. I can't—can't breathe. I can't."

"I know. I know. Listen to me. Do you have something with your address on it?"

She nods and clutches her chest. "Pl—please get ... I need to get out."

"I'm going to get you out of here. I just need your address."

"'Kay. Okay."

I wipe the tears from her face, and she nods and digs into her pocket. "Good. Good ..."

Blackness takes over, and everything is silent.

"Please. I think ... I think when he hit his head, he did ... did damage. He needs a doctor. Help us. We need help. I need to get out. We need to get out. I can't breathe. I don't want to die." She's panicking. I try to open my eyes, but they're so heavy. "I have ... have water. I think he's waking up."

"Are they coming?" I ask, rubbing my head. "Are they coming? Tell them we're in a … we're in a … um, we're in an elevator." I open my eyes and finally sit myself up. Aaliyah's on the phone; her makeup is running.

"Are they coming? Can you send them to help? We need help. The walls are getting smaller. AHHHH!"

The elevator groans in protest as it drops. I grab Aaliyah and hold her tight in case we crash to the bottom.

But it stops. I open my eyes, and it's completely dark. "We can't move. Aaliyah, don't move," I tell her. "Do not move."

Her body shakes in my arms, and I can hear the dispatcher on the phone from the opposite side of the elevator. I know if we move, there's a chance we'll fall more.

"I want my … my mom. I want my mom. I want to go home."

"Okay. Okay. Don't move. We can't move. Did you give them the address?"

She tightens her arms around me. "Yes."

"Okay. They'll be here soon. What did you get for lunch?"

"Tacos," she whispers. "'Cause it's Tuesday."

"I love tacos. It's my favorite food. I like chicken tacos. What kind did you get?"

"Chicken. I want to get–get out. Please."

"Listen to me, I don't want you to move. I know you're terrified, but help is coming, and I'll get you out of here. And when you do, I think maybe you should move somewhere on the first floor."

"I want to go home. I'm scared. I don't … don't like elevators. I don't … I didn't want to get in."

"So, you're afraid of elevators? That's okay. Most people are," I tell her.

"I don't like elevators or cars or airplanes or tunnels. I need to get out. I need to–to get out." She shifts to move, but I tighten my arms around her.

"Okay, no. No. Don't move. Aaliyah, listen, we can't move because the elevator isn't stable. Just sit with me. Let's talk. Why are you afraid of all those things?"

"I can't get in small … small places. They–they … I can't breathe in here. It's too small."

"I know. You were brave for coming in to help me. I bet after this you're not gonna be scared of shit after this. I–I can the timers gonna go off." My thoughts are fuzzy as my head grows tired. "My head is … I think my … they're gonna save you." I let my head fall back, wishing I was still at the skatepark, practicing, but I'm glad I met Aaliyah.

"Sh–should I get the phone?"

"No. It's not safe. I just … want to sleep for a little bit." I close my eyes. "My mom is outside. I just want to sleep …"

"No. No, don't go to sleep. You have to stay awake, please." Her voice is faint, but I lift my head to try to stay awake. "I'm gonna try to get the phone." She pushes herself up, and as much as I don't want her to move, I'd like to know how close help is.

"Slow. Move slow," I tell her, and she does.

The elevator creaks, and she pauses. "Okay. Okay." If it wasn't for the light being on the phone, I wouldn't let her try this.

"Careful. Careful." She has a hold of my hand, and once she grabs the phone, I slowly pull her back to me.

"Are they coming? Is help coming?" The phone is no longer connected, but at least they know where we are.

"It's okay. Hey, it's okay. They'll be here soon, and you'll get out of here."

"Yeah. Yeah. We'll get out of here." She lays her head against my hurt shoulder, and I close my eyes.

This shit hurts, bad. I can't remember the last time I fell off my board and was in this much pain.

"I hate being so scared. I hate it. I was locked in an elevator when I was twelve. I don't … I thought I was gonna die. I didn't get out for almost four hours cause nobody knew I was in there. It just stopped working. I need–I need to get out of here."

"I'm sorry. You must've been so scared."

"Yeah. I swore I'd never get in an elevator again, but it turned into so many other things. I've never been in an airplane. I can hardly get in a car. Small spaces terrify me. Like, it's hard to–to breathe and … I just want to get out. I just want to go home."

"I want to get you home. I promise I'll get you out … out of … of–shit."

"What? Are you okay?" She pushes herself up, and the elevator creaks. Again, we're falling, and she's screaming. I grab her and pull her back, holding her against me.

The elevator stops, and I take a deep breath. "Shit. Don't move. Listen to me, whatever you do, don't move."

"I'm sorry. I'm sorry. I'm sorry." She tucks her head into my side, and her arms are wrapped around me.

My phone rings, and I take it out of her hand and slide the green button.

"It's Kelly. Your call keeps dropping. I want you guys to know that help is on the way. They're about fifteen minutes out."

"I don't know how long this elevator is going to hold. It keeps falling. It keeps—"

Again, the elevator starts to slide, and Aaliyah screams. I close my eyes, expecting the worst, but it creaks to a stop.

"Okay. It's okay. They need to hurry."

"Please. I–I can't die here. Please. Please."

"Shhh. Hey, listen. They're nearly here. You're gonna get out of here, and you're gonna stop … stop being afraid to live and … and I want you to promise me that you're gonna do things you want and not be afraid."

"It's getting–it's getting smaller. I want to get out. I want to get out!"

"I know. I know. They're almost here."

"Pl–please. Please. Help. We need help. They need … they need to–to hurry."

I tighten my arms around her and close my eyes. I wish she'd stop crying.

❧ • ❧

"Can you guys hear me?" There's a voice, and I lift my head up.

"Yeah. We're in here. Aaliyah, hey, they're here. Aaliyah …"

"Mommy …"

"No. Hey, it's Orion. Help is here." I try not to move because I don't want the elevator to move.

The top of the elevator slides open, and light comes in. "Hey guys, how are you doing in here?"

"She needs to get out right away, but if we move, the elevator moves," I tell the guy.

"They're here?" Aaliyah moves to pull away, but I hold her against me. "I need to get out."

"Okay, hey, don't move. They'll get us out, but we can't move until they tell us."

"Listen, we're going to get these doors open while one of my guys tries to secure this thing. Keep still."

"I told you they were coming. You ready to get out of here?" I don't know why, but I kiss her head."

"Yeah. Thank you," she whispers.

The top opens more, and the firefighter sticks his hand in. "Listen, we're gonna have to pull you out one by one. We have to be quick. This thing isn't as secure as it should be."

"Aaliyah, listen, I need you to grab his hand and let him pull you out of here."

"I don't want to move. We're gonna fall. I don't want to fall. I–I can't. I know it's gonna fall. No. No. I can't."

"Yes, you can. It's gonna be okay. You got this. He's going to pull you up, and you'll be able to go home. I need you to trust me. You can do this."

She shakes her head, and I tighten my arms around her.

"Aaliyah, grab his hand. After we get out of here, we'll go get tacos. Okay?"

"No. No."

"I know you're afraid, but you have to. We can't stay here. You can do it. I know you can. You were brave when you jumped in after me. You're strong, and you can overcome this fear. Reach out and grab his hand, please. Please, Aaliyah. It's okay. You're okay. You're almost home."

She loosens her grip on me and turns to face the firefighter.

"Slow. Don't move too fast."

The way out is small, but I know she can get through. I need her to get out. I don't want her to die here.

She slowly stands and grabs the firefighter's outstretched hands, and they start to pull her up.

"Not too fast."

As soon as she's out, I can breathe. I lean back against the wall and listen to her crying, safely in the hallway. I pray she lets me see her after this mess is over.

"All right, you ready?"

I nod and slowly stand up, but the elevator shifts, and I fall forward, and someone from above screams loudly before everything goes dark.

The Admiral
Returns to Ship

Travis West

Ira Caplan sat at the piano but did not play. He gripped the edge of the piano bench, his eyes closed, and listened.

The music, voices of presenters, and applause traveled from the auditorium through corridors, down stairwells and narrow hallways, until they reached his dressing room as an indecipherable drone no more than a vibration. He wondered who they were cheering now, although, truth be told, he barely cared; he was still coming down from his own subjection to grandiose idol worship. They fed his ego—and also made him feel unclean.

The Lifetime Achievement Award. Were they kidding? Lifetime achievement recognition was for the dead or nearly dead, and, as far as he was concerned, he was neither. He figured he had at least four, maybe five more plays left in him. He was only sixty-seven; he could push himself to ninety, at least.

And yet, who was Ira Caplan to refuse the inaugural Cole Porter Lifetime Achievement Award? He had more than paid his dues, enough to earn his own dressing room, a luxury not afforded to most of his peers, another perk of a Cole Porter recipient.

The door opened and closed behind him, and he silently sighed to himself. He had been clear to the staff that he not be bothered; he would ring out should he need anything. He turned to face the intruder.

"I explicitly stated to your employer that I was not to be interrupted. How clear do I—"

The man in the doorway smiled. "Hello, Ira."

Ira stared, mouth agape at the man's face—one he had seen many times over the years across auditoriums but not up close and personal for nearly a quarter century. Brown skin now pinched around the eyes in a fan of craggy wrinkles; laugh lines ran deep on either side of his mouth, forming the borders of jowls.

"Crispin Matero. What the hell are you doing here? I told them no visitors allowed. Apparently, nobody got the fucking memo."

Matero chuckled. "Special *Matey* privileges, I suppose. It's good to see you too, Ira. Captain."

The room chilled at the mention of the nickname.

"Quit with the *Captain* bullshit. I'm still sore at you, you know."

"You're still holding a grievance with me? Ira, it's over twenty years on."

"You left me high and dry. Straight out of college, we started writing together, and you severed all ties with a fax. A twenty-five-year partnership—they called us the modern Rodgers and Hammerstein. A *fax.*" He turned his back on his old partner and fussed with the papers on the piano's music desk.

"Well, you've done quite well for yourself in the interim," Matero said. "The first ever Cole Porter Lifetime Achievement recipient, Tony Award winner, Oscar winner. You didn't need me."

Ira harrumphed. "Maybe I didn't need a partnership, but maybe I wanted one. You left me to swim in a sea of trepidation at a time when I was doubting myself the most. I was spitefully outed by an ex-beau right before opening night for *Hopscotch Avenue*. Six months later, my agent delivers your fax to my office. I couldn't help but wonder if the press coverage of that revelation scared you away."

Matero sat beside Ira on the piano bench. "Ira, you really think I left because you're gay?"

"How could I not? Those people you hear cheering out there? They don't care. They accept me for who I am. But, as you know, we're a very small community, we theater goons. We're a bubble. The rest of the world? To the rest of the world, I'm just the Jew fag who writes the song and dance numbers."

"I honestly doubt that's all they see of you. For the record, I never judged you for being who you are. That's who you are and part of the reason I loved having you as my business partner and my friend. I couldn't have cared less who you were sleeping with."

"Then, why did you leave, Crispin?"

Matero sighed. "Because no matter how badly we wanted it, we were never the next Rodgers and Hammerstein. We were the Captain and Matey."

It was Ira's turn to chuckle. "Bah! A bunch of *schmegegge* from the Broadway press."

"Regardless, the names stuck, and I was the Matey. At least you got to be the Captain."

"They were only plays on our last names. Silliness that didn't mean anything."

Matero issued his own harrumph. "They could have at least made me an officer too. The Captain and the Colonel would not have sounded so bad. The Captain and Sarge, I could have handled. But Matey is … lesser than. Aye, aye, Captain."

"Gimme a break. Lesser than? You've won your own share of awards in the intervening years, if I recall correctly, Tonys included."

Matero nodded. "True, true. But they make movies based on your musicals—'major motion picture events.'"

"They made movies from two plays we wrote together: *Tulips for Xochitl* and *Cigarette Reveries*. Both of which earned quite the reception, if my memory serves me well."

"In the eighties. Long, long ago. I had to prove I could do it on my own, write a play. Had to show myself and the world I had the talent to succeed on my own merit, that I was more than someone's matey."

Ira placed a hand on Matero's shoulder. "Well, you showed 'em. You are definitely more than a matey. You've been captain of your own ship for a long while now."

"Thanks, Ira." Matero smiled at his long-estranged friend. "I've missed us, you know. I'm sorry for leaving the way I did."

Ira waved a dismissive hand. "Forgotten water under the bridge. Honestly, it gets exhausting holding all these grudges."

"So, what's all this?" Matero asked, reaching for the sheet music. "Working on a new play?"

"I am, yes. Untitled, as of yet, but maybe you can help with the christening."

"What's it about?"

"A couple of composers so used to working with one another they can't imagine writing alone. Then, one day, one of them up and walks away without giving a reason."

"Bullshit!"

"No bullshit. The narrative is split, telling the individual journeys of both men. All I've known of you the last twenty-plus years is whatever found its way to me through the various grapevines, so maybe you can write your half?"

"You're serious?"

Ira warmed at the expression of surprise on Matero's face. "As can be. What if we called this one, *Captain & Captain*?"

"You're already the Captain. But I like the sound of Admiral. Can you play me a little of what you've already written?"

"Sure thing, Admiral."

Ira Caplan placed his fingers on the piano keys and began to play.

Fantasy Lover
Catherine A. MacKenzie

Fantasy Lover and I arrange to meet in the Crow Bar, a pub in the Thames Hotel in Jamesville. Although the name sounds like a prosperous vintage hotel, the Thames Hotel is actually an old, dilapidated motel, and the Crow Bar is the usual nondescript, smoky bar. The bar has a reputation—and not a nice one—but it is a place I'm not apt to see a familiar face, which is the reason for picking this location. Fantasy agrees.

My name is Hungry Lion. Not my real name, of course. Neither is her real name Fantasy Lover, but she hasn't revealed her true name to me yet.

I enter the hotel. Anticipation brews inside me. Warily, I glance around, ready to duck if I see someone I know. Should someone surprise me out of the blue, I have a prepared answer: *I just happened to be in the neighbourhood and came in to use the washroom facilities.* That will work, won't it?

The lobby, thankfully, is deserted except for the young woman at the front desk.

"Just going into the bar," I mumble, with a slight smile.

Disinterested and barely glancing up, she nods.

I'm an hour ahead of schedule. We arranged to meet at eight o'clock, but I need some sustenance—the alcohol kind—before I meet her. Hungry Lion is about to meet Fantasy Lover. Yes, I'm hungry like a lion, and I don't mean food-hungry.

I told Maxine, my wife, that I have a late-night meeting. She knows I'm involved with an acquisition this weekend. However, the shareholders from Germany aren't arriving until tomorrow morning, but what Maxine doesn't know won't hurt her. Later tomorrow afternoon, the directors of Lincoln Oil will hold the annual board meeting, followed by dinner. I advised her I might be late then, too—in case Fantasy Lover and I hit it off.

I sneak into the washroom where I stare in the mirror. While I splash cold water on my face, I notice creases and thinning grey hair. Have I lied about my looks? I told Fantasy I have a teeny bit of grey, but I have a whole head of it— where I have hair, that is. I'm balding on top but keep my hair long on the sides and down the back. Maybe I'm trying to recapture my youth. I wish I had bought some Grecian Grey, but that would have aroused Maxine's suspicions. Maxine, my wife of over thirty years, still tells me how handsome and sexy I am. I would reciprocate with compliments if I could, but I can't lie. Maxine is old. I'm old, too, but women age faster than men, and women look older than men the same age.

We have two wonderful sons. Both are adults, having moved out years ago. One is married and living in Las Vegas; the other is single and lives in Los Angeles. We don't have grandchildren yet, but I anxiously await that glorious occasion. Grandchildren would keep Maxine busier, affording me more free time. She'd fly out to visit them and would likely be gone a week or more, leaving me plenty of time for extracurricular activities, hopefully with Fantasy Lover.

I love Maxine; I do. But I'm a man, and I need to feel alive. We're in a rut. Maxine isn't as interested in sex as she once was. I'm not, either, to be honest—at least not with

Maxine—but a fling might help in that department. Get me back in the mood. Who knows, I might appreciate Maxine a little more. And an affair would bring excitement to our dull lives. That's my excuse for cheating, not that I consider it cheating, not in the 'cheating' sense.

I take one last look at myself in the mirror, pat down wayward hairs, straighten my dress pants, and adjust my grey sports coat, before leaving the restroom. When Fantasy told me she'd be wearing a grey jacket, I decided to wear my grey one, too. The same colour theme will give us a touch of unity.

The Crow Bar is a fairly large room, but it is cosier and warmer than it first appears. It has rustic wood textures and a gas fireplace in the corner. Numerous paintings of boats line the walls. The bar is in the centre of the room. Booths line two walls, and square tables are scattered about. Four young males sit at the bar, and several individuals occupy booths and tables. The room is quiet, but it'll liven up.

I glance at my cell phone: 7:15. I slide into an empty booth at the far wall where I have a clear view of anyone entering. I'll recognize Fantasy Lover before she notices me since I didn't post a photo on the website as she did. She told me she'd wear a pink blouse under her grey jacket. I informed her about my slightly grey hair and matching grey jacket.

I order a beer. When the server returns, I ask for an order of wings with honey-garlic sauce.

Everyone is pretty laid back, but it's early yet. It'll be a rocking place later, especially on a Friday night. Perhaps Fantasy and I will end up in one of the hotel rooms.

By the time I finish the wings, I'm on a second beer. It's now 8:10. Several more people enter the lounge, but there's no sign of Fantasy. Where the hell is she?

I don't have her phone number. Have I been stood up? I can't believe that's the case. We hit it off so well, and she promised she'd be here.

LoversUnlimited.com boasts numerous photos and profiles of all ages. The website is geared toward married couples looking for discrete sex, but I noticed numerous singles. I stumbled upon the site one night when I couldn't sleep, and for the fun of it, I set up an account and profile. I never knew such a site existed and was shocked to find numerous individuals from my area. I browsed through the males' profiles for an idea of my competition. Everyone uses anonymous names, of course. But what about the photos? Were they fake, too? Some looked too good to be true, what with muscles and pristine teeth.

I spent a considerable amount of time searching the females' profiles, but no one caught my eye until about a week later when I discovered Fantasy Lover. Younger than me, her profile stated she was in her midfifties, but she looked like a fortysomething model. Hot! No other word to describe her. Her sexy smile and attractive features screamed for attention. Almost as if she were tailormade for me. I immediately sent off a message, and the rest was history, as they say.

I was elated when I received her quick reply. For some reason, I didn't expect to hear from her. Immediately, I wrote her back, and we exchanged emails every day for a week. Finally, I asked when we could meet.

And tonight's the night!

Fantasy is also married, but her profile says she's bored with her workaholic husband, which suits bored me to a T. I'm entitled. I'm a man, after all, and I've paid my dues. Thirty years of marriage should do it.

The ringing of my cell makes me almost jump onto the table.

It's Maxine. Oh hell in damnation. Why is she calling?

"Charlie, how late are you going to be?" she asks.

"We're still tying up loose ends. Then we're going to dinner. It'll probably be after midnight before I get home."

"Oh, okay. Just wondering. I'm bored. Wish you were here."

I catch a flash of grey at the door and get rid of Maxine as fast as I can. "I'll see you later. Don't wait up."

Is that Fantasy? Doesn't look like her, but it's hard to compare from the memory of a small computer photo. She's wearing a grey coat but with a black turtleneck underneath. Maybe she spilled something on her pink blouse and changed at the last minute.

The woman lingers at the door, peering around the room.

I walk over.

"Fantasy?"

"Pardon?"

"Are you Fantasy?"

She looks at me as if I'm an alien.

"Fantasy? What kind of name is that? No, I'm not Fantasy."

"Oh, sorry. I guess I've mistaken you for someone else."

Her eyes flash. A look of lust. *Some other day we can get together*, I want to tell her, but right now, Fantasy Lover is on my mind.

When I look up, I see Fantasy—the real one! She's walking toward the open door of the bar, and she's even more attractive than in her photo. Besides her gorgeous face, she's tall and slender. Her grey skirt matches her jacket and, as promised, wears a pink blouse. Her skirt, above her knees, is shorter than I expected. Black stockings, black shoes, and a black purse complete the outfit.

"Fantasy?"

"Hungry?"

"Yeah, that's me. Hungry. Nice to see you. My table's over here."

Fantasy follows me across the room and slides into the booth across from me. She places her handbag beside her and drops her coat from her shoulders.

"Want to hang it up?" I ask.

"No, it's fine here. Thanks anyways."

"I thought you weren't coming."

She smiles. "Sorry. I got held up." She begins to explain.

I'm not interested in the details. I'm just glad she's arrived.

"What would you like to drink?" I ask.

"A chardonnay, please."

"Would you like anything to eat? I've just finished some wings, but I can order more."

"No, thanks."

Oh no! I'm certain I have garlic breath from the wings. How will that go over? Darn. Should've ordered barbeque wings.

"I must apologize," I say. "I ordered honey-garlic wings while I was waiting. Guess my breath ain't too fresh."

Fantasy glares at me as if I'm from Mars, just as the mistaken Fantasy had. Did I overdo it? It sounded as if I was planning a sexual encounter before we exchanged ten words. But that's what we're here for, aren't we?

After the server takes our drink orders, we idly chitchat. This is all new to me, and I'm not sure how to proceed. I've already put my foot in my mouth.

"You're prettier than your photo." I hope for redemption. Flattery should get me everywhere.

Fantasy blushes. She looks like a decent woman. Why is she here? Oh yeah, her workaholic husband. Then again, I'm a decent gentleman, and I'm here.

"So … where do you work?" I ask.

"I'm self-employed. I'm a hairdresser. I have my own business in my home."

"Oh." Hairdresser. Not what I expected. Thought she'd have a professional job.

Fantasy stares at me as if she knows exactly what I'm thinking.

"I love what I do. It's very rewarding transforming people."

I mumble something and change the subject. Weather's known as a safe topic. "You looking forward to beach weather?"

She glances at me, and then examines a crack in the wood table.

I want to say I'm not a good conversationalist, but I don't want to admit meeting women is new to me, so I ignore her expressions.

We talk. I find out she is married for the second time. She has one child with her first husband. Her daughter is married and lives in the same town we do, as does her ex.

"I haven't any grandchildren yet." She smiles. "But I'm hoping someday soon."

At the grandmother remark, I imagine her standing beside flabby old Maxine and compare the differences. What happened to Fantasy's ageing? Must have shut down somewhere along the line; she's only a few years younger than my wife, yet Maxine looks twenty years older.

I think back to when we married. We were in our late twenties when we tied the knot. We had known each other throughout high school and dated off and on. After graduation, we went our separate ways, only to meet again several years after we graduated from university, at which time we fell madly in love. Young love, right? We wondered why we'd lost touch for so many years. Our first child, Jimmy, arrived the following year. Tommy followed two years later.

They're both good kids. They went to college. Graduated. Have good jobs. As far as I know, they're happily married. Their wives are the daughters I never had. Maxine and I wanted another child, but she had problems with Tommy's delivery, and we heeded the doctor's warnings about another pregnancy.

Is that when the romance ended?

As I reminisce, I realize this is the moment I should be consumed with guilt. Here I am, thinking of my wife and kids while I sit with a woman I'm going to have an affair with, and I don't feel the least bit guilty.

I shake my head and concentrate on Fantasy Lover. I'm about to ask if she wants to check out the rooms when a shadow falls over me. Thinking the server is back, I look up to tell him we're fine for now.

But it isn't the server.

It's Maxine.

She looms by the booth. Her face is contorted, and I see—and feel—the fury about to explode from deep inside her. Her mouth opens. Then closes.

Mine does the same.

Her mouth moves.

Fantasy glowers at me, grabs her purse and jacket, and races toward the exit. I want to run after her and pull her into my arms, but I'm frozen stiff. Thunder pounds against my ears. I hear only bits and pieces of Maxine's rant.

"Can't believe … Cindy called … Thought she saw you … Wondered where I was … So, this is what you do … Liar … Cheater … I'll get you …"

Hell! Cindy? That woman I thought was Fantasy? She did look familiar. Only met her once when she came to the house to pick up Maxine for some sort of female outing. I'm usually good with faces. How did I not recognize her? How did she recognize me? What I perceived as lust in her eyes must've been her look of recognition.

Cindy didn't waste any time in contacting Maxine. Hell in damnation. The bitch!

What am I going to do? What's Maxine going to do? She's still standing by the table, but she's quiet. I can't look at her. My life flashes in front of me—what happens when you're about to meet your maker, at least, that's what people say. In other words, when your life is over. That's exactly how I feel: my life is over.

Done.

Caput.

Fini!

The thundering silence overpowers me until Maxine throws her wedding ring into my half-empty beer glass and dashes toward the door.

Good toss, I stupidly think.

I grab my coat, gulp the rest of the beer, and spit the ring into my hand. I toss several bills onto the table before I chase after her. I pray I've left enough money, although that should be the least of my worries.

I have a lot of explaining to do. I don't want my marriage to be over. I love Maxine. I just wanted a bit of excitement. I'll talk to her. She'll understand.

When I get outside, she's nowhere in sight; neither is Fantasy. I hate to admit it, but I was hoping Fantasy would be waiting for me.

I stand like a fool. A tender loving will make me feel better. But when? With whom?

I sigh and saunter down the street to my car. It's gonna be a hard night. *Hard.* I snicker at my punch-drunk pun while the Beatle's tune "A Hard Day's Night" choruses through my head.

The Black Mark
Sunanda J. Chatterjee

She felt the crash before she heard it. Her head snapped back, and her neck ached from the whiplash when the vehicle hit her. She had been stationary at the stop sign near his house, figuring out an excuse for being late.

Momentarily stunned, she turned around in her seat to look through the rear window. It was Paul's car! The black Bentley. Surprised, she opened her door and stepped out. "What happened?"

"I'm sorry," he said, getting out of his car. "I thought you were about to drive out of the crossing."

The foggy evening had darkened, and the streetlights turned on, flooding them in orange cones of light.

She said, "But I hadn't moved. I … I was thinking."

Paul looked apologetic. "I was distracted from before …"

She blushed, warm with guilty pleasure at the memory of his body entwined with hers just minutes ago. Then her chest tightened as she eyed her misshapen rear bumper with the jagged black mark across the silver gray. "Oh no! I'm in so much trouble." She tried to scrape off the black paint without success.

He shifted his weight from one foot to another. "I'll get it fixed."

A blue Miata slowed at the intersection, and then sped past without stopping. She hid her face in the hood of her sweatshirt. She dared not be recognized near Paul's house. "I don't have time. Eric's expecting me home."

"Hey!" he said, holding her by the shoulders. "It's okay. He won't find out."

She pointed to his dented front bumper. "What if he does? He knows you have a black car."

"I have an idea."

He had her follow him to the mall downtown where the parking structure was being renovated. A row of black and white zebra poles had been erected to prevent people from entering. The construction crews had left for the day, and the structure was empty.

In the darkness, she followed his instructions and backed hard into one of the poles. Both got out of their cars to examine the result, their footsteps echoing. The air was suffused with the smell of fresh paint.

"See?" He pointed to the black and white paint on her car and the gray marks on the pole. "That's your story."

She nodded and drove home, her hands trembling. Eric was opening their mailbox when she pulled into the driveway. She rolled down her window and said, "I had a little accident."

"My god! You okay?"

The concern in his voice sent guilt stabbing through her heart. She blurted, "I backed into a pole in the parking structure in the mall."

He looked at the bumper and tried to dust off the streaks. "This can be fixed. Honey, I'm just glad you're safe."

She smiled gratefully.

His voice was thick. "What were you buying at the mall so late?"

Her hands froze, and her throat constricted. "Um … I wanted to get you a surprise for our anniversary but I–I didn't find it."

He leaned into the passenger side window. "You're so sweet. And I haven't thought of getting you anything. What would you like?"

She forced a smile. "Surprise me."

"I will. Hey, don't worry about the car. It's okay." He reached out and tapped her nose affectionately.

She pulled into the garage and turned off her car as beads of sweat formed on her forehead. Then she went inside and took a shower to wash off Paul's musky cologne and be the good wife again.

Eric turned on the lights in the study, tossed the mail on the desk, and picked up the phone. "It's fine, babe."

The anxious voice at the other end said, "How do you know?"

"She lied about the accident."

"So, she didn't see us?" she said. "My Miata is conspicuous."

The Thirteenth Bell
Callie Rae Sutton

The room was small, and though you could smell the cheap coffee the chief was drinking, there was also the stench of drunkards and blood from previous interviews lingering in the air.

Chief of Police, Charlie Gott, gulped down some room temperature coffee, set the mug down, then sat himself in the chair across from the lady. "Miss, let's go through this one last time from the top." He checked to ensure the recorder was on. "Today is November twelfth. The first victim …"

"I wish you'd stop calling them that. All the people I have killed had it coming."

"I doubt any jury of your peers would group a 'cheating boyfriend' into the same category as the others that you so called 'provided justice.'"

The woman shrugged. She was deceptively quaint. Her mousy-brown hair was wrapped up into a neat, low bun. Her clothes were on the verge of frumpy, and, as expected, her demeanor was shy. But now, she was an open book, as if she had been praying for someone to catch her and rid her of this—whatever it was.

"Well?"

She narrowly glared at the chief with a cut-throat smile. She placed her cuffed hands on the table and leaned forward to talk even closer to the recorder. "My name is Melanie Zander, your humble librarian of Brookburn, Maine, and I killed David Ross."

David Ross was *the* guy, one who someone like shy little me could only dream of. He was tall, dark, and handsome. Enough nerd to have common ground with me but enough jock to make him sexy and desirable.

We met at an end-of-the-year festival on campus. I was next in line at the taco truck, and he was talking to his buddies and walking without paying attention. Of course, he ran into me, making his drink spill all over my dress. Instead of walking away and laughing like his friends did, he stopped and did his laughable best to pat me down with the napkins that he clumsily grabbed from the food truck's counter. In the midst of patting my breasts down, he looked directly into my eyes with his bright blues, and we both busted out laughing.

"I'm so sorry," he said.

"No. Not at all. Really, this isn't the first, and I'm sure it won't be the last."

"Even still. Would you allow me to buy you your meal?"

I blushed. My cheeks got so warm. But I thought, who does that? Only a nice person, right? So, I said, "Sure."

He bought my lunch and we picnicked on a nearby bench. That was our first date.

Our relationship grew quickly after that. The summer break was something I had only read about in romance novels. We had picnics by the lake almost daily. We played like children at the park. And he took me to some fancy restaurants. I even had to go shopping and find something more elaborate than what I had in my closet. David Ross treated me like a queen, something that I had never experienced in my mundane life.

Fall classes eventually started, and naturally, we both got busy. Sometimes we wouldn't see each other until the weekends. That was hard. Really hard. So hard, in fact, that I decided to surprise him one night at his dorm room. He had mentioned a study session with some of his classmates, but everyone's got to eat, right? So, I packed up our little picnic basket, ran up the stairs, tiptoed to his room, and quietly opened the door with the key that he had given me.

The lights were off, but I heard sounds. Then it hit me. I turned on the light, and there he was, butt-naked in his bed, with this blonde cheerleader-type bimbo.

"I thought you were different."

"I did tell you I was unavailable tonight."

"Yes. You are right. You did. You told me you were studying. Tell me, David, what subject is this?"

The bimbo reached for her glasses and sat up, bringing the covers up with her to cover her naked body.

"Technically, Women's Studies. She is the professor."

"Your degree is in engineering. You aren't even taking that class."

"Sure does look like he is." The blonde smiled and reached down to his nether regions.

"You disgust me." And I stormed out.

Chief Gott reached for his coffee mug but decided against it when the mug was now cold. "Tell me about the night of the murder."

"Well, it was Halloween. Everyone was dressed up. David, like myself, loved the holiday, so I knew he was going to dress up. I figured he would go on the bar crawl like most of the college students did. I decided to dress up in a different costume than what I had originally picked out with him. This way it would be easier for me to follow him. He was dressed as a pirate. I went with the grim reaper."

The chief scoffed. "Isn't that ironic."

"Glad you can appreciate it." She gave a curt smile, then said, "May I continue?"

"Please do."

We went from one bar to the next. He had no clue that I was even there. None. Which was great. To be honest, I don't really know why I chose to follow him. But I did. There was a chill in the air, and the wind picked up. The moon was out. I don't know, maybe that's what got to me.

Anyway, he went down an alley by himself to take a piss. I stayed in the shadows against the wall. I could hear bells. One, two, three, four … I got a little closer. Five, six, seven, eight, nine … There was a pipe that I almost tripped on. The bell struck ten, eleven, twelve … I reared back and swung with all my might. I swear I heard one more chime, then I honestly felt like I was soaring. I kind of blacked out a bit. I woke up the next morning in the bell tower of our fine town, Brookburn, with all the pirate's jewelry from David's costume, his dad's class ring that his dad had given him before going to college, and his keys. I went home, saw his death on the news, and didn't look back.

Chief Gott stood up and grabbed his coffee. "No, you certainly did not. But you sure did look forward. Your next victim …"

"Rapist," Melanie corrected.

"We'll talk about that after I refresh my coffee. Would you like a water?"

"Please."

Melanie looked out the window. It was a bit blustery, as she could see the trees sway and leaves form mini tornadoes. It was late afternoon, and she was surprisingly calm.

The chief came back in with a bag of chips for himself, his coffee, and a water. He handed the water to Melanie.

"Thank you."

He nodded his head. "Adam Mitt."

Melanie screwed the cap of the bottle back onto the bottle, swallowed, and scooted back into her chair.

Adam Mitt. What a shit-for-brains little boy in an adult body. My roommate, Abby, and I were getting ready for our dorm's Halloween party, which was actually the day before the holiday, as Halloween was on a Monday. That year we dressed together as sexy fairies, which was a bit out of my comfort zone, but I wasn't alone at least. We heard a knock at the door, and she answered it. I couldn't hear much, other than some mumbling, and then Abby shouting, "No!" Then the door slammed.

When I asked her about it, she just said that this guy had been asking her out, and she kept telling him no. We went about getting ready and headed downstairs to the common room. We danced all night and drank a lot. Abby and I went our separate ways at some point during the chaos. I woke up in our room but just kind of sat there in bed when Abby came in. She almost looked like a zombie.

"Are you all right?" I asked her.

She didn't answer. She took another step, but then she collapsed.

I turned on the light and went to her. Her lip was busted, one of her eyes was puffy and black, and her bottoms were all in disarray. I cried as I felt I already knew what had happened. I got her some water, draped a blanket over her, and carried her to the clinic. Abby, my best friend, had been raped. She refused to talk to the authorities or the medical personnel.

When she was released later that day, I took her back to our room. I propped her up in her bed and put on a show for her while I made some soup. When I brought her the soup, she grabbed it, reached for the remote, and turned off the TV.

"I don't want to make a big deal about this, but …" She started to tear up. "I have to tell someone. Can I trust you not to tell anyone?"

"You can count on me."

She nodded. "The guy who came to the door last night was Adam Mitt. He has grabbed me in the past and tried to steal a kiss. I slapped him. He came last night to attempt an apology but got too close and decided to grab my wrist as I started moving away from him." She wiped her tears, but continued, "After you and I separated last night, he found me. I was wary, but he got me a drink, and we talked. I remember getting tired, like, really tired. I woke up this morning, in his bed. He was in the bathroom. My head was pounding. Adam came out and said, 'I hope you enjoyed last night as much as I did. I told you I'd have you.' I started getting choked up. He said, 'Oh, are you going to cry now? You bitches are all the same, thinking you are here for more reasons other than to please the working man. Please.' I shook with fear, hate, and sadness. I leaped up to hit him, but he got to me first. He just kept going. Then stopped and said, 'I have to go to class now. Don't even think about telling anyone. You know they won't believe you anyway.' That's when I came back to the room."

My heart sank for her. No one asks for something like that, let alone deserves it. I knew what had to be done. I stayed with her until she fell asleep, grabbed a knife, then went out. I started to hear the bells again as I reached his dorm room. But this time, I had a feeling of empowerment, and I embraced it. It was raw but oddly justified. I knocked on his door, and he opened it. Adam turned on his charm and tried grabbing me by the waist and said, "One fairy last night, and another tonight." On the tenth bell chime, I thrust the knife into his gut. I smiled as I heard the thirteenth bell and noticed I was flying. I went over his head as he fell to the ground, and flew out the window.

I was soaring in the sky with the stars and clouds. It was thrilling. I found myself going to the church bell tower. I looked at my reflection in the bell and saw myself as a crow. I went back to the body, as no one had found it yet, and I found myself attracted to his watch, his 'douchey' diamond earring, and a gold chain around his neck. I brought them back to the bell tower and stayed to admire my collection until the sun peeked through, and I noticed my talons turning back to feet. Soon the reflection in the bell was little old me, Melanie Zander, and no longer the vigilante 'Crow,' as you all so appropriately named me.

"A pretty realistic name given how I finally caught you, but we'll get to that. We have one more victim … my bad … one more 'villain' to discuss before we get to your most recent endeavors."

"Ah, yes. Julie Price. You guys dropped the ball on that one for sure."

"Hard to put together a case when no one has found the body."

"Maybe so, but I'm sure she would have cracked had you kept on her. You could tell from her baby shower that you and I both attended, as you may recall, that she was already having some trouble during the pregnancy."

"I didn't really notice anything."

"Go figure."

"Enlighten me, then."

"That I will."

Julie had asked me to help her put together a book list for the baby, and I was all too happy to oblige, as my new position at the library made me feel at home. I gathered some of the classics and some new ones and put them into a lovely basket, then showed up at the baby shower. Lots of people were already there, but I couldn't find Julie at all.

I took it upon myself to look around the house when I heard crying from the upstairs bathroom. I knocked on the door, and Julie answered, "Just a minute." There was some shuffling of stuff, then the door unlocked, and there she was. Her eye makeup was leaking down her face, and her eyes were a bit bloodshot from crying. When I asked her if she was all right, she just broke down again. I guided her back into the bathroom and asked what the problem was. She said something along the lines of, "I'm not ready to be a mother. What if I am horrible at it? What if this was a mistake?"

Knowing that she and James had been trying for years, I figured it was just the hormones. Not that I'm a mom and would know, but since I am adopted, I'm sure my birth mother had her reasons for giving me up.

Anyway, I did my best to reassure her that everything would sort itself out. She left the bathroom to join the party, and I stayed to go to the bathroom, or at least, that's what I told Julie. In reality, I snooped. And what did I find but none other than the duo abortion pill—a.k.a mifepristone and misoprostol. Granted, as far along as she was, I'm not sure how effective it would have been, but I am sure it would have caused problems regardless.

After that day, I kept my eye on her, just to be on the safe side. And I didn't see any other red flags until after the baby was born. She came into the library a few months after giving birth on a Saturday. I asked her how the baby was doing, but she seemed to be in her own zone and walked right past me. Soon she brought up some books on postpartum depression.

I truly felt bad for her. I know James was a hard-working man; therefore, he normally left Julie at home alone with the baby all that time. But now, knowing her mental status, it worried me even more. I asked her if there was anything I could do, but still, no answer. I finished helping her check out, and she left. After that night, I made it a point to check on her every night. And every night, I saw James, Julie, and the baby, usually in James's arms, at the table having a nice family meal.

One night I stopped by the house a little later than normal, as I had to reorganize the backstock shelving at work. I noticed the light in their bedroom turn off, so I assumed they had gone to sleep. But then I saw a light come on in the baby's room. It was Julie. She was holding the baby in her arms, rocking back and forth. She leaned over and put the baby into the crib, then turned to leave the room. I guess the baby started crying though because Julie turned back around. This time she grabbed a pillow from the rocking chair and held it over the baby's face. I went into shock. I felt like I couldn't move. I should have knocked on the door and prayed she'd stop in time. But then I saw her remove the pillow and pick the baby back up, rocking it back and forth, making me believe that she hadn't gone through with it.

At some point, I made it back to my apartment, but I couldn't tell you how I got there. The next morning, I saw Julie on the news, stating that she went for her morning walk with the baby, turned around for a moment to get something out of her purse, and the baby was gone.

❧

"I still don't understand why you didn't come to the cops about what you saw."

"Chief, knowing what you know now, about me, and my crow-like self, would you have believed me?"

"I don't know. But it would have given us more to go on. More of a focus."

"Chief, I wasn't a hundred percent sure that what I saw was what I saw. For all I know, she put the pillow in the crib with the baby, then picked it back up and continued to rock it to sleep."

"If you were in doubt, then why did you kill her?"

"I saw her with the body of the baby after the news report."

❧

It was still bright on Halloween, but given the night's reputation over the past few years, thanks to yours truly, there was a curfew for trick-or-treating. Kids were all dressed up, giggling and running about. The crinkle of candy wrappers could be heard, usually followed by the parents saying, "Not yet."

I decided to take this year and not go on any wild adventures—i.e., 'not murder anyone'—as I wanted to enjoy my few hours as a crow. Still human, I wandered the streets as the kids went up to strangers' doors and asked for candy. Then I saw Julie with a bundle of clothing behind her house while James was passing out candy on their porch. Remember, this was a month or so after the baby went 'missing.' I found my way to her and followed, again staying in the safety net of the shadows. She went down a few blocks and into the woods where the town witch, Narissa Cloud, lives.

She walked down to the creek back there and threw the bundle of clothes into the stream, then ran back into town. I followed the bundle, but it was in the middle of the river, and it was going too fast for me to catch up. Before I lost sight, I saw a little hand unravel from the bundle.

I ran back to town as fast as I could. The town had fallen asleep early again; you're welcome. I went to Julie's house and let myself in through the window; it was cracked open just enough. It was surprisingly nice weather for it to be the end of October. James was in his room, but Julie had been sleeping in the nursery. I picked up the same pillow that I had seen her with that night with her baby and held it over her face. She was shocked to see me sitting on her, rightfully so, I suppose, but you know the saying, *Karma's a bitch*. You'd think she'd expected something to happen. Then I heard them. The bells. Like music to my ears. She stopped flailing, and on the thirteenth chime, I was my crow-self again.

"And that's when you took her wedding band, a silver baby rattle, and her locket with the picture of the baby inside."

Melanie nodded her head. "Once again, justice was served."

"Hum," the chief grunted. "Finally, we come to …"

"Mr. Kent Court. The perfect husband to Mrs. Natalie Court, who just happens to be one of my coworkers and friends. This one is easy enough. Kent was a highly sought-after lawyer, but he was fired a few months ago when the company noticed he was keeping two financial books. He was blackmailing his wealthy clients to pay him more to ensure a not-guilty charge, even though any jury could tell that his clients were dirty. That alone would qualify for my services if you ask me, but he took it further. A man with that big of an ego who was knocked down to nothing decided to pick up a new hobby of drinking and hitting Nat. A few weeks ago, she came into work with a busted tooth and some ribs that I was sure were broken. I knew exactly what to do."

"Trick-or-treating was observed the day before this year."

"Gee. Can't imagine why."

Melanie rolled her eyes with a cockeyed smile. "No clue. Anyway, I was walking home from the library on Halloween and saw Mr. and Mrs. Court at the new Italian restaurant across the intersection from the library. I strolled by and saw their hushed conversation was pretty intense. That meant tonight was the night, with my perfect alibi and all."

"Or so you thought." The chief had a big ol' grin plastered on his face.

"Yea, yea. We get it; you caught me. Can I finish my story?"

He gestured with his hand for Melanie to proceed.

"I grabbed a hoodie and my gun from my car, then waited for them to leave the restaurant. I ran over before they got to their car and grabbed her purse. Even though Mr. Court was an asshole, I knew the hero in him would help a damsel in distress and follow me to the alley."

"That is when Mrs. Court came back into the restaurant where she had remembered seeing me and my wife. I followed her out, but by the time I got to the alley, all I saw was Mr. Court on the ground, a bullet through one eye and claw marks on the other. Then, out of the corner of my eye, I saw a crow with shiny little knickknacks in its beak and a talon. Some of my best work, if you ask me. I took his cufflinks, watch, and the wedding ring that he didn't deserve. I didn't see you until dawn. I had decided to stay in my bell tower that night. When I turned back to human, you cuffed me and took me in. Congratulations, Chief Gott. Must be proud of yourself for such a win. A serial killer had been on the loose for too long."

"You came in so easily. Makes me wonder if you wanted to be caught."

Before Melanie could answer, there was a knock on the interrogation room door. Clerk Gavin Thorne came in. "Sorry for the interruption, but there is someone here who says they have some insight into the case."

"Who is it?"

"Narissa Cloud."

"I'll be out in a moment."

The clerk closed the door.

"I'll be right back."

"I'll be right here. Hey, you have the time?"

"Why? You have an important date? Am I keeping you?"

"Just curious." She shrugged her shoulders.

Chief Gott chuckled but checked his watch nonetheless. "Looks like we have been talking for a while. It is eleven forty-five p.m. By the time I come back in, I'll have to restate the date on the recorder to November, Friday the thirteenth."

"Wow, time flies when you're having fun. Before you leave, it is getting a bit stuffy in here. Do you mind opening the window?"

He raised an eyebrow.

"Halloween is over, and you have me cuffed. You really think I can leave?"

"I suppose not. It does get rather stagnant in this building." He opened the window just a crack and left.

Mrs. Narissa Cloud was waiting in the chief's office. She had long white hair, emerald eyes, and a soothing voice. She certainly fit the 'town witch' description, but she was actually quite a nice lady and had been a part of Brookburn for quite some time.

"Mrs. Cloud. How can I help you?" The chief sat in his chair, and Narissa Cloud began to speak.

"More like how I can help you. You see, my family goes back generations in this town. So far back that we were the starting point of the infamous witch trials. It was said long ago that our daughters would be cursed with a tormented life, and on top of that, the mother who would bring the child to witching age would then die soon after."

"That is quite a tale, but how is that helping me with the Melanie Zander case?"

"Chief." Mrs. Cloud shifted in her seat. "I am Ms. Zander's biological mother."

The chief all but fell out of his chair.

"You see, I fell in love, something that our bloodline was warned against, as it usually leads to babies. You see, our bloodline had also continued, despite such a curse, because there were no girls born. I was the first daughter in the family for generations. Most everyone had been lucky enough to have a son. My mother, unfortunately, wasn't so lucky. She passed when I was eighteen, the witching age in our family. Eventually I fell in love. And I fell hard—too hard based on what my mom had warned me about. The love blinded me.

We got married and got pregnant soon after. When we found out it was a girl, I panicked. I told my husband that the best point of action was to try something new. I suggested adoption. That way I could skirt the curse's bylaws of raising a daughter to the witching age, in hopes to save myself from an early death and the torment destined to my daughter."

Chief Gott's jaw dropped so far it looked as though it might fall to the floor.

"My husband agreed. The Zander family picked her up from the hospital, and a week later, my beloved died. My loophole had cost me to lose the love of my life. However, I was able to watch my Melanie grow into this beautiful young woman with a caring soul. On her eighteenth birthday, I stopped by the bell tower and waited for the thirteenth bell to toll, signaling her first transformation. Sure enough, she showed up. A flapping frenzy of feathers. The process takes a few years to get a hold of. As much as it was a joy to hold her and care for her, I cried, as my plan hadn't saved her from a life of torment. It only prolonged my life to watch everything unravel before me."

"Did you know the killings were from her?"

"Not at first, no. The first two were outside of town at the college. Part of me thought that if she left, it would do her well. To be away from the bell tower, you know? But when she came back and the killings continued, I suspected. Then I saw her behind my house, following that Julie woman, only to hear of her death the next day."

"You said on her birthday, she changed? I thought it was only Halloween."

Mrs. Cloud gazed down at the floor. One, two, three, four … The church bells echoed through town.

"Mrs. Cloud?"

Five, six, seven …

Narissa peered up and cracked the slyest of smiles. "Chief Gott. We can change only a few times a year: Halloween, our birthday …"

Eight, nine, ten, eleven …

"And Friday the thirteenth."

Twelve.

"Don't you move." The chief sprung out of the chair, practically leaping over the desk, down the hall and opened the interrogation room door.

"Thirteen chimes, you've run out of time." Melanie cackled and shrunk into a magnificent crow.

The chief attempted to get to the window before her but to no avail. She squeezed right through the crack.

He ran back to his office to find his window wide open, papers flying everywhere. He ran out the building and looked up at the moon, shining bright. Two crows flew over the town's horizon.

Reefer Madness
Sheena Robin Harris

A year at most, the words rattled around, back and forth, slinging their foreboding weight while I sat in the car, eyeing the brick-clad building in front of me. The place wasn't at all what I expected, but then again, I wasn't sure what I expected. The building stood tall, no windows. The sign above the door read GREENER THERAPUTICS. No blatant pot leaves, no flashing neon signs, no red-eyed zombies lingering in the lot.

Well, at least if anyone sees me going in here, I can proclaim ignorance. This place looks more like a pharmacy than a weed shop. At my age, natural confusion wouldn't be such a far-flung perception.

Before I talked myself out of it, I gave the surrounding vehicles one last scan for signs of someone I knew, slipped on my rain bonnet and sunglasses, and creaked my way out of the car. I moved fast—fast for me, anyway—my arthritic legs crackling and sending warnings up my spine the entire twenty steps to the door.

"Hi, there, and welcome to Greener Therapeutics. Can I see your ID?" a very non-hippy young man said as I stepped across the threshold.

"What? What do you need that for? I—I'm not comfortable with that," I said, eyeing the non-hippy suspiciously. His oatmeal-colored slacks and button-up green shirt made him look quite dapper but made me quite uneasy. This already felt off—where were the beads, braids, and scruff? Tie-dye? Peace signs? Back in my day, we knew the ones that went after the devil's lettuce, because, well, they looked like they fell right off the Woodstock bus.

"No worries, ma'am. We require a quick look at everyone's identification to enter the dispensary. It's just state policy, nothing more," he said, handing me some kind of pamphlet. "This explains some general laws and rules that first-time customers find helpful. I assume this is your first visit?"

"My doctor told me I need to take weed," I blurted out the lie, wringing my hands on my shouldered purse strap. I couldn't help darting my eyes back toward the parking lot. Why hadn't I parked farther from the door? My old practical Buick stuck out like a sore thumb, and right at the front of the building. *Damn these old joints!* With the sound of the heavy traffic on the highway, my heart felt like a myocardial infarction was well on its way. *Highly possible.*

"Well, it sounds like you have a wise medical provider. I assure you, we only use your ID to verify your age and keep track of purchase limits."

I snorted. *Age?* If this young dope dealer couldn't tell that I had one foot knee deep in the grave, maybe he *was* high. And purchase limits? What had I gotten myself into? I should've known better. Of course, the government kept track of who was buying the dope. They probably had a plot to figure out which seniors were getting reefer so they'd have a reason to deny their Medicare claims. *Well, at least I don't have long to worry about those.* That stark thought had me pushing my shoulders back and lifting my chin. *Seriously, Marjie, facing death and still worried about what people think.* How many things had I missed out on because I was afraid of what people would say or think? *No*—I shook my head in quiet rebuttal. *This stops now.*

"The name's Mrs. Marjorie Carter. I'm seventy years old, and I want to buy weed." I pulled out my wallet and presented my driver's license. "My doctor *is* a wise man, but he didn't tell me anything." I removed my sunglasses and looked at the young man right in his widening eyes. "I made that up," I confessed after rediscovering my newfound death-facing bravery.

The young man's smile grew wide and he nodded. "Well, that's perfectly fine as well, Mrs. Carter. We're happy to help you get what you need either way." He scanned the back of my license and handed it back to me with a smile. "My name's Kenneth, by the way, and keep your ID handy. Catrina inside will scan it again when you make a purchase."

"To monitor purchase limits, yes?"

"Correct. The nice lady behind the counter inside, that's Catrina. She'll help you find whatever cannabis products you want to try," Kenneth said as he swung open the next set of double doors. "I really hope you enjoy your visit."

"Thank you, young man." I patted a bemused Kenneth on the arm as I shuffled my way past him into the weed store.

The corner of Catrina's mouth lifted when I approached, surely as surprised to see someone her great-grandmother's age standing across the counter as I was surprised to be there. Incredible how much things could change when you were told you wouldn't have a life at all much longer.

Catrina's red-violet hair shimmered under the overhead lights. Like Kenneth, she wore an emerald-green button-up, but her rolled-up sleeves revealed an entire garden's worth of colorful rose blooms tattooed on her porcelain arms. *Maybe I'll get a nice peony tattoo.* I couldn't help but admire how the little jewel in her nostril complemented her sparkling sapphire blue eyes. *I could get one of those too—a ruby one.* Her thick eyeliner came out to a perfected winged point, and her lips were painted a deep shade of red that made her look absolutely stunning.

Go wash that smut off your face—you look like a harlot. I could still hear my mother scolding me from all those years ago. I'd only ever dared wear loose powder and the slightest rouge after that. All these years and not a single shade of red lipstick. *I think it's time for some new makeup.*

"What can I get for you today?" Catrina asked, pulling me from my accidental misstep into another epiphany.

"Hello, Ms. Catrina. The kind young man at the door, Kenneth—he's just lovely—he advised me that you can help me purchase marijuana."

Catrina's half smile became a full one. "Absolutely, happy to help, and you can call me Cat. Do you know what strain you wanna try? We just got in an elbow of Grandaddy Purp from one of our local grow ops that everyone says is fire. Def won't last long though—got a QP left. It's one of our top mid-range THC cultivars. Pretty heady, but the body vibes are legit, and you'll want *all the food.*"

Dear God. What is she talking about? What was an elbow, and why did people think Grandaddy was on fire? Heady body vibes? That sounded like a seizure. *I'm in over my head.* "Grandaddy who?" was all I managed to ask. "I'm not sure who that is," I muttered as I shuffled for my reading glasses in my purse. Images of my own Grandad wafted in. The old man looked like he was made of wax tucked into that silk-lined box. The first and last funeral I'd ever attended. That glued-in-place smile still made me cringe fifty years later. *Definitely going with cremation.*

Catrina giggled softly and waved her hand at a shelf of clear jars behind her filled with what looked like little clumps of still-green hay. "Well, you may know it by its more formal name, Grandaddy Purple Kush." She plucked one of the little jars of hay off the shelf and reached for another nearby. "Oh, and if you want to go a little more therapeutic, we've got a Lilac Diesel hybrid that's bombed with CBG. The hit's totally skunk but the back end tastes a lot like cherries and sage. Sounds like a weird combo, but I promise, it's stellar." She placed the two jars in front of me.

I leaned in a little closer to read the labels. Right there in black and white, *Grandaddy Purple* and *Lilac Diesel.*

When Catrina lifted the lids from the jars, the odor that infiltrated the air between us was so pungent I stepped back. There was no mistaking what was in front of me. I'd never laid eyes on the reefer, but I sure did remember the smell.

"No, Marjorie. You don't want to go in there," Randolph said on our honeymoon in the city. We'd taken a late-night stroll after dinner. I'd purposely guided our steps toward the sound of music and laughter a few blocks from the restaurant. Finally married, finally out from under my mother's judgment, I'd been ready to experience everything, and a dance hall sounded fun. "That's no place for people like us. It's crawling with dopers, whores, and drunkards." As I'd stood there entranced by the sounds, a couple our age burst from the front doors, laughing. Her lips were painted as red as her sequined red dress, and she looked so happy, so free. *Harlot,* my mother whispered.

Just as the couple strolled by, that smell slipped into my nostrils. Randolph coughed and pinched his face in disgust. "Good grief, Marjorie. See what I mean? We're not going in there. The whole place smells like reefers." He tugged my arm, steering me away.

"Reefers?"

"Yes, reefers. You know, dope, marijuana. People go insane when they smoke it, even kill people. Haven't you heard of the reefer madness? We've got to get away from here. It's not safe."

"Are you looking to wake and bake or blaze and daze?" Catrina's question pulled me back to the present.

"Oh, no. I don't bake in the mornings anymore. Now, when my husband was alive and Gentry was just a boy, I baked every morning. My guys *loved* their biscuits. These days, I'm just as satisfied with bran cereal and a cup of black coffee." Catrina's eyes narrowed, and then a sharp chuckle slipped out before she used her hand to hold it back. I didn't understand why she thought I was so entertaining, but I smiled back at her. I couldn't help it. I liked her. Her lightness was contagious even though I didn't understand half of what came out of her mouth.

"No, no. I mean … um, I guess I should ask, what kind of experience do you want to have? Oh, wait—is this your first time?"

"I'm afraid so, yes. My doc—no, *I* decided that I would like to try the reefer. I've always wondered what it was like, and being that I was just informed that I've only got a few months left, I figured there's no time like the present."

Catrina's eyes softened. "I see. I'm really sorry to hear that, Miss …?"

"Mrs. Marjorie Carter, but you can call me Marjie if you like." I liked the sound of that—*Marjie*. The only person to ever call me that was my best friend in grade school. My mother insisted that shortening my name made me sound less educated. *This is Marjorie, not Marjie. She hates to be called that.* Yet I never hated the shortened version at all. I actually found it more endearing. Even Randolph called me by my formal birthname, something I'd grown to dislike. So formal, all the time. Not a single *Dear, Darling,* or *Sweetheart* in almost fifty years of marriage.

"All right, Marjie, are you a smoker, or would you prefer an alternative method of consumption? If you're brand new to the effects of cannabis, we should probably stick with something a bit less potent than Grandaddy Purp. And if smoking's not your thing, we have edibles, drops, and even THC capsules if you prefer."

Twenty minutes later, I walked out of the weed shop with something called a White Widow pre-roll, which sounded like it must've been made for me, and two peach-flavored gummy rings that Cat told me would be 'the bomb' for my arthritic hips. I wasn't certain if I liked the sound of that, but she swore it only meant that I wouldn't feel an ounce of pain after eating just one.

Two Hours and One Gummy Ring Later

The trill of my phone startled me where I sat wringing my hands on the armchair. I'd eaten the ring, just as Catrina instructed, but nothing was happening. *Just my luck, I decide to try reefer for the first time, and the dope dealer sells me a dud.*

"Hello?" I answered on the second ring.

"Hey, Ma, listen. I left my wedding ring sitting in a cup in the kitchen sink. I'm in the driveway. Could you grab it for me and bring it out?" Gentry said over the line. *That boy would lose his head …*

"Yeah. Give me just a minute." I hung up the phone and lifted myself to a stand, checking my new bright-red lipstick in the mirror. *You look like trash,* my mother sneered. It was right then when everything started to feel … *askew.* But that odd sensation could've easily been a change in blood pressure. "Give it a rest, Mother," I grumbled as I stepped into the hall, feeling something weightless slip into my consciousness.

I found myself repeating the phrase in my head the entire walk to the kitchen because my thoughts were getting a little harder to grasp. *Sink in the kitchen.* Gosh, this house was so long when your legs felt like lead weights, and I was so thirsty. My mouth felt like it had grown hair it was so dry. *Sink in the kitchen.* And, that noise—what was that? It sounded like a bug buzzing in my ear, except the noise was everywhere. I felt it in my skin. It was on my teeth. My tongue even tingled. *Sink in the kitchen.* After what felt like days, I stepped from the hallway into the kitchen. *Sink into the kitchen.* I took one giant step away from the protective walls in the hallway, but my foot dipped farther than I expected. *Wait, what am I here for?* Another step. I dipped even lower. *Crap! I'm sinking into the kitchen.* That's why I was there. I was sent to the kitchen for this, someone had told me so. Slowly, step after grueling step, I was becoming part of the kitchen floor. I froze, unable to go any farther. I was under the table now, still sinking.

"Ma, what the hell are you doing?" My son's voice radioed from somewhere far, far away, and the sound jumped around in my ears for what had to be minutes before I realized I should answer.

"I'm sinking, son. Sinking into the kitchen," I murmured, studying the grout lines on the tile floor under my feet. The tiny flecks of silver on the tile sparkled in the shadows. *Just like stars*, I thought. I would be one of those stars, right there, a part of the kitchen floor. Everyone would walk all over me.

"Oh, God. Ma? What's wrong? Are you … having a stroke? Why are you under the table?" His voice was closer now, so loud I winced and closed my eyes because the volume made them burn.

"They said to sink into the kitchen, so I …" I couldn't finish. The buzzing was just too loud. "What's … where's that noise coming from?" I kept my eyes closed but tilted my ear toward the sound. The problem was, the tilt sent me whirling so badly that my legs gave out, so I sunk farther into the kitchen floor.

"The fridge? It always makes that noise, Ma."

"Such an odd word … you ever noticed that, Gentry? *Sstaaarrr. Kitchen Ssstaaarrr.*" I said as the cold of the tile slipped into the bare skin of my arms. "I'm a twinkle, twinkle star." I felt the cold sink farther into my legs now. *This is it. I'll be in the kitchen forever.* I laughed out loud at the thought.

Someone else laughed. That sound, the way it bounced up and down like a rubber ball on concrete, I felt it everywhere. Another stream of unstoppable giggles glided out, but I couldn't figure out why it all was so funny.

"No, Ma. You're not a freaking star," Gentry said between his heavy breaths and laughter. "You're high. How in the world did you manage to get weed? That's it, ain't it?"

"Yes. I always wanted to try the reefer," I answered, now gazing at the underside of the kitchen table. "Cat gave it to me."

"Who's Cat? Why would she give you weed? Good grief, Ma, come here. Let me get you off the floor." I felt the warmth of my son's arms around me as he slid me across the kitchen floor, and then lifted me to my wobbly feet.

"I'm dying, son." I heard the words tumble out of my dry mouth before I could stop them.

"No, Ma. Trust me, you're not going to die. You're just extremely stoned. It'll wear off in a few hours, and you'll be as good as new." He laughed again as he guided me to the bedroom. I loved that sound, but somewhere in my fuzzy head, it registered that he didn't catch my confession. I chose not to correct him and just laughed with him instead. He laid me on the bed and began unlacing my shoes. After pulling them off, he pulled a blanket over me and kissed me on the forehead, just as I had done to him those many nights so many years ago.

"You're going to be OK, Ma," he said, still smiling. I was so proud of the middle-aged man that stood over me. In spite of his gray hair and crow's feet, he was still the baby boy that brought me so much joy. He was the only one in my life that never tried to make me into their idea of who I should be.

My eyelids drooped heavily as I heard his footfalls growing quieter down the hall. I could hear him talking to someone, his voice low. "I'm not sure, but she's a little freaked out. She thinks she's dying." He laughed softly. "I'm going to stay here with her for a while."

Dying, I thought, and then I laughed too.

<u>*ONE YEAR LATER*</u>

"We've gathered here today to celebrate the time we've had with a special lady and say our goodbyes," the suited man said to the small group of people gathered in the room. "Some people make an impression no matter where they go, so they're hard to forget. After so many years here with us, I have no question she will make an impression in the next chapter, and I know she's on her way to a good place. Unfortunately, the place is so far away."

Gentry stood at the back of the small group, thoughtful and quiet while the man spoke. He felt a bit out of place among his mother's friends, but because he knew how much it meant to her for him to be there, he would not have missed it. A few others in the group wiped stray tears from their eyes in spite of their smiles. Catrina shook in quiet sobs.

"And, while saying goodbye is always hard, goodbye in a place like this is always followed with a special introduction to someone new." The door in the corner of the shop opened, and a small-statured senior lady stepped through. Bright fuchsia hair glinted under the fluorescent lights and contrasted sharply with the emerald-green shirt. Her lips were painted a deep shade of incredible red, which matched the sparkling ruby piercing in one of her nostrils. But that sparkle was nothing like the blaze of life in her eyes or the contagiousness of her broad smile.

"Everyone, while we send Catrina off on happy trails on her next cannabis adventure, I'd like you to give a warm welcome to our newest budtender, Ms. Marjie Carter."

Marjie stepped forward and gave the small crowd of employees—and her son—an excited wave before taking Catrina into her arms for a tight hug. "Best of luck, young lady," she said with a smile before kissing her on the cheek. "You will be *stellar*, no—*fire*, no matter where you go. You are *the bomb*."

"Marjie, as we always do with newcomers at Greener Therapeutics, I'm giving you the floor to tell everyone here a little about yourself. Even though we've grown to know you quite well over the last few months." The man in the suit gave Marjie a teasing smile. Several employees in the group laughed.

"Well, let's see, where do I start? I'm seventy-one years young, and I know I may seem like an odd addition to the team. But, not long ago, I was told I was dying, and that brought me to this lovely place to see you fine people." Tears made her blue eyes sparkle. "I'm happy to say after a year of the best *reefer* in town, I'm currently in remission. And, even if I wasn't, I'd be tickled pink to be spending my last days here with you folks."

The room erupted with claps and hoots of welcome. Gentry stepped forward and squeezed his mother's hand. "Proud of you, Ma." He leaned in close to her and whispered, "I told you you weren't going to die."

Marjie threw back her head and laughed, almost madly.

The Majordomo
Marlon J. Hayes

Chauncey believed in sticking to routine, no matter what obstacles might appear. It was the main reason he'd been employed as the butler for Maurice Jameson, a curmudgeonly, reclusive millionaire. Chauncey was used to Mr. Jameson and performed his duties with pride and skill. He knew his job wasn't easy, but he to loved it. It was solitary work, and he was well paid.

Every morning, Chauncey woke up at six o'clock, without the aid of an alarm. He'd been employed as the butler for twenty-five years, and for the last five, he'd been the only help remaining. The others had either retired or been let go, and they'd never been replaced. He was now responsible for every aspect of Mr. Jameson's life. He was the cook, chauffeur, secretary, gardener, and, of course, the butler, which was why he called himself the *majordomo*. Majordomo sounded much more majestic to him.

When lawyers called, he answered, because Mr. Jameson no longer talked to them. He didn't want to be bothered. There were no creditors, because the old man never believed in having debts. In fact, each of his three ex-wives had been paid off handsomely in the divorce decrees, with the only condition being he never heard from them again. Each marriage had produced a child, and just as with everyone else in his life, Mr. Jameson held no affection for any of them. He paid for their schools, riding and elocution lessons, and when each reached their majority, he gave them huge trust funds. He viewed the money as insulation from the unwanted duties of being a father. His children reciprocated the lack of affection, and they sent cards for his birthday and Christmas but never for Father's Day.

Chauncey rode the lawn mower on Mondays, and since the pool had been drained and covered, there was no need for a pool boy. He handled everything, which suited him perfectly. He himself had no family, and he spent his days seeing to all the needs of Mr. Jameson. The only vacations he took were in his daydreams of foreign destinations. Lately he'd started contemplating his own retirement.

The only pleasures Chauncey allowed himself were long drives throughout the countryside and his devotion to the gardens of the estate. He knew he would look funny to others if they saw him adorned in his wide gardening hat and overalls. He wouldn't have cared, even if someone ever saw him, because the tending of his roses, lilacs, and tulips gave him pleasure. He was out there every afternoon, even during winter, planning expansions and dreaming of how beautiful his garden could be. Except it really wasn't his.

There would come a day when he would own a small villa, maybe in Spain or Italy, where he could grow flowers in his own garden. He knew the time was growing near when his heart's desire would have to be realized. Of course, there comes a time in everyone's life when *someday* becomes *today* or *tomorrow*.

Today started off just like any other day. He woke at six, prepared coffee before showering and dressing, then cooked a small breakfast, before opening the curtains and to allow the sunshine in. After eating, he stood gazing at the beauty of the garden with a happy expression on his normally stoic face. When he finished his coffee, he started his routine.

Chauncey walked down the winding driveway to the mailbox to retrieve the mail. As he walked back to the house, he sorted it into categories, some to be opened and responded to and others which would go into the trash. After that, he walked into the parlor, where he pushed Play on the answering machine.

Chauncey answered the phone between eleven a.m. and three p.m. The calls he missed were reviewed daily, to either be erased or returned. There were calls from telemarketers, and he erased each one. The monotony of the calls allowed him to not really listen, as he daydreamed of his future garden. His reverie was interrupted by the next call, and his attention was riveted to the message from the night before.

"Hey, Dad, it's me, Morris. I know it's been years since you and I have spoken, and it's time that changed. I'll be in your area tomorrow, and I'll drop by in the afternoon. There's a proposition I'd like to discuss, and it'll be good to catch up. See you soon."

Chauncey rewound the message, listening to it again, while thinking of the reason behind the call. Morris was the youngest of the three children and could be described as a ne'er-do-well. He was spoiled, irresponsible, and full of get-rich-quick schemes. His trust fund should have lasted two lifetimes, and Chauncey was sure it had been squandered. The purpose behind the impromptu visit was probably to beg. Chauncey knew Mr. Jameson's response would be an emphatic 'no.'

But just as sure as he knew the old man's response, he knew Morris would keep trying, with the persistent nature inherent to most losers. Chauncey had the gut feeling his own dreams of the future were nearer to fruition than he planned.

He would notify Mr. Jameson of Morris's impending arrival after he tended to the garden. Then he would start making his preparations.

Chauncey performed his duties, then busied himself with preparing for the unwanted visit. The finest bottles of liquor were brought out, because Chauncey knew Morris would want a free drink of fine spirits. There were bottles of expensive cognacs, scotches, and bourbons, some valued at more than $20,000. He prepared the parlor for the reception of the visitor, dusting and polishing until it sparkled, chiding himself for not doing it often, despite the excuse of Mr. Jameson no longer frequenting the room.

That afternoon, Chauncey stood staring out of the windows which overlooked the driveway and the county road which went past the isolated estate. Mr. Jameson owned about four thousand acres and liked its location because of the sparse population of the area. In fact, they had not received a visit from anyone in years.

Chauncey went outside and busied himself in the garden. Once he was satisfied with his efforts, he returned to the inside of the house, where he cleaned himself up and waited.

Around three, a black Cadillac sedan turned off the road and began the ascent up the driveway. Chauncey watched as the car stopped outside the front doors. It was beautiful, and he found himself wondering how it drove. He could envision himself behind the wheel. He shook off the vision and paid attention to the man exiting the car.

Morris was close to thirty and looked like a handsome man gone to seed. His face was the ruddy complexion of someone who spent too many nights drinking, and his paunch bespoke a lot of unhealthy living. His suit was rumpled, as if it had been at the bottom of a suitcase. Chauncey wrinkled his face in distaste, then hurried to open the door to keep the man from ringing the doorbell and disturbing the quiet. He opened it as Morris was extending a hand toward the button. The man's fingernails were bitten to the quick, adding credence to Chauncey's thoughts about the visit.

"Good afternoon, Mr. Morris," Chauncey said.

"How ya' doing, Chauncey?" Morris said, stepping through the open door, and waited as Chauncey closed the door.

Chauncey walked toward the parlor, positive the man was behind him, carrying his hat in his hands, as befitted a beggar. He walked into the room, then glanced around to make sure everything was as it should be, before turning around and speaking.

"Your father will be down in a while to receive you. He doesn't get around well these days. I'll go upstairs and help him, but first, I need to make sure you are comfortable."

Chauncey motioned toward the sofas in the room, and Morris sat down on the one nearest the windows. Chauncey watched the man look around with an appraising look on his face, as if he were gauging the value of the furnishings and paintings. Chauncey forced his face to remain stoic. It required effort, because he did not approve of anything about the man. He walked to the credenza, where he'd put liquor, a glass, and a bucket of ice.

"Would you like a drink while you wait?" he asked.

Morris looked at the label on the bottle, then nodded in approval. Chauncey lifted the bottle of Louis XIII cognac and turned his back on the young man to prepare the drink.

"I'm sure you are nervous about seeing your father," he said. "This drink will calm you. Because this is a fine cognac, I will not diminish it by adding ice. I have a glass of ice for you on the side, and you can desecrate it if you wish."

Chauncey picked up the two glasses and moved toward the man. He placed them upon coasters on the side table, then waited as Morris sipped the cognac. He nodded appreciatively.

"This is delicious," he said, licking his fleshy lips.

"Indeed. It will take a while to get your father, so feel free to drink as much as you'd like, as we rarely imbibe. By the way, is that car a rental?"

Morris downed the cognac in a gulp, heightening Chauncey's disapproval, because it was supposed to be sipped in appreciation, not gulped down as if it had not been cultivated for seventy-five years prior to being bottled. He did not know whether to blame the man for being a barbarian or Mr. Jameson for failing as a father. Either way, the result was disappointing.

"It's mine," Morris said. "It was a gift from a girlfriend, who shouldn't have put it in my name. When I left her, it was in a car she'd bought me."

The man slapped his knee, laughing, and Chauncey pursed his lips. He nodded, then left the room, leaving the man alone. He walked slowly up the winding staircase to the second level. He opened the door to Mr. Jameson's suite and walked toward the windows, ignoring everything else. He gazed out at the spectacular garden, and he marveled at the colors painted in the sky by the approaching sunset.

He was lost in his musings for a few minutes, before remembering his duties. He shook off his thoughts, then started preparing for the reunion of father and son. He returned to the lower level, where he glanced in the parlor where Morris had imbibed a quarter of the cognac. Chauncey shook his head in disapproval, but he was not surprised. He walked to the back of the house, in the direction of the French doors which led to the garden. He stepped outside, sliding on his gardening gloves, while looking up at the dying sun. Everything was as he'd left it, and he found himself whistling as he made his way back to the parlor.

Morris was slumped against the back of the couch. His eyes were open, unseeing in a frozen stare. Chauncey was sure the paraquat had done its job, but he put a gloved hand against the man's neck just to be sure. He felt nothing. He patted the man's pockets, removing a wallet and car keys. The wallet held forty-seven dollars in cash, identification, and a few business cards. Chauncey removed the cash, then returned the wallet to the man's pocket. He pocketed the cash and keys, then took a deep breath. He was glad he was in shape, because Morris weighed about two hundred pounds. He scooped the man up in a fireman's carry and walked towards the open doors leading to the garden.

In the five-by-four hole he'd dug earlier, he dumped in the body. The sun was almost completely down, but Chauncey did not need light to see what needed to be done. He was slightly out of breath and sat on a nearby bench to let his breathing calm down. It would be a shame to make all of the preparations for the future, then collapse from a heart attack while burying the past.

Once his breathing returned to normal, he began his task in a methodical way. He replaced the dirt he'd removed, shoveling it first onto the face of Morris, because he didn't like him staring back at him. As he heaved the dirt into the hole, he thought of how funny life can be. Patience was a virtue, and sometimes things happened which changed everything despite a person's best intentions. Even though he'd prided himself on being the captain of his emotions, he regretted actions which were spurred by anger instead of logic.

When the hole was almost filled, he put the rose bush back in place, then put mulch around it, disguising that a hole had been dug. He went in the house and turned on the floodlights. The moon wasn't a factor yet, and he wanted to look at his handiwork before turning to his next tasks. He stepped outside again and looked at the garden.

The rose bush looked natural, as if it had never been moved. If his calculations were correct, father and son were separated by a few feet, as the elder Mr. Jameson resided beneath the lilacs, which Chauncey had planted two years before. Every one has a bad day, and Chauncey sometimes regretted his own response to a harsh criticism from his former employer. He'd stuck the sharpened trowel in the old man's eye before he knew it, and that was that. He had not panicked, and everything went according to plan, until Morris had decided to pay a visit. Chauncey stepped back inside the house and looked out at the garden, before turning off the floodlights and returning it to darkness.

He started whistling, thinking of everything which would happen in the days ahead. Being the majordomo for a reclusive millionaire had its perks. An off-shore account awaited him, and with money, one could disappear if needed. There were countries with non-extradition laws, and it would be a long time before anyone looked for him. He'd taken advantage of the power-of-attorney privilege conveyed upon him by Mr. Jameson (even though the old man wasn't aware of it) and paved his way for retirement. He would discontinue the mail and because of the seclusion of the estate, no one would be curious, at least not for a while. In the morning, he'd drive the Cadillac formerly owned by Morris to the airport, where he would leave it in long-term parking, before catching a flight to where his new life awaited him, as well as a garden of his own.

He chuckled to himself, thinking of stories and movies where the answer to the questions were always the same: *"The butler did it."* It was apropos for this situation, with only a slight difference. Chauncey was, or had been, the majordomo.

Playing in Concert
Bonnie Olsen

I adjusted the maestro's stand to the angle he prefers and checked my work with a protractor—yes! twenty-one degrees, exactly. We members of the All-City Teenaged Musical Association take our responsibilities very seriously.

We get to skip school every Wednesday and, instead, assemble at Symphony Hall. There, we 'set stage' for the Philharmonic Orchestra, after which we become its audience for that day's rehearsal. It's a novel collaboration between the city's school district and its arts commission. There's never enough money to fully support the symphony, and we All-City musical teens can be a shining jewel in the school district's crown—better, anyway, than the considerably duller jewel that's the All-City football team. For one thing, we talented young musicians aren't bumbling musclebound morons. And for another, we can actually play together in concert.

We arrive early in the morning, sweep the floor, set up chairs, (basses get stools), arrange music stands, then place sheet music upon those stands in the exact order scheduled and open to the correct page. For a final touch, we place two brand-new bonbon-shaped cakes of rosin two-and-one-half inches from either edge of every music stand in every string section—twelve first violins, twelve second violins, ten violas, ten cellos, and five basses. That's a lot of rosin cakes.

At school, rosin is a rectangular block of shiny brownish amber, but it's shiny only for the first chair violinist on the first day of school. After that, the same block gets passed from hand to hand of every single high school string player, getting more worn and less clear as the year goes on. But for the professional musicians we serve, each string player gets a shiny new cake of rosin at every rehearsal, because the Philharmonic gets shipments of real, imported French rosin, shipped in by the crate.

We teen associates were supposed to work under the supervision of a Philharmonic employee, Mr. Crowley, but we didn't get to be all-city teenaged musical associates by being slap-dash or unreliable, so 'Growly Crowley,' as we secretly called him, didn't have much to do. He'd just sign for the day's shipment of rosin, then leave us to our efficient, reliable selves to get the job done.

So, the day Growly Crowley didn't show, Lance, our teen association's percussionist, simply signed for the crate himself and took over the task of distributing rosin to the rest of us— after which, quite naturally, the Philharmonic's rehearsal went on without a hitch. The work rehearsed that day was, if I remember correctly, Mendelssohn's "Symphony Number 4 in A major," a fitting celebration for our first, glorious, Crowley-free day.

Weeks later, Growly Crowley had yet to show, had yet to be missed, and Lance was handling rosin distribution with seamless aplomb. And because Crowley was no longer there to shoo us away after the real Philharmonic's rehearsal, we took to bringing our own instruments and conducting our own impromptu rehearsals in the empty hall. What a thrill it was to play from our heroes' stage, and the acoustics there were marvelous. Crowley would have had a fit, but Lance, of course, did not. Like the rest of us, Lance was a serious young musician.

And then Lance showed up in shiny new black leather pants, a skintight skin over his already skinny legs. He'd let his hair go all bushy, and he wore his shirt unbuttoned to the waist. To put it bluntly, he looked more like a rock and roller than a serious young musician. It made us whisper.

How can a kid like us afford leather pants? / Because he's a percussionist, stupid!

This made sense. The flutists and violinists among us might earn a few bucks playing the occasional wedding, but Lance was a percussionist, and every rock and roll band needs a drummer. The world fairly teems with rock bands; and rock bands, unlike classical orchestras, earn real money.

Then Priscilla started whispering about how Lance was looking dragged-out and reedy these days—red-rimmed eyes, hollow cheeks, lost weight—but Priscilla was a hefty girl, and next to her, anyone looked reedy. Anyway, Priscilla played the viola, and no one expects much from a viola player. I mean, know what's the difference between a viola player and a vacuum cleaner? Give up? A vacuum cleaner has got to be plugged in before it sucks.

Besides, even in black leather pants and red-rimmed eyes, Lance was one of us.

And then Tom, Ed, and Bruce—brass players all, pointed out that Lance had been ducking out of Symphony Hall during long stretches of rests in the percussion part. And then Hal, our bassoonist, pointed out that Crowley's—and now Lance's—crates just had to contain more than rosin, and we string players had to agree. Even professional Philharmonic musicians can't need *that* much rosin.

So what—besides rosin—might be in those crates shipped all the way from France?

Drugs, of course, French drugs, like in the movie, *The French Connection*.

The very next day, Burt, our third chair trombonist took a cigarette break—trombonists do tend to think they're way more suave than the rest of us—and he discovered Growly Crowley's body, the horrible stink behind—not within—the always-stinky dumpster behind Symphony Hall.

Burt's discovery led to a lot of questions from police detectives, though never about the Philharmonic's supply of rosin. And when it turned out that Crowley had actually been *stabbed* to death, the questions stopped. I mean, who ever suspects helpful, earnest teenaged musicians of stabbing? Not these cops.

And who did the helpful, earnest, teenaged musicians suspect?

Lance. He might be one of us, but rock and roll? That had to make a difference.

A big difference, and if there was any detecting to be done, we'd have to do it ourselves. So, we planned for next rehearsal to include a selection of Mozart minuets, which of course don't call for percussion, and when Lance slipped out, we slipped after him, whispering among ourselves.

Won't he notice the music's stopped? / Well, goofball, if he has, he obviously doesn't care.

Together we huddled in the entranceway and watched Lance practically drag himself over to a parked car and slump there beside it, shoulders hunched.

What's he doing? / Waiting, I guess./ Sure doesn't look like he wants whatever it is he's waiting for. / Well then, why doesn't he just turn around and go back inside? / Maybe he's making a contact. / Right out here in the open?/ Well then, maybe he—

From out of the shadows, a mean-looking guy approached, the nastiest, wildest rock and roller you ever saw. His hair was twice as bushy as Lance's, and his black leather pants, twice as shiny. As for this guy's open-to-the-waist shirt, that was nothing compared to the spike-studded black leather vest he wore over it. He was twice our Lance's width and half again his height. And Mean Guy had a knife—well, we were pretty sure it was a knife—at least some sort of menacing object concealed in a holster-like sheath at his hip.

Could be a gun. / No, stupid, a knife. / Gun. / Knife.

Priscilla the violist whispered something to the cellist beside her, and both girls slipped back indoors.

Over at the car, Mean Guy kept advancing—actually, more like looming—and our Lance was pleading like crazy, you could tell.

Here in the entranceway, the two girls returned and whispered to the musicians around them. Those musicians slipped back, returned, and did more whispering.

Lance's pleadings got more frantic, and Mean Guy kept right on advancing and looming.

Someone was whispering to me when Mean Guy pulled his knife—it really was a knife—gleaming dangerously in the sunlight.

As one, we gasped. As one, we froze.

Then Priscilla the violist raced forward, looped a D string garrote-like around Mean Guy's throat, and yanked for all she was worth. And Priscilla, remember, was a hefty girl.

Mean Guy was struggling like crazy, but Priscilla's fellow string players bound his limbs with C strings and A strings and E strings. Then the woodwind musicians with their sticklike flutes, clarinets, and oboes jabbed him hard with their instruments, while brass players and bassists bludgeoned him with their heavy instrument cases.

See? We all-city teenaged musicians do perform well in concert.

Her Father's War
Gabby Gannon

Anna's mother calls, telling her she needs to come home and visit. With no further questions, she packs a bag and tells her boss she will be working remotely for a little bit.

As she drives through familiar streets, she reminisces about her father. A career military man, he instilled certain beliefs into her.

Adages such as: if you're on time, you're late; if you're early, you're on time; and no matter their age, it's always yes sir or no ma'am, and many others are ingrained as a part of who she is as a person. Anna's entire childhood, her father worked and did his best to protect his family and serve his country. Her entire adulthood, he has spent paying the price for that service.

Pulling into the driveway, she remembers long drives, listening to classics by The Big Bopper, The Temptations, The Righteous Brothers, and many more oldies' artists. She thinks about all the time she spent playing with various magnets he collected during his duty travels and kept on the metal roof of his old truck.

As her footsteps thud up the stairs to the porch, she considers the memory lapses he began experiencing when she was in junior high. The aversion he developed to fireworks when he loved the pyrotechnic displays on holidays and at theme parks. His overall struggles dealing with aspects of himself he's never shared with his family.

She walks slowly across the porch, stopping at one of the rocking chairs that are as much a piece of her childhood home as the walls. When her mom called, she told Anna she is going to visit her sister to allow for father/daughter time. Her mom explained she plans to leave after a nice family breakfast.

Anna drove through the night in order to arrive when she knew her mom would be finishing cooking. A smirk spreads across her face, turning to a full smile. One thing her parents will always be is predictable. Almost on cue, her dad opens the front door, not because of a security system's alert but an innate knowing that his daughter is home.

For as long as she can remember, her dad has been able to know when she is at the door. She attempted to trick him numerous times as a kid and delighted in never being able to fool him. In her teenage years, it prevented her from ever being able to sneak in or out of the house. As an adult, it's a comforting trick she'll always cherish.

"Hey, kiddo, your mom's just getting breakfast on the table. Get in here and eat before it gets cold." He places his hand on her shoulder, guiding her inside and to the dining room.

"I still say it's unnecessary for you to have come all this way to babysit me while your mom visits your aunt." He attempts to look annoyed, but she catches his smirk as he lowers himself into the same seat he's occupied at the head of the table her whole life.

"I couldn't pay enough to actually have someone babysit you. The hazard pay alone would bankrupt us." Her mom takes her own seat, raising an eyebrow at her husband.

He takes a bite of eggs as a boyish grin breaks out across his face. The three relatives share easy back-and-forth conversation through the remainder of breakfast. Anna's mom leaves shortly after.

"I was thinking, it's been a long time since we've gone out to the camp." She turns to see his reaction. "Since mom's gone for the week, why don't we go? It's less than two hours' drive."

Light radiates through him as the biggest smile Anna's seen in years spreads across his face. "That actually sounds fantastic. Let me pack a bag, and we'll set out."

She busies herself cleaning the few dishes in the sink and unplugs the coffeepot since it won't be needed for a few days. As she hangs the dish towel on the horizontal handle of the stove, she thinks back on aspects of her childhood.

Knowing military time and the phonetic alphabet is mandatory. Waving to neighbors, even strangers, is customary. An ID at the age of ten is a rite of passage. Always knowing the directions of the flag to face quietly at 1730 during retreat is second nature.

Camaraderie, patriotism, pride, respect all builds the foundation of military family life.

Standing in awe of fireworks display yet expecting the ensuing nightmares. Knowing how to avoid serious questions and important conversations after sunset. Walking on eggshells during an 'episode.' Flinching into defensive position when an unexpected bang is heard. Missing the moments that create lasting memories. Being physically present while mentally traveling through hell.

Anxiety, fear, pain, anger are the lasting remnants of securing freedom.

His deliberate footsteps shake her out of her reverie. "You ready, kiddo?"

"Could Allen Toussaint eat crawfish every day?"

As expected, he chuckles at Anna's nod to the New Orleans musician and one of their favorite songs.

Force of habit has him climbing behind the wheel, and she skeptically slides into the passenger side. They exit the quiet neighborhood, and she eyes the white-knuckle grip he has on the steering wheel as large trucks sidle alongside them. A horn blares in the distance, and she watches as her father flinches, and his eyes lose focus, no longer seeing the three-lane highway they're barreling down.

She clears her throat. "Snacks. Can you pull over right up here so we can get snacks and drinks?"

Flexing his fingers to relax his grip, he straightens in his seat. "Not much of a road trip without mother-not-approved junk." He pulls in the tiny lot of the convenience store, parks, and they head inside.

Loaded down with two plastic bags, they headed back to the car.

"Dad, why don't I drive? I don't think I've ever gotten to be the one to drive out there."

Unspoken understanding overrides his reluctance to hand over the keys. Anna's mom has told her that he has been struggling when behind the wheel because of the varying noises and hectic traffic. For the remainder of the drive, Anna keeps one eye on the road and the other surreptitiously watching her dad as he tenses and fidgets uncomfortably in the passenger seat.

A distant relative meets them at the boat launch. The small pirogue barely looks fit enough to float, let alone carry three adults down the bayou. She knows from experience the vessel is sturdier than it appears. They sit strategically to even the balance and set sail.

As the small town fades into the distance, her father visibly relaxes as the briny air puts his anxiety at bay. Calm washes over Anna seeing him peaceful if only for a moment.

As they venture farther down the bayou, they are swallowed by the moss hanging from looking cypress trees that are ever present in swamp country.

The thicker the vegetation grows around them, the thicker her father's Cajun accent becomes. Anna warms as she inflects her own Cajun accent in her speech.

They tie the boat to the pier and carefully exit one floating vessel for the floating dock. Their cousin waves farewell as he unhooks the boat and goes back to town.

Her father inhales deeply, closing his eyes, allowing the air to begin working its magic. They trod down the pier and cross the overgrown lawn to the structure barely able to be classified a home but has been a steadfast getaway since before Anna can recall. He unlocks the door to the house and enters through the screened front room. The lock on the door is more to secure the dwelling during storms rather than from potential intruders. Every property along the bank is owned either by blood relatives of friends that have become extended family.

Stagnant air begins to stir as the breeze enters the house. Humidity is inescapable due to the lack of air conditioning. Anna remains outside while her dad brings their bags inside and checks things out. Out here she has always preferred being outside because being inside with no power makes her feel trapped.

Here electricity is only for the necessities such as keeping beer cold and typically runs off generators instead of a power grid. Outside she knocks webs off the hammock that has hung between these same two trees as far back as her memory reaches. Sitting in just the right spot, she keeps her feet on the ground to rock back and forth.

Sticks and rocks crunch under foot announcing her father's approach. "I'd say you needed this as much as I did."

Squinting against sunlight breaking through the trees, she turns to see the father of her youth. Lighthearted and at ease, not the tense retiree from recent years.

"I forgot how beautiful it is here … and quiet." She rocks her feet back and forth, swinging lightly.

He sits in one of the wooden chairs to the side of the hammock. "I know your mom told you about my episodes getting worse. I know that's why you dropped everything to come babysit." Anger reddens his cheeks while he averts his eyes.

She leans to the side and rocks the hammock. "Can't a girl want to spend time with her dad in one of the most relaxing places?"

His voice tightens despite the smirk on his face. "She's told you about my temper and lack of paying attention, hasn't she?"

Already predicting her father's tactic, she arches one eyebrow. "No, Mom told me you haven't seen any of your friends in weeks. You stopped working on projects around the house. You've been on guard and distant."

He waves his hand dismissively. "I've just been tired and a little off since my last surgery."

She reclines back in the hammock. "All right, old man, that's bullshit." She side-eyes him, knowing her language will make him pay attention. "Your last surgery was five years ago. You stopped physical therapy two years ago and haven't talked to your best friend in six months. You haven't stopped to get beignets since the last time I took you. When I called last week, you asked how the overtime was going, when I'd already told you I had my normal hours back minutes before." She pauses to look him full-on. "You need to talk to someone."

"Apparently you've already talked to everyone." He rolls his eyes like a temperamental teenager.

Anna laughs. "That's what happens when you live forever in the same small town, gossip galore."

A small chuckle escapes before he turns serious. "Everything is fine. I don't need to burden anyone with my problems."

"If it helps you sleep and cope, it's no burden. Besides, there are people literally *paid* to listen to people's problems."

Speechless, his irritation boils below the surface. He gets up and walks away, leaving his daughter softly swaying in the gentle breeze. She hears his heavy footsteps along the pier. She stays where she is, choosing to pick her battles over the long, bound-to-be-emotional weekend.

She lifts her arms behind her head, relaxing into the netting. Her eyes slide closed as her mind travels back to one of her earliest memories as a small child.

~⦿~

Dad lays flat on the floor as Anna runs up to him.

"Airplane!" Her childish voice echoes with excitement.

Easy laughter creases her father's face. He bends his legs, keeping his feet flat. She leans her belly against his lower legs and reaches out with her hands, instinctively knowing his will be there to hold onto. Gripping her tiny hands in his, he lifts his legs in the air.

Her giggles warm his heart as he shares in her joy.

The memory changes, and she's a few years older. Her father assesses the strength of the rope with a narrow board tied to one end, the other secured to the thickest branch of the oak tree. Anna vibrates beside him, impatient to get on the makeshift swing.

She barely listens as he explains how to tie the rope around the board the safest way. He releases the rope, and she launches herself from the ground. She pumps her legs to make the swing go and promptly falls to the ground.

Her father looks down at her and instantly scolds her. Tears fill her eyes, not from pain but from the anger flashing on her father's face. Her mother recently told her to be patient with her dad because he was still adjusting to being home. Her eagerness to play made her forget to be careful.

"You can't just jump on things and play all the time. People get hurt or *worse* when people don't listen." He looks down at her, sees the tears in her eyes, and drops to his knees. "I'm sorry, baby. Daddy didn't mean it."

The memory morphs again, and she ages to her preteen years.

"What do you mean, I'm grounded? You told me I could ride my bike with my friends." Confusion clear on Anna's face, she holds her hands out in front of her.

Red faced, her father's anger evident as his knuckles whiten around the belt in his hand. "You know better than to back talk."

Eves wide, she backs up. "But you told me I could go."

Another transition brings her to her teen years.

Underneath the new-to-her car she'll be driving. "I turn this?"

"Yes, but be prepared. Oil will begin pouring out."

She does as he says, and as the oil pours into the pan positioned underneath, they slide out from under the car. Anna wipes her hands on the rag her dad hands her, pride on his face, watching his daughter learn a needed life skill.

A boom echoes through the air, and he hits the ground in a defensive position. "Take cover!"

She lowers herself beside her dad. "It's just the neighbors old truck backfiring."

A pit forms in her stomach as she recognizes the sheer terror emanating from him.

Sweat trickles across her skin as memories of different signs of her father's struggles flicker through her mind. Some of the scenes are seemingly insignificant on their own. Others trigger shivers as she attempts to shake off some of the larger altercations that occurred over the years. She reflects on the role and persona she developed as her own way to cope.

She mulls over each instance she saw a crack in her father's armor. Replays every fight and remembers every tear shed … on both sides.

The breeze picks up, bringing the scent of impending rain. She sits up in the hammock and places both feet on the ground. She blocks her eyes against sunlight reflecting off the murky water. Her dad approaches her, his steps heavy and slow.

"Rain's about to start. We should move inside. We can have lunch." He turns to head toward the house.

"I figured rain was on the way. I stopped being the mosquito buffet." She quickly follows him inside.

"I called my sister and told her we were coming so she stocked the kitchen."

"I knew she would. She knew all we'd bring was snacks. Mom will be happy we'll have real sustenance."

Her dad slams down the butter knife he was using to spread mayonnaise on slices of bread. "I'm perfectly capable of deciding and providing adequate food. You didn't give me time, and we only stopped at a gas station." His voice gruff as he turns to grab a napkin to wipe up dropped condiments.

She sighs. "Dad, no one thinks you're incapable. It was more your sister's predictability."

He closes his eyes for a brief moment, loudly inhaling and exhaling. "I know. I'm sorry."

She leans her hip against the Formica counter. "I really think it'd do you good to talk, get things off your chest." She makes eye contact with her father and sees true, undeniable fear.

"I–I don't want y'all to think differently about me." Tears thicken his words.

She reaches over and covers his hand with hers. "Not gonna happen." He opens his mouth to protest, but Anna cuts him off. "Ain't happenin', Dad. You've lived, loved, fought, retired … It all makes you–*you*. But that does not make you less just because you need help understanding and getting through your experiences."

"It's my job to protect you and your mom. Knowing what I've seen won't do that."

"You've succeeded at your job. Relieving your pain is *not* a failure. Sharing your experience and healing your trauma is *not* weakness."

"Enough!" Anger boils out of him as he slams his hand on the counter and storms off, leaving his daughter standing alone in the tiny kitchen.

Defeat weighs heavily on her. Her father has done so much for not just her but so many others. She only wants to help him but knows he must seek help first.

❧ • ☙

He stomps down to the water's edge and inhales the musk indicative only of the swamp. This place has always held a special place in his heart. It's where he escaped to as a teenager, brought his wife to introduce her to family, taught his daughter to swim. This camp isn't financially rich but sentimentally irreplaceable.

He takes deep calming breaths to temper his anger, allowing the flow of the water to match settle his pounding heartbeat.

Anna's dad spent his life in service to defend and protect his family and country. It has been his purpose. The last thing he has ever wanted is to become someone else's purpose by being a burden. But even with all that he can't deny the episodes he's been having and his worsening patience.

Over the years, he has felt pieces of himself slipping beyond his grasp. Losing memories that he cherishes and at the same time not being able to forget the horrors he dreads. Anna knows he needs a connection to his past to push him to connect with his present. Recognizing what is slipping away is the only way to make him seek help.

Her father struggles with letting go, with being the one taking orders he doesn't understand versus a precise plan. His military career was spent with a clear path; there was nothing to question because when his superiors ordered it, he did it.

He sees it as accepting help is questioning what he did and why. Questioning that leads to questioning who he is and every belief he's held during his life.

Watching the ebb and flow of the bayou, he begins to consider the things he's missed out on because of his own stubbornness.

He missed several games of Anna's through the years to avoid the crowds.

He opted out of certain vacations his wife tried to plan because of the memories that may be triggered.

He cowered away from friends in lieu of explaining his odd behaviors.

The breeze blows through the moss dangling from the cypress trees and cools his heated skin. He walks to the old hammock Anna loves so much and lets his body settle in the aged netting. Raindrops break through the leaves on the branches above him, and he moves inside to the couch in the screened-in porch to avoid another confrontation with Anna.

Darkness surrounds the unit of soldiers. The canopy of trees conceals any light from the moon above. They were told this was one last mission before they could go home. The humidity thicker than any experienced back home presses down on them.

He strains to hear beyond their labored breaths and the dull cadence of their boots on dry, packed dirt. He tilts his head, seeking any comforting sound of nature, but there were no chirps or hoots to be heard. Even the animals know to avoid the danger before these men.

They approach a break in the tree line, and each of their pulses skyrockets, unsure of what awaits them at the campsite ahead. They were told it was a rescue mission to be done in the dead of night. The intel provided to them said it should be straight forward. Nothing could have prepared them for what lay ahead even if they had known all their intel was wrong.

Explosions reverberate, drowning out every other sound. Flashes of light cast gruesome shadows. Gunpowder and death cling to his nostrils. Every image, scent, and sound sears into his memory, burned deep for the rest of his life.

The bodies of friends are indiscernible from those of enemies.

He takes a step to offer aid to an injured soldier and stops in his tracks. Beside his boot is a charred teddy bear. Under burns and dirt, the child's companion is identical to one that resides on his daughter's bed.

Anna's protects her from the shadows at night. This one lays among atrocities he would die to protect his daughter from experiencing or know exists. Another explosion sends him flying for cover. He hits the ground, and everything goes black.

∞⤴•⤵∞

He jerks awake, covered head to toe in a chilling sweat, as his heart beats a blistering tempo. Fans whir, stirring the cloying heat, and his eyes dart in every direction, seeking the danger. He sits up, taking deep breaths to slow his racing heart.

Silhouettes of ghosts dance on the edge of his vision. Gunfire blasts farther in the distance than ears should be able to hear ring in his head. Muscle memory has his body tensing to defend himself until the softness of the couch beneath him connects him to the present.

Times like now, in the solitude of night, the past intrudes on the peace he so brutally fought for. Unspeakable images still imprint on the back of his eyelids.

Bones creak as he rises and walks to the kitchen to grab a glass of water. He heads to the screened porch, then outside to feel the warm breeze on his skin. He hopes the wind can cleanse his thoughts.

Every mission he participated in has varying classified status, but more than that has kept him silent for decades. Concerns for his family has always been a stronger incentive to keep his memories to himself. He served and fought to allow them naivety of the world's evils. He bears the weight of so much in solitude, not just because he was trained to do so, he does it to protect all those he loves.

His physical scars are easy to tend with; the mental scars are harder to carry. His duty did not end when he retired; it simply changed.

No longer wearing a uniform … still a soldier.

The sweet scent of cypress sprinkles with the decay of the bayou both do nothing to erase the putrid tone of his thoughts. Closing his eyes, exhaustion makes it hard to fight the memories warring in his mind. Embracing the memories will transport him back to a time he would rather forget but will always find a way to the surface.

Lost in his mind, he doesn't hear the soft footsteps of Anna approach. As she lowers herself in the chair beside him, the creak of the wood jolts him. She sits silently, allowing him to settle back in his own seat.

Her voice gentle, Anna keeps her eyes focused on the moon's reflection on the water. "Dad, you've held it in for so long. It's time to share."

The surrounding shadows shorten with the arriving dawn as chirping birds chase away the secrets of night.

He looks at his now adult daughter, recognizing something in Anna he's never noticed before, and a wave of peace he never expected flows through him. He did his duty. He fought so she didn't have to. The memories he's always hammered down would no longer hold power over him if they weren't solely his to bear.

His gaze travels back, and his shoulders relax. "It was near the end of my last tour. My unit was sent on one last mission."

Big Girls Don't Cry
Amy Hunter

Gracie kicked an empty box, creating a shallow dent in its side. Sighing, she grabbed one of her favorite dolls and tossed it in. Her mother would be home from work soon, and she would expect half of her daughter's toys to be packed and ready for donation.

Tears pricked Gracie's eyes at the mere idea of losing her beloved toys. Grief lumped in her throat, threatening to choke her. Helpless and alone, she did the only thing she could; she plopped onto the carpet in the classic crisscross-applesauce style, snatched the doll from the box once again, and hugged it to her small frame.

She didn't understand. The kids at school didn't have to give away their toys, so why did she?

Before she could journey too far aboard that train of thought, the room darkened, and a boy's laughter pierced the silence. "Oh, Gracie! Time to watch your favorite music video …"

Gracie whimpered. Her brother knew she was afraid of the dark, so he exposed her to it every chance he got, and the fact that the video scared her was just an added bonus.

"No, Mason. Please don't!"

In the darkness, he grabbed the remote control from her bedside table and switched on the television. Gracie stood and charged at him, illuminated only by the staticky television, tears streaming down her face. It was no use. She tripped over the donation box and fell to her knees. By the time she could stand back up, her brother had slammed the door.

Slowly, she turned and faced the television. Just as she expected, the scary video played on the screen, with the distorted man singing about eating her soul.

"The boogeyman is going to get you," Mason mumbled, laughing.

Gracie pressed her back against the door. Mason did this to her at least once a week, so she knew the drill. She closed her eyes and placed her hands over her ears, desperate to block out the music.

Since her room had once been a garage, the switch was outside the door, in the kitchen. If she could only pry the door open, she could flip on the light. Maybe then the scary man on the screen would go away. But no, Mason had locked the door.

Gracie sunk to the floor and hugged her knees, rocking her body in self-soothing motions. Her mom would be home soon to punish the boys, she told herself. Oh yeah, they would regret messing with her.

As time passed, she yawned. Then, before she nodded off, she could have sworn she saw a faint red glow from under the bed …

❧ ◦ ❧

"But, Mama, I put a doll in the box …" Gracie trailed off, knowing her mother wouldn't believe her about the missing doll. Her brother had undoubtedly stolen it so she would get in trouble. Typical.

"*A* doll? Just one?" Her mother rolled her eyes. "Dammit, I was going to let you choose which toys to get rid of. Now, I guess I get to choose."

One by one, Gracie's mother picked toys off the floor and tossed them into the box. Toys that Gracie loved. Toys that were irreplaceable in her eyes. Toys that were her only true friends. And, with the toys, so went her heart.

"Pout all you want. It's time to grow up."

Gracie cried herself to sleep sometime before supper and woke hours later, tucked into bed with a gnawing pain in her stomach that wouldn't subside. She reached to turn on her bedside lamp and gasped. The missing doll that she'd planned to donate now nestled beside her on the pillow without its shoes or bonnet, but otherwise intact. She hugged her toy, grateful for its safety.

Who knows? Maybe her brother had grown a conscience and felt bad about torturing her. Maybe her mother had a change of heart. Maybe …

All thoughts stopped when she heard her music box come to life, playing its dreamy nocturne louder than usual against the dead silence of night. Her eyes searched the shadows to locate who had flipped open the lid, but the box sat alone on her desk, its ballerina spinning.

For the remainder of the night, Gracie lay in bed, sleepless and staring at the music box.

The next day came and went, and before she knew it, she was ready for bed again. Gracie's mom tucked her in and leaned over to kiss her forehead. The tender moment lasted mere seconds.

"Goodnight," her mother said, already crossing the room and heading for the door.

As she reached for the light switch, Gracie called to her, "Mama, can you leave the bathroom light on? Please?"

She knew better than to expect her mother to oblige. Still, when the expression on her face morphed from loving to stern, Gracie winced.

Here it comes …

"You're too old for this, Grace. You're a big girl, and big girls aren't afraid of the dark."

Well, big girls are stupid, she thought but didn't say.

"Get used to it, kiddo," her mom said, unfazed by Gracie's plea. She switched off the light and left her daughter immersed in darkness. "I'll see you after my shift. Your brother is in charge, so mind him."

The shadows danced as the moonlight spilled in from Gracie's window. They seemed to beckon her. She knew they weren't alive, logically, but all logic was lost in the face of darkness. She closed her eyes and counted to three before reopening them to see the shadows twist and bleed together, then separate into even scarier claw-like shapes.

She closed her eyes, then opened them. Closed, opened. Each time she opened her eyes, she experienced what felt like a mini heart attack. And each time it was as though she had to get used to the dark all over again.

With sweaty hands, she felt along the bedside table for her cup. At this point, she'd do almost anything for a sip of water—anything but step foot out of bed. The floor might as well have been lava. Still, a drink might have been the only reprieve from her panic.

Gracie closed her eyes one more time and counted to three, but her eyes shot open when she heard the nocturne again. The sorrowfully sweet song drifted around her room as if the notes themselves could waltz.

She squeezed her eyes shut again and counted. She even tried praying, although at this moment, she couldn't really remember how to pray. Nothing worked. The haunting music persisted and nearly made her heart pound out of her chest.

Suddenly, the nocturne stopped. She took three calming breaths and opened her eyes, peering between her fingers and into the darkness.

She saw the red glow of his eyes first. Time seemed to slow, and Gracie didn't know if she was the one screaming or if the shrill sound had come from another part of the house. All she knew was that eyes weren't supposed to be red, and people shouldn't have fangs.

The screaming stopped when the creature in front of Gracie covered his eyes with one clawed hand, peeking out at her from between his fingers, the way she had just done. He seemed almost innocent.

"Who—who are you?" Gracie stammered. "Are you going to hurt me?"

His voice sounded almost childlike. Shaking his head, he said, "Water. For you."

The monster extended his other hand to offer her a small bathroom cup of water, and she accepted, trembling but still grateful. Maybe he wasn't a bad guy, after all. Looks can be deceiving.

"Th—thank you, mister," Gracie said with a grin. "What's your name?"

He shrugged. "I guess I don't have one. I don't need one where I'm from." The monster pointed toward the underside of the bed.

Gracie's mouth formed a big *O*. The pieces were falling into place. "Oh. Well, do you want one? I could give you one."

He shrugged.

"How about Jack? Are you a Jack?"

Just as he shrugged again, Mason kicked the door so hard that the doorknob bounced off the adjacent wall. He entered the room with balled-up fists. "What the hell is your problem? Why are you screaming?"

She didn't have time to reply. When Jack noticed her cower, trembling, that was it; he pounced, claws extended and fangs bared. Mason didn't know what hit him.

Gracie giggled and added two imaginary lumps of sugar to her plastic teacup. "More tea, sir?"

She didn't wait for Jack to reply. Instead, she filled his cup with imaginary 'tea' and offered him a scone.

He accepted and delicately held the fake pastry like it was precious, but he also wondered what to do with it.

Gracie giggled. "You eat it, silly! Not really, 'cause it's fake, but you can pretend to eat it."

He watched her for a moment. "Thank you," he said, raising his voice to talk over a low moan that came from where Mason lay on the floor, bloodied and unconscious.

Gracie ignored her brother and his pain. After all that he'd done to her—after the years of torture—he deserved what he got. Nothing less.

"One lump or two?" Gracie asked her monster, grinning.

Mason could wait.

One Small Slip
Melissa J. Rodgers

The pole slipped, biting into Brody's shoulder, and he hissed, teeth clenched. "Blast this Ark!"

"Hold true, Brothers." Lachlan grunted, face rigid and red. "The summit is but a stone's throw." Days had passed since the men had a full night's rest, but their crusade, although disorganized, was important. The fate of the world rested on their shoulders, so if Lachlan had to drag them up that last stretch of the mountain alone, he would.

Finlay stumbled over the loose rock and pebbles and came down hard on his knee. "Geoffrey, if ye'd hold yer share of the load, I wouldn't be strugglin' so!"

Arms shaking, Geoffrey lifted the pole above his shoulders to aid his grumpy partner. "On your feet, you bumbling fool. You'll pull the lot of us down the mountainside, for sure," Geoffrey yelled in a thick French accent.

Brody groaned, readjusting his hold as the weight shifted. "I don't remember volunteerin' for this."

Of course, Brody would bring that sore subject up, and Lachlan couldn't spare the breath to laugh at his audacity.

"The day you accepted that white mantle, you pledged your loyalty and service to the Crimson Cross. Now move."

As they crested the mountain, campfires blazed in the night, and the striking of axes pierced their ears.

"To the tent," Lachlan said as the wind picked up and ruffled his hair.

Dark clouds sailed past a Hunter's Moon, and rolling thunder shook the ground under Lachlan's feet. He jolted as jagged bolts of lightning cut across the sky, and the hair on the back of his head stood on end from the thick charge of energy left in the air. A storm was brewing. But not a typical storm, the sort that struck from below, not from above. Lachlan could feel it down deep in his bones.

With the last of their strength, the men plodded through camp, pushed past the flaps, and eased the Ark to the ground.

Geoffrey hunched, hands on his knees. "Why … does it have to be … so heavy?"

"Aye." Finlay wiped his brow and flinched when the sting of salt touched the open blisters covering his palms. "It's one thin' to protect the contents, and another to carry it within somethin' so leaden."

"Not lead, but layers of gold. You blasphemous buffoons know as well as I … no light shall enter the Ark of the Covenant, so what better way to protect such precious cargo? Why must I always remind you of the importance for which we toil? I tell you, that alone is exhausting." Lachlan shook his head and rapped on the Ark. "Enough of these sinful complaints of sore hands and burdened backs. Night is upon us, and it's time to sup."

Later they rested near the fire, platters of roasted vegetables at their sides.

"Will they ever stop chasin' us?" Brody snapped a twig and tossed the pieces into the flames, where the pine crackled and hissed.

With a simple flick of Isadora's wrist, bedrolls, blankets, and chainmail hovered in the air, yet her gaze kept returning to the only hiding place left. The Ark. Legend had it that God struck down those who touched it. But it mattered not. She had her orders—grab the Grail and get out.

"*Demito.*" The items floated back to the ground, seemingly undisturbed. Isadora inched closer to the Ark's golden cherubim poised on top, hand outstretched, fingers trembling, and swallowed down the building dread. She had trained years for this monumental moment, so why did fear of the unknown wreak havoc on her now? God or no God, she had to pull it together, so she focused on the lid and dug deep within her soul. "*Aperio.*"

Nothing moved.

Isadora clenched her hand and scowled, mumbling a litany of curses under her breath. She could not fail. All depended on her.

It was common knowledge that the Church thought women insignificant, so of course, they chose her, just as the Sisterhood predicted. Those bishops expected Isadora to test the waters, and if she drowned while doing so, only then would they dispatch the Almighty man. But unbeknownst to them, they recruited a witch. Hypocrisy at its finest.

Isadora's eyes rolled back, and glowing white replaced the blue. "Spiritual sisters and all diabolic devils and demons, I implore you. Grant me thy will to overcome my weakness. Take thy fear from my wretched soul. Replace it with courage and the power to prevail in all that is unholy." Pushing frustration aside, Isadora held her breath and touched the Ark.

The earth didn't quake, and the skies didn't fall.

Since magic proved worthless, Isadora snatched her dagger and kneeled beside the Ark. She wedged the enchanted blade under the lid, and the forged steel bent each time she pried upward. Again, the lid wouldn't budge.

As an exasperated sigh fell from her lips, a voice mumbled from behind, "Damn you, Lachlan. Always right."

Isadora spun, taking aim with the knife and a hex on her tongue, but her heart settled when she encountered a sweet smile and a set of green eyes—hypnotic, breathtaking eyes. Some would call him devilishly handsome, but a plan was a plan, so attractive or not, he had to die. "Where is it?"

"It?" He cocked his head.

Teeth bared, Isadora kept her voice low. "Fool, you know I talk of the Holy Grail."

"Ahh, that old thing." The young man rocked back on his heels and flexed his toes.

Isadora twitched her head toward the Ark. "Open it."

"You understand why they desire it, yes?"

He was stalling, and she knew it. "Aye, eternal life from one small sip. Now do as I say and *open the Ark*." Her voice lowered, and Isadora's eyes burned into him as she used the Power of Suggestion—a spell she had grasped long ago. It always worked on the weakest of minds, and men were just that—weak.

"Why would anyone want that?"

Damn him. Isadora slammed her fist down on the Ark. "Who wouldn't?"

"I would wish it on no one." He frowned. "It takes the strongest of wills to endure loneliness of that nature."

"Pfft, loneliness? Even I, a lowly woman, shall drink before relinquishing it." She cackled. "Even my sisters shall sip before putting the Grail into the hands of those we despise. No, sir, I fear no loneliness."

"So, you are no better than they are. How sad."

"You dare to compare us? For years, those who considered themselves disciples of Christ slaughtered my kind. White magic, dark magic—it mattered for naught. Burned alive at the stake. Drowned. Any way they saw fit." Isadora twirled the dagger around her knuckles and caught the handle in mid-toss, the sharp end pointing straight between his eyes. "It is our time for retribution. We'll take their gold before bringing them all to their knees. With our new immortality, the Sisterhood shall rule the world."

"But with immortality comes a blood toll. Do you not see—"

"I do not care to see, only succeed." He had wasted enough of her time. Isadora charged, grabbing his tunic and pressing the dagger to his throat. "Open. It. Now." Keeping the blade in place, she dragged him to the Ark.

With a hand resting on each side of the Ark, the young man bowed his head and whispered, "I beseech you, please, walk away before—"

Isadora thwacked the back of his skull with the butt of her dagger, and he groaned. "Enough of your pointless prattle."

"So be it." Rubbing the knot on his head, he reached under the lid, and the seal cracked open.

"Out of my way." Isadora shouldered past, pushed the lid over, and searched inside, brow furrowing. "I come for a chalice, not these burdensome tablets. Do the templars not carry it?" She snorted, lifting a pair of worn boots and tossing them to the side. "Does it even exist?"

"Things are not always as they seem."

Isadora's shoulders slumped, and guilt swelled in her belly. Even though she failed in her mission, leaving loose ends could spoil the sisterhood's next attempt at eternal life. Any other day, she wouldn't give a damn about the unfortunate fate of an innocent, but on this given night,

Isadora pitied this man who would die by her hand. Life was not fair, it seemed.

Isadora faced him. "I'll have your name, young knight."

"Knight? You think I'm one of them?"

"You speak in the manner of a templar, all noble and such, all holier than thou."

The corner of his mouth curled up. "I give you my word. I am no knight, noble or not."

"Then I'll have your name, young sir." Isadora drew the last word out.

"My name?" He raised his eyebrows and tilted his head to the side. "Shall I whisper it in your ear, my lady?" he softly said.

"I think not." She held the dagger in a death grip, and the candlelight caught the sharp edge of the blade.

He stalked closer.

Her hand glowed as the magic built within. "I warn you, stay where you are. Halt, I say!"

With his next bold step, Isadora directed her power at his chest, energy rippling from her palm in a stream of blue fire. She smirked, eyes reflecting the flames licking up his neck and nipping at his flesh. Now he could experience what her kind had endured for years. But her evil grin faded when he patted his clothing and smothered the flames. He even had the gall to lick two fingers and snuff the last spark out between them. To hell with magic. Isadora spun in the air, gown rippling in a cyclone of linen and lace, and lashed out with the dagger, slicing his neck.

Blood spurted, soaking his singed cloak, yet he continued to close the distance, expression now impassive.

Mesmerized. Enchanted. Breath caught mid-throat. She couldn't push him away when he cupped her cheek. Isadora's power drifted away, merely out of reach, leaving her arms, legs, and mind heavy and numb. The knife slipped from

Isadora's grasp as his wounds mended before her eyes, and the green of his gaze swirled until glowing emeralds stared back. Perfect white teeth, behind flawless full lips, elongated into a pair of fine-tipped fangs.

"They call me Grail"—he touched his nose to the pulsing vessel on Isadora's neck and inhaled—"but holy … I am not."

Baseball Dreams
Wendy Vogel

Joey would have beat me bloody if he knew I joined the search for that missing woman. Carrie, her name was, and she left her work at the Backyard Bar one night and just didn't come home. They found her car in the river, so they started the search there, and we all lined up while a cop told us what was important and what was garbage. It seemed to me that anything other than a dead body was probably garbage, since we weren't looking for beer cans or used condoms, and that's pretty much all you got in this part of the riverbank where the kids go to hang out.

Joey and me used to hang out there, too. Back when I was a cheerleader, and he was heading for the minor leagues. We'd come down here after baseball practice and drink with his buddies. He was a different guy then, full of hope and big dreams. He never hit me before the wreck. But I was different then, too.

The cop said if we saw anything, we should stop right there and not touch it. Just yell for him and the dog to come check it out. I wouldn't be touching a dead body if I found one, not that it was likely. Just because they found her car there didn't mean they were going to find Carrie anywhere nearby. If you were going to dump a body near a car, why not just leave it in the trunk? But she wasn't in the trunk, so we shuffled through the woods by the river, step by step, everybody looking down like we were hunting for shells on a beach.

Joey took me to the beach one time. In Florida, where they let you drive your car right onto the sand. There weren't any shells, but there were a lot of people. Joey didn't like it when other guys looked at me in my bikini, but he's the one who said how hot I looked in it. I wore a T-shirt when I went down to the ocean, and a ballcap. He got really sunburned when he fell asleep by the pool, and we didn't have much fun after that.

We didn't find Carrie, and that's okay. I didn't think we would. But I thought I should go, because I knew what she looked like, and not just from the pictures on the news. Joey hung out at the Backyard Bar, and sometimes he took me. I didn't like how he looked at our waitress. It reminded me of how he used to look at me. Before the wreck.

He wouldn't have liked me looking for her, but he was at work. Summer was the busiest time for a guy who drove a concrete mixer for the city. Plenty of roads to fix. He wouldn't be home until dark, so he'd never know I was here.

My left ankle ached from the walking by the time I got back to my car. That was old pain, from the screws holding my foot on. It was almost ripped off in the wreck, but they did a good job putting it back together. It only hurt if I walked too much or if the ground was uneven and I turned it funny. I can't wear high heels anymore, and Joey hates that. Sometimes I put them on for him, but only when I'm lying down. That makes him happy for a little while. Especially if the lights are down and he doesn't have to look at my face. The scars make him sick, and he tells me all the time. I think they remind him of that night he drank too much and our dreams both shattered like the windshield, crumpled like the front end of a Camaro.

And honestly, I was the lucky one. My ankle and my face were nothing. His elbow was everything. The doctors did everything they could, but his pitching arm was never going to pitch again.

Things went bad after that.

He didn't get addicted to pain meds or anything. But when you have this one dream from the time you're a little kid, and you work every single day of your life to make that dream come true, and it feels like it really will happen, then it's just gone, well, that's gonna leave a mark inside you. And the scars on the inside are way worse than the ones on the outside.

His truck wasn't there when I pulled up in front of the house. If I timed this right, it would never pull up there again.

My hands were shaking as I unlocked the front door. It was an overcast day, and Joey always kept the blinds shut in all the windows. The front room was all shadows on the old, stained couch. What little light there was reflected off last night's crushed beer cans. I counted fourteen on the coffee table in front of the TV, and I left them there. The dogs were outside in the back yard, barking up a storm as usual. Probably an opossum in the woodpile, or maybe a snake under the shed.

I'd seen it first thing when I came down for breakfast. Almost washed away, but there was no mistaking the print of his size twelve work boots. The smudge was still there now, of course. Joey doesn't clean much. That's women's work. Most of the time. There was another stain on the doorframe that led to the basement. I didn't clean that one, either, but it sent ice right down into my stomach.

I didn't want to go down there. But it was safe without Joey home. And I had to see. Had to be sure. It could have been a nightmare, and I'd look a fool if I wasn't sure. Way worse than a fool. Mangled and broken, if I were lucky. Cold and stiff if not.

It was an old house, and we always kept the basement door shut, because it was just splintered wood over a dirt floor down there, and it always smelled like damp and mold. When the dogs got down there, they liked to dig and made an unholy mess for me to clean up. Joey never went down there unless I was in big trouble. And he always made me go first. It was cold and wet, and sometimes I was down there for a long time. Three days once, down in the dark with the water bugs and the mice, chain wrapped so tight around my bad ankle that I couldn't walk for two weeks after. But he never went down without me.

The top three steps squealed under my weight. I held onto the handrail as I descended the first few steps in pitch black, feeling over my head for the cord that turned on the bare bulb at the bottom of the stairs. It clicked on, turning the black into more shadows.

There wasn't anything to be afraid of down there. Not when Joey wasn't home. But it still felt like a million eyes were watching me as I left the bottom step and stopped on the rotting floor planks. Probably spiders in the walls, all telling me to go back upstairs and get out of here before it was too late. The washing machine and dryer were down here, an old yellow top-loader we got secondhand when Joey bought the house. The last people who lived here left a bunch of tools, all rusty and covered with spiderwebs, hanging on an old pegboard over a metal worktable. Joey wasn't into woodworking. But the tools had certainly come in handy.

More blood down here.

Joey's baseball bat was shoved in the corner, same as this morning, partly hidden under a bunch of moldy shop towels. And fresh dirt was all over the floorboards. The ones that were still attached.

I knew what was under the other ones. The boards in the corner where the ground sloped down at the back of the house.

Her face was pummeled way beyond anybody recognizing her from a picture. A baseball bat will do that.

I should have called the cops first thing this morning, after Joey left for work, hungover and dragging ass from the weekend. Carrie's name was all over the news, and even though the body under the floor didn't look like her anymore, there was no doubt whose blood was all over the bat.

But I had to see who came to search for her. Who had red eyes from crying about her. Had to see their faces before I made the call that would destroy them like that bat destroyed her.

No more waiting. I called the cops. Told them what I found in the basement. What I could see when I lifted up the floor plank. Blond hair mashed in with so much blood. I didn't touch the baseball bat.

Oh, Joey.

Things should have been so different. You should have been a major league pitcher by now. I should have still been beautiful, instead of the scarred, twisted mess the windshield left behind.

But it wasn't different. It was this.

When I heard the creak of the top stairs, I thought it was the cops. They come quick when you find a dead body in your basement.

It was Joey.

He called down from the top of the steps. "Marnie, what you doin' down there?"

I didn't answer. I should have. He wouldn't have come down if I'd just said I was doing laundry. But I froze up too long.

He was right in my face before I knew it, staring down into the little space in the dirt under the floorboards.

"Jesus Christ, Marnie. What the fuck did you do?"

When he looked back at me, it was that look I knew so well. He was gonna hurt me bad. I shouldn't have lifted up that floorboard. Shouldn't have let him know that I knew what was down here. But it was too late.

He shoved me away from the hole in the floor, and I stumbled, crying out when I rolled over my bad ankle. I crumpled to the floor, feeling splinters lodge in my hands and knees.

"Jesus, Marnie, what the fuck?"

He came at me again, boot raised to kick me, and I scuttled backward, right into the worktable. I hauled myself up, looking for anything I could use.

Screwdriver.

It was stuck to the pegboard, but I pried it loose and turned around just as Joey got to me. I buried it in his shoulder, and his eyes got so wide. But it didn't stop him. He grabbed me by the arms and flung me over, right over that missing floorboard. I scrambled back as he pulled the screwdriver out of his shoulder in a shower of fresh blood. And still he came. He'd come close to killing me a bunch of times since the accident changed him. But this time it was for real. This time there'd be two bodies under the floorboards.

My hands found the moldy shop towels and the bat underneath it. When I pulled it out, even in the dim light, I could see it still had long blond, bloody hairs stuck to it. I pushed myself up and raised that bat, looking like he used to look a million years ago, when we were different people.

"Police! Drop your weapon!"

I dropped the bat. Joey whirled around and started babbling on to the cops on the stairs about how he didn't know nothin' about it and how I attacked him. But I was limping, and we were both covered in blood, and there was a dead waitress under the floor of the house he owned. I still had plenty of bruises from the last time he beat me, and he knew it.

The cops cuffed him, and he turned a look on me that should have made me roll up on the floor and cover my head. But this time was different.

As they pushed him up the stairs and a kind, gentle cop told me it was all going to be all right, I caught Joey's eye under that bare lightbulb.

I gave him just the tiniest smile.

No more beatings. No more chains in the basement. No more waitresses he thought I didn't know about.

And now, no more Joey.

Fortune Cookie
Carl D. Jenkins

San Francisco. The name alone conjures images of many things—trolley cars, bridges, Chinatown, road construction. It's where I'm from.

It was in a small factory on a narrow road. The workers there mostly spoke Chinese, when they spoke at all. But the wisdom we were born to reveal was in a different language, an often choppy language. We never knew what wisdom we carried until we found our destinies, but I saw many siblings meet theirs in the shop.

He who would go far see many thing before arrive.

I took that one for my purpose when it was ejected onto the tray beside me. I do not know if my sibling left empty or if she was found out, but I honor her memory for the gift she granted me. It offered courage as I traveled in the world. I hope she found a path that made her happy.

The air was still sweet as I was packaged into a cellophane pouch and tumbled into a large box with dozens more. I do not know how long I slumbered in that sweetness before harsh light brought me back to wakefulness. I gazed up at the youngest human I had yet seen as she smiled upon us. I felt the wisdom tickling at my insides and somehow knew my purpose had to do with her.

But my time was not yet come. This human scooped many of us into a bowl and closed the lid again, leaving me to slumber. Each time the light came, I wondered. Sometimes it was the young, smiling one looking in on me, and other times it was a craggy thing whose lips creased more than us. I wondered what wisdom she locked inside and if any would ever benefit from it. I hoped I would not be waiting as long as she.

Oh, lucky day when the smiling face finally pulled me from the box. Her fingers were light upon me, almost as gentle as the wrapper that kept the air around me sweet.

I watched from my perch as she walked through a place that looked far different from the factory. I liked that bowl. It let in the light, and my slumbers were shorter.

"Bing Gan!" the voiced boomed, and the young woman turned. There stood a man in an apron no longer bright. I could smell him from inside the bowl as we drew near. His hand dipped into the bowl, rough and acrid from burned things. I was horrified that this might be my end, but his hand withdrew with another and left me at the very bottom of the bowl.

I watched with terror as the man tore open the pouch and did not even look at the wisdom my sibling contained before casting it away. Bing Gan did not look at him, but his lips leered agape, any wisdom he may have contained long spent; I pity whomever he may have passed it on to.

I enjoyed those days in the bowl, watching people come and go. Many hands approached me, some attached to people so short I could not gauge how they guarded wisdom. But Bing Gan remained the one I felt connected to.

Every time the bowl grew depleted, I grew happy that my turn neared; but every time, the bowl was replenished. The sour woman always stirred the bowl, and the dirty man would always interrupt Bing Gan to dip his smelly hand into our midst.

After some time, I realized the young woman would stay close to me when a particular young man was in the shop. He always sat in the same place. She watched him when she was near me but barely glanced up when she was near him. He always smiled at her, but they kept their wisdom close.

I began to watch him too and realized his gaze would often follow her when she was with other customers. I wondered at this custom as I saw other patrons sharing their wisdom with one another. That these two so clearly wanted to but did not made no sense.

The days grew long, and the air in my pouch began to lose its freshness. I worried that I might never get my chance. But chance eventually appeared in a most intriguing way. Bing Gan herself reached into the bowl one day, her fingers coming straight to me. She pressed me to her lips, nearly as soft as her fingers had been.

She placed me on a tray with some sort of paper, a contract perhaps, and placed me on the table beside the young man. He smiled as usual, and still she refused to meet his eyes. I heard him say, "Thank you," as he signed the paper and placed me inside his pocket.

Oh, sweet slumber. I probably needed it, but it was warm in a pulsing way. I think it was short too, as I found myself in a pile of things that included several old siblings in a very tiny facility that moved quickly, and I could not see those we passed. It pulsed loud and faster than the man. When it was still, a variety of people passed, and I could see them all, some sharing wisdom and others either silent or all shared out. But only the young man ever entered.

Occasionally, he would reach for one of us, and I would hear him speak the wisdom aloud. The slips of wisdom and empty wrappers surrounded me on the dash.

Do not chase happiness – create it
Share your happiness with others today

It's taking a lot of wisdom to fill this one up. Perhaps that was it; he did not yet have enough wisdom to share. I did not want to see him turn into someone like that dirty man, empty of wisdom and smelling of dead things.

My days continued to be long, and I missed Bing Gan. The young man was not around much, and there were no others to provide distraction. But sometimes, when he visited Bing Gan's facility, he would park where I could see inside. Every time, it was the same. He would smile, and she would be looking away.

I noticed, too, another pattern. The cookies he saved were the ones she gave him. When she was not there, he left the wrapper and the fortune on the table. I looked at my siblings beside me in his facility. Not many remained.

The usefulness of a cup is in its emptiness
Each new song begins with a single note

Finally, I see him prepare to leave, and he stands to talk with her. She finally looks back and returns his smile, the same bright smile she gave to all of us many times when she filled the bowl. Even when deciding which of us was to go to whom, the sour woman never looked and let fortune fall where it would.

The man was excited for the next few days, and he often looked to where I sat on the dash.

One door closes so that another open
Success come soon

I am now alone, but I have seen the beginning. My Bing Gan and this young man have begun to share their wisdom. It can only grow from here, and I see it will take many more destinies to awaken them completely.

We are out front of Bing Gan's facility now, but it is dark. I wonder why we have come, and I am fighting against slumber. Only the tiny light above and the music are keeping me from it. I can barely see the man in his seat. A door opens on the facility—not the big one I can see through but a small dark one I never noticed before.

Then she appears—Bing Gan. She looks around before approaching. She opens a door beside me. I have not noticed this door before either. He always enters from the other side. So many new things. This must be her door. I am overjoyed that she has her own door. He offers her gum—a limp, fragrant wafer that provides scent instead of wisdom. He unwraps it more often than he does my siblings but always spits it out, leaving the smell to keep me company. I barely remember the sweetness of the factory, and I'm afraid he notices.

He asks if she would like to go someplace called 'the lake.' She is looking at me when she agrees.

They do not talk much on the way, and what they do say does not sound a lot like wisdom, but they are sharing. She keeps looking at me. Finally, they stop, and she gathers all the empty wrappers and places them someplace I cannot see. They take turns reading the slips of paper to one another before they disappear as well.

"But this one," she asks, and I feel her fingers on me once again, "why do you still have it?"

"That one is special."

"How so?" I hear teasing in her voice. It is a new sound, a dangerous sound.

"That is the one you kissed."

Her eyes go wide, and her color changes. She looks away again, and he places me to his own lips. They are rough, but his touch is as gentle as hers.

He offers me back to her, and I am torn. I realize I have accepted that my destiny lies with him.

"Share it with me?"

She sits still a moment, coloring deeper and deeper until I worry she will burst into flames. I look out over the lake. It is vast, dark and shimmery at the same time. I do not know what is out there. I know not what even to imagine.

I feel her fingers on me once again, along with his. I feel my wrapper gently pulled away. The sweetness of the factory air, nearly exhausted, makes way for new smells. It does not smell like death. The smell of gum fuses with the fragrances of almond, vanilla, and orange I am used to. I smell what must be the lake. I feel their pulses synchronize as they pull open my shell, the final tickle of wisdom released first from one half, and then the other.

Her teeth bite first as he reads aloud, then his, before I drift off into slumber, my destiny finally fulfilled.

Good things take time

The First Step
William Thatch

Walt Haynes stood front and center on the big stage he had dreamed of playing on since he had first picked up a guitar. A surreal, otherworldly feeling overcame him—something he hadn't felt in years—like the first time they had had opened for bigger acts on the country-wide rock-and-roll tour that first put his band, Southern Love, on the map and propelled them into superstardom. For that moment, Walt felt as if he had become one with music—an antenna tuned to the universe's artistic frequency, with no purpose other than to welcome and disseminate the cosmic radio waves. A sea of ten thousand heads banged along to the rhythm of Nick's drumming as Walt belted out the final lyrics of the band's first number one single, "The Wayward Son," since their debut in the early '90s.

Walt abandoned the bass guitar, letting it hang from his neck, as he grabbed the microphone still in its stand, bent at the waist, and turned, holding the final note as the veins in his neck and arms popped due to his intensity. When his lungs had depleted their breath, the guitarists, Johnny and Danny, played their final notes, and Walt dropped the microphone stand to the floor. The band stood tall and peered into the thousands of eyes locked onto them, raised their hands, and welcomed the roar of the fans.

It marked the first time in years that Walt had felt a natural high. It had been there for most of the first national tour, until the days on the road had become routine and monotonous and the notes had lost meaning in their repetition. Something reverberated in the air Walt needed that night, a reminder of why he continued the path he'd chosen in life.

As he stood before the legion of fans chanting their name, Walt's skin tingled like an electrical current coursing through him. At that moment, he had ten thousand fans, ten thousand friends, ten thousand people who had taken time out of their day and money from their pockets to experience his art. He felt more alive on stage than ever in his life.

But tonight, Walt Haynes never felt more isolated and alone, as if the stage had turned on him. For years, the crowd's adoration and the thrill of performing had meant he spent a night with the love of his life—music.

Tonight, however, the love he received felt wrong, as if he were a lothario only looking for his next night of passion and had tricked a woman into believing he wanted more than to get off, as if he'd uttered, 'I love you.' He didn't deserve their approval. It felt like every finger in the room was pointing at him, shaming him. His reason for waking up every day for years, living out a wild dream come true, now filled him with a cold, empty feeling that terrified him.

Walt recoiled from the crowd even as Danny, Johnny, and Nick took the time to throw drumsticks and guitar picks to them. He beelined for the backstage area, ripping the bass guitar strap from around his neck, and shoved it into a roadie's hands.

He assumed Danny, Johnny, and Nick would follow him soon after, but Walt didn't care enough to check. He needed to get as far away from the stage as possible.

Walt had become enamored with the stage and performing since the summer before he started grade school when his parents took him to Nashville to visit his grandfather Ernie. There, in a local bar, he watched his grandfather croon on stage for the half-empty room while strumming his guitar. Walt's father explained that once upon a time, Ernie Haynes had even released an album when vinyl was the medium of choice. But his career had never taken off, and Ernie settled into a comfortable profession as a session musician for more prominent names in country and blues.

So many years later, Walt remembered the feeling that night as the barflies gave the aging Ernie a standing ovation but also his grandfather's beaming smile and the energy Ernie Haynes was imbued with after the show. The old man Walt had just met, moving slow and gingerly as age took its toll, became rejuvenated after every show.

From that point forward, there was no questioning his destiny. Not only did Walt want to perform on stage, he needed it. In the days that followed, he would be reprimanded every other day in school for jumping onto the teacher's desk and tunelessly belting out an incoherent string of words. Eventually, as he grew older, his parents also rebuked him for neglecting his schoolwork in favor of studying and practicing his music, listening to every album he could get his hands on.

The guilt from the stage that night followed Walt like a ghoul, chasing him through the venue's hallway, where he stopped only to grab a bottle of beer from a cooler. He burst into the dressing rooms and threw himself into the shower, still clothed.

The cold water was a welcomed shock to his system, distracting him and reminding him that he hadn't stripped down. Piece by piece, Walt peeled off the clothing to wash the grime and sweat he had accumulated during his performance as the water slowly warmed.

But the guilt wasn't washing away.

Walt's heart pounded, his breathing hastened, and his brain raced as everything he felt that night, which had built inside him, crashed down, sending the weight of his world onto his shoulders. A strangled cry escaped him, muffled by his hand over his mouth and a swig of the beer, and his eyes burned. Walt didn't know if there were tears. They were lost in the water rolling down his skin if there were any.

I have to get a hold of myself.

They had a half hour between the show's end and the meet and greet with fans.

Walt slapped himself across the face with all his strength. Unprepared for the drastic action, he recoiled into the tiled wall. Righting himself, Walt tensed and struck again, this time with his off hand. His face stung as blood rushed to the stricken areas.

"I'm okay," Walt whispered. "I'm fine."

Stepping from the shower, Walt heard the band in the locker room. Going out and dealing with the three of them filled him with renewed dread.

The band had been dysfunctional from day one. Upon meeting Nick, his instincts had told him the two wouldn't work out, but living in rural Wyoming, the teenagers who would form Southern Love had been excited to have assembled a full band. More communication, debate, and concessions regarding the band's direction had occurred then, but in hindsight, they were obviously living on borrowed time as a group. Walt's influences included his grandfather's genres, mixed with a little rock and roll. Nick, meanwhile, kept pushing for heavier, louder metal. The longer the band continued, the more they fought over the little decisions.

Danny, having played with Walt for years before the band's formation, often sided with Walt, while Johnny, a few years their junior, remained loyal to Nick after Nick had left a band that had refused to let Johnny jam with them. Caught in the middle was the now former bassist of Southern Love, Cody Davis, as the middleman trying to balance the peace and decide tiebreakers.

"Maybe Cody had the right idea," Walt muttered as he collected his soaked clothing from the tile.

Cody had gotten fed up with the fighting a few weeks before. It had been during a rehearsal before the show that night when Walt and Nick had shouted at each other, barely cognizant of the fans there. Walt couldn't even remember what it had been about anymore. Not that he and Nick needed a reason to start in on each other. Cody had loudly declared, *"Fuck it, I'm done,"* and had walked out. The band's manager had tried talking him out of quitting, but Cody had his fill of the endless fighting.

No one in the band had heard from him since.

Walt entered the locker room, and the *THWAP!* of a rubber band firing from somewhere greeted him, connecting with his right testicle. Walt groaned as a torrent of laughter filled the room.

"Nice one!" Nick extended a closed fist to Johnny.

Proudly, Johnny accepted the offer of a fist bump.

Walt glared at Danny. He expected that of Nick and Johnny. He had followed Nick around like a puppy dog ever since Nick's original band with Johnny's older brother had broken up over a disagreement about Johnny's inclusion in the band. Nick's decision to side with the more talented brother had earned him almost unquestioning loyalty from Johnny. Danny, however, had been one of Walt's closest friends since grade school.

Grunting through the pain, Walt hobbled to his suitcase and discarded his wet clothing on the bench beside it. He threw open the suitcase, rifled through, grabbed some shirts, and gave them a sniff test, discarding them one by one as they reeked of sweat and filth from weeks on the road.

"Didn't you change your shirt last week?" Danny asked.

"Yeah, but I need a new one," Walt replied.

Although said under his breath and behind his back, Walt heard the bench creak under Nick as he leaned toward Johnny and muttered, "Prima donna."

Walt clenched his fist but thought better than starting another fight. Everything ached enough—physically, emotionally, and mentally. He couldn't take another battle right now.

As he grabbed his last clean shirt, an envelope caught in the folds fell into the suitcase. He stared at it, then his trembling hand covered it with the dirty laundry. He pulled on the clean shirt, revealing it to be one donning the band's logo.

"Oh my god," Nick groaned. "Are you seriously wearing one of our shirts?"

"Fucking mark," Johnny chimed in with a grin.

"It's the only clean one I've got!"

"Mark," Danny said, masking his comment with a cough into his fist.

Although Walt had heard Danny's comment, the words felt as if they had come from someone driving past at ninety miles an hour; the words lost any meaning or point to the wind. With a still-unsteady hand, Walt zipped his luggage closed, grabbed another beer from the cooler, and left the dressing room.

Walt traversed the backstage area on autopilot, fixated on the floor ahead of him and nothing else. The world around him had been stripped away as the standard 4x9½ envelope with his name neatly printed on the front took precedence over everything else hanging around his neck.

Southern Love had been on the road for a few weeks by the time he had found the letter from his parents tucked into one of the luggage's front pockets. At first, he had found it strange, as he had visited his hometown of Riverton before leaving on tour. Surely his parents could have said anything they had needed to then.

At first, the letter, written in his mother's unmistakable print, had told him how proud of him they were, that he had worked hard for the success he had garnered, and that he deserved all the adulation he received. It was nice to hear, as his visit had not been pleasant, and Cody had already quit the band by this time.

And then the tone changed.

For the rest of the page, and a couple thereafter, Walt's mother—and presumably his father, judging by choice wording—explained how disappointed and disgusted his parents had grown in the man they raised and how his antics were unacceptable. Listed among his wrongdoings were instances where his parents felt he had been rude or disrespectful to the people back home. They made a point of addressing how, perhaps to the rest of the world, he was a rockstar extraordinaire, but to his friends, family, and community, he was an 'asshole'—one of the choice words that let Walt know his father had helped with the writing. It wasn't out of the ordinary in the conservative rural town for men to have more coarse language in the workplace, but it stayed there.

Other transgressions listed included his own use of language, his almost constant state of drinking, being loud and boorish, and the time he had tried return food at a community barbecue for not being cooked to his liking.

As the letter listed each item, Walt scoffed and argued against it in his head. *They're just words. Fucking get over it. Yeah, I drink, but I can handle it. I just wanted some seasoning on the chicken; that's not unreasonable!*

That was the broad list of issues. It continued onto specific instances and complaints from townsfolk, often only whispered around Riverton but sometimes directly to Walt's parents. The elementary and high school students had petitioned him to talk to them about pursuing their dreams and hard work, but Walt had blown it off because of a hangover. When the pastor had asked if Walt would be attending church services on Sunday, Walt had acted disgusted with the idea of being up that early. His bawdry tales of life on the road had affronted some of the men who, while Walt was sure they had enjoyed the stories he told them, felt it was inappropriate in public.

It was just dreadful to hear them talking about when you got thrown out of the bar in Hudson, his mother wrote.

But that's what rock stars do, Walt argued to himself.

That had become the expectation of Southern Love when they came to a town. They sold out a show, met with fans afterward, and if anyone wanted to continue the party, a bar would always be open until they shut it down. It started on their first major tour with an established band. The five had been trying to keep pace with the rock stars who had made it in the business.

It's part of the job, Walt told himself firmly. *She doesn't understand that.*

The letter also mentioned the rumors about what they had been doing on the road: *No one needs a watch that costs that much.*

I don't even have that watch anymore. It broke when I jumped into the Bellagio's water display.

I've heard that you boys have left bastard children all over this country.

If we have, I haven't heard about it.

I expect that behavior from Nick, but the rest of you know better.

A little cocaine never killed anybody.

As with any celebrity, the rumors often held a kernel of truth, but like a game of telephone, they would end up blown out of proportion.

As Walt crossed the threshold into the venue's vestibule, he gave the letter another dismissive excuse. *She just doesn't understand this life.*

Walt had tried to make it a point to be responsible regarding the partying. At first, he had sworn he would never drink on show day, which he later revised to not before a show, then only when he was partying. But the party never seemed to end.

In the lobby, Walt heard the cheers from the two hundred fans who had stuck around to meet with the band and get some autographs. He smiled wide, gave them a resounding greeting, and tried not to let on that anything had been wrong that night. Every fan there, however distant he felt in the moment, had paid good money for a performance—both on stage and off—and Walt intended to ensure it was money well spent.

Walt stalled for a moment until the rest of the band caught up to him, and they sat behind wooden tables. As it had been for quite a while, Danny and Johnny ensured to sit between Walt and Nick to give them as much distance as possible. For the next couple hours, their hands danced across shirts, jewel cases, and a fair number of breasts.

One fan unrolled a poster. "Hey, can you sign this?"

"Sure thing." Walt laid his hand on the picture to flatten it out and poised his pen before taking stock of what he saw.

The artwork was an expanded version of the cover art for Southern Love's latest album, featuring details that couldn't fit on the small CD booklet. The artist, having drawn it in a comic book style, had a scantily clad, busty, blonde woman seductively licking a crucifix dominating most of the picture. To make the image that little bit more sacrilegious, the image of Jesus Christ on the cross, complete with a depiction of a crown of thorns around his head, was winking at the woman. Other art on the poster depicted the band on a stage, in the background, amid a nuclear mushroom cloud, playing to a mosh pit of teenagers. Although easy to miss at first, there were implications of a few lewd acts within the chaos of the pit, and a couple people had their arms tied off as they injected themselves with heroin.

Walt had approved the artwork, both album and poster, as he had felt it encompassed the band's theme of rebelling against authority and society's norms and hammered home with the aggressive title of the album, *Take That, Society*.

He loved the artwork but couldn't help but wonder if it wasn't a bit much. The letter his mother had penned pointed out that despite how highly regarded the boys had been for their success, the local music store had placed a large price sticker containing the band's name over the artwork.

No one wants this smut in their children's hands, his mother had written.

Many parents back home had forbidden their children from buying the latest album. At the time, the news had caused Walt to smirk; it was great marketing. The parents say no, the band becomes more desirable when merely listening to them becomes an act of rebellion, and the kids find a way to do it anyway. But the artwork, upon closer inspection, shouldn't have been in kids' hands. Walt agreed with that in hindsight.

Walt signed the poster and thanked the fan, then moved on to more autographs and fans telling him how much the music meant to them. Little by little, the line of fans cleared out, until only the band and two fans who had purchased the VIP package to hang out on the tour bus remained.

Normally Walt would take the lead, keeping the conversation flowing with the VIPs—in this instance, two women named Shannon and Charlene, who had brought their own cooler stocked with cans of Eisberg beer—but Walt couldn't shake the artwork.

Of course, everyone would have a problem with that. They're a 'church on Sunday every week' sort of people. The thought kept circling until Walt remembered a promise he and Danny had made to their mothers; they'd maintain attending church every Sunday. He couldn't remember how long they had kept up with that, but he suspected they hadn't carried the promise throughout the first tour.

He used to look forward to the community gathering on Sundays, especially the part where they would sing the hymns. He wouldn't have ever considered himself devoutly religious, but he had attempted early on, even if only because his parents had expected it of him.

By the time the group had reached the tour bus, Walt had forced himself to refocus on being social. The fans were important; without them, he wouldn't be living this life, and everyone in the band knew that. As often as the band was at each other's throats, they made a point to be professional in front of the fans—even Nick.

For the next hour, Walt, Nick, Johnny, Danny, Shannon, and Charlene drank, told stories, and asked questions of one another as cans and bottles piled around them. Despite his smile and the obvious flirting from both women, everything happening around him felt a million miles away. It was one of the most incredible moments of being a rock star in Walt's eyes—getting one-on-one time with the fans and learning how his music had affected different people from different walks of life.

But the more intimate setting of the tour bus felt no different from the stage earlier that night. It felt wrong. He didn't want to be there. He wanted to want to be there, but his heart wasn't in it.

Walt exited the bus with a bottle in one hand and a half-empty pack of cigarettes in the other, claiming he'd forgotten something in the venue. Ensuring he was out of sight so as not to have anyone disturb him, Walt moved to the back of the bus.

The first drag of the Red Apple cigarette calmed the anxiety that had built in the pit of his stomach all night. Walt's eyes wandered to the night sky dotted with thousands of stars. *When was the last time I looked up at the stars?*

It'd been a long time, he knew. But he didn't have the time anymore. Everything churned along so fast these days. He couldn't recall the last time precisely, but he remembered the most significant time.

His friend Thomas—the band's original drummer with Walt and Danny before they had found Nick and Johnny—stole the keys to his father's truck and took it for a ride, along with a bottle of booze. The pair drove into the middle of a field, south of Riverton, where they reclined against the truck's windshield, gathering a buzz, and stargazed and discussed their plans.

"Man, fuck this town," Thomas said.

"I don't know," Walt muttered. "It's all right. I don't mind it."

"No, *fuck* this town. What is there to do here? Not a goddamned thing."

Riverton was one of the smallest towns in the least-populated state in the country. If you liked the simplicity of it, it was quaint and beautiful, and life moved along at just the right pace. If you wanted more, as Thomas wasn't shy about expressing, it was where hope went to die.

"Yeah, I mean … I guess I can't stay here if I want to make it big with the band," Walt said.

"Exactly! No one will hear all the great shit you guys are making. I tell you this now, the second I graduate—and I mean the *second* I graduate—I'm gone. I'll just take my dad's truck to somewhere better."

"I think he might notice the truck being gone that long."

"Fine, then I'll take a bus or something. Point is, I'm not staying here. There's nothing here. I want to see the lights of a city, man. I want excitement. I want to make money—like, real money—the sort of money where you never have to work again."

"That'd be cool," Walt said, his primitive teenage mind contemplating the life he could lead if the band took off: loud music, partying, everyone knowing his name. "I want a number-one single. The money you get from that must be insane."

"Yeah, now you're talking. Big time, big bucks, big-titted women," Thomas said, eliciting a laugh from both teens.

"Ah, I don't know. I'm just happy making the music."

"No, man. You gotta think big. If you don't, we'll be stuck in this one-note town the rest of our lives."

Thomas sat upright on the truck's hood, taking a swig from the bottle of amber liquid. "You and me, right now, we're making a pact."

Walt sat upright, a little lightheaded as the booze took hold.

"The two of us are gonna make it big, and we're gonna make it rich. We're bigger than this little town, and we're not gonna let it dictate what we deserve out of life. We deserve it. You deserve it."

Walt nodded. "Yeah. I deserve it. I'm working hard on the music every day. It's gotta count for something."

"Fuckin' picture it, dude. You on stage in front of ten—no, no!—twenty thousand screaming fans. Every song you put out is a number one hit. Women are throwing themselves at you, and record labels have bidding wars over you."

"Yeah …" A dreamy smile spread across his face. "Yeah, yeah, I like that. What about you?"

"I don't know. I'll figure it out. But we're gonna make it."

"Damn right we are."

"No, yell it, man. We're gonna make it in this world."

"We're gonna fucking make it!"

Thomas stood on the truck's hood, took another big drink, and shouted into the air at the top of his lungs, "We're gonna fuckin' make it in this—whoa!" The alcohol had taken hold of Thomas's sense of balance, sending him crashing off the truck to the hard ground below with a thud.

"Oh, shit!" Walt crawled gingerly to the edge of the truck, aware of his waning motor functions. "You okay?"

All Thomas could do during the coughing fit was give a thumbs up.

That night, for Walt, it wasn't just about the music. There was a goal, a mission, a pact to fulfill. He envisioned the life of a rock star, and it wasn't enough to be known in town as the kid who was good at the guitar and good at singing. He wanted the whole world to know.

Thomas had made it out of Riverton first. It hadn't been upon graduation, however. Thomas had flunked out, but he had taken that bus to Las Vegas. He was out of everyone's life—no word from him, no phone calls, no big newspaper stories. One day, after five years, he returned, disheveled and desperate, with tales of making it in Vegas. He'd gotten a lucky streak at the tables and had turned it into millions, until he had lost it all at the same tables that had made him.

While Thomas was gone, Walt and the others had chipped away at their dreams, writing and performing as often as possible, until someone in the business discovered them. It wasn't long after Thomas returned that the band was leaving to pave their chapter in rock-and-roll history.

It's the same old rock-and-roll story, Walt had penned in his lyric book at the time. He had seen the next ten years unfold in front of his eyes every night—the sex, drugs, and rock and roll—the path of a rock star painted clear as day in all those who had walked the hundred miles of hell before him, but still, he had driven down the same road.

All these years later, however, the same stars stared down as indifferently at Walt as they had that night, not knowing or caring about higher aspirations or success. They existed as burning stars somewhere in the universe, while Walt concluded that maybe his star had finally burned out, that he had lost everything on the same stage that had made him.

I just wanted to make music. Why'd everything have to get more complicated?

The music part was fun. Music had always been fun. But then Walt had to get the others involved to make the band happen. He had to get agents and managers and lawyers, had to sign contracts and tour, and he got to play that music, but so much more came with it.

Walt took another drag off the cigarette, blew smoke into the night air, and paused to look at the burning end. He hadn't smoked as a teenager. That had only come while touring when the life of a rock star had taken over. He'd always shied away from it. He'd lost his grandmother to lung cancer and had sworn never to start.

Walt sent the cigarette flying across the parking lot with a determined flick. "I don't want this anymore," Walt said to himself.

It took a moment for those words to sink in. He had said it about smoking, but something felt right about the words. Like they were a truth he had denied for a long time, it felt good to finally get it off his chest and admit it to himself.

"I don't want this anymore," he repeated, this time more confidently.

Walt took a deep breath and held it. He could reconsider, step back on that bus, and keep going.

But he didn't.

Walt had reached his decision—not in his mind or heart but in his soul. Some things in life were more important than being the rockstar extraordinaire, and he was losing those things the longer he deprived himself of them.

His grandfather was just one state over. Walt's wallet was with his luggage, but he wasn't going back for it. If he did, he'd never get away. The rockstar life had taken its pound of flesh from him, and he wouldn't let it take any more from him. He'd walk to his grandfather's if he had to.

And then, as Walt had written about in the last song with Southern Love in honor of Thomas, "The Wayward Son," Walt began walking away from it all.

Away from the tour bus.

Away from the laughter on board.

Away from the fighting and the arguments, the stress of the road, the pressure of management, the sex, the drugs, the booze, all of it.

Walt peeled off the Southern Love shirt, dropped it to the ground, and kept walking away from the life he had built.

His nerves were alight with anxiety. He couldn't promise it was the right decision.

But he promised himself he wouldn't look back.

The DeLorean
Mika Spruill

The voices in my head were right; stealing that car was the only sane thing to do. Why else would the shiny stainless-steel DeLorean arrive outside my apartment exactly one year after my world fell apart?

It's fate, one voice whispered.

The only way back to your life with Veronica, another said.

To find the man who stole her away, the third said.

I couldn't argue with their logic.

My neighbor, Oscar Ward, had bought the car weeks ago. I'd heard him through our shared wall discussing the logistics of its payment and transport. We lived at the end of the Windsor Hills complex dedicated to lonely middle-aged men—the divorced and the dejected—where the conditions proved almost as sad as its residents. Though we rarely spoke, I knew the arrival of the DeLorean was the culmination of Ward's life mission; he had little else.

You need this more than he does, the voices said. They were stronger now. The three years I'd spent with Veronica was the only time my mind had ever been completely quiet. *Don't wait. Do it tonight*, they urged in unison.

As a two-bit teenage thief, I would have chosen the classic screwdriver smash-and-start, but life—and a cherry-red Mustang with a silent alarm that landed me in juvie—had taught me a few things. For one, work smarter.

Ward was as predictable as my morning shits. He arrived home at 6:00 p.m. every night, his microwave dinner caused all the lights to flicker by 6:15, and he left for a walk and a smoke by 6:30, without the telltale jingle of his keys in the deadbolt. It was 6:32 p.m. when I heard his fat feet clomp down the hallway to the courtyard.

I skulked from my door to his, trying not to look guilty. I found it unlocked, just as I'd suspected. His living room was a jumble of game controllers, headsets, and cords connecting his massive flat-screen TV to the single gaming chair in the center of the room. Shelves of unopened action figures lined the walls, and in one corner lay a heap of empty Hungry Man cartons and Mountain Dew cans. His keys hung on a hook just inside the foyer. I snatched them and turned for the door.

Too easy. Keep looking. Maybe he has something valuable.

Do him a favor. Set a fire and watch this shit-pile burn.

Fuck, he's coming back. Hurry up before we get caught.

I made it out just as Ward turned into the hallway, lost in a conversation on his phone.

He knows.

He's calling the cops.

You might have to kill him.

"Of course, I love you, Min-Ji," Ward said, passing me without a glance. "I know. It's just that I was saving that money to fly you over here so we could meet. But I guess if you need it for your children ..." He disappeared into his apartment.

I wiped the sweat from my brow and ran to the car. The locks made a satisfying *pop*, the door raised just like in the movies, and the forty-plus-year-old engine purred like it was brand new.

Let's make like a tree and get out of here.

Dumbass. It's 'Let's make like a tree and leave.'

I know, but that's the line from the movie, fuckface.

It's wrong though, tit-wit.

Yeah, but it's in the movie that way.

I hit the gas to drown them out. The car lurched forward, past the point of no return.

As I drove through town, Veronica's face filled my mind, forcing my heart to leap and sputter. I would have returned in an instant to spend my life with her, but I couldn't forget how it ended—finding my wife in another man's arms. Granted, I'd been piss-ass drunk, and they were both a bit hazy, but I know what I saw.

Once a whore … the voices reminded me.

Veronica had vehemently denied everything, of course; there was no other man, and I was crazy. That one word had made my blood boil. I'd seized her by the throat, lifted her off her feet, and threw her into the bedroom wall. *'I'll show you crazy,"* I had yelled. By the time her limp body had crumpled to the floor, the man had disappeared like a ghost—not escaped but vanished—and no one would ever believe me. I lost everything that night—everything but the restraining order, a pending divorce, and the empty black hole I would never escape.

The voices broke through my reverie. *Find him, the man who stole your love …*

Your whole life …

And destroy him.

As the DeLorean careened into the empty lot outside Walmart, I racked my brain for bits of the movie I'd forgotten. Something about plutonium, a stopwatch and …

Maybe this wouldn't work.

Nonsense. Eighty-eight miles per hour, that's all you need.
You can't stop now.
What does Hollywood know anyway?
"There's nowhere to set a date," I said out loud. "How will I get back to the right day?"
Concentrate. Concentrate hard and we'll do the rest.
"I don't know."
Haven't we been helping you this whole time?
Don't you trust us?
If we're wrong, you can just dump the car and walk away.
They were right. I'd come this far; I couldn't give up now. Vengeance was within my grasp. I mashed the gas pedal and white-knuckled the wheel as the speedometer lurched past forty, sixty, eighty mph. Just as the dial neared ninety, the DeLorean veered out of control—a sharp left into the path of a light pole. I couldn't avoid it. Metal crunched, glass shattered, then time expanded and sent me on my way.

I had made it. I had actually traveled to the past. Our bedroom looked just as I'd remembered. Veronica stood by the bed, one leg propped while she lathered lotion into her golden skin. The sight of her stole my breath. I ached to touch her, to hold her one last time before the inevitable hell broke loose.

I closed the distance between us and wrapped my arms around her waist, leaning my head against her back. Her hair smelled like jasmine and vanilla. Even as I brushed it behind her shoulder and kissed her neck, she didn't turn, didn't even notice my presence.

A man burst through the bedroom door, and our eyes met.

I recognized him instantly, haggard and disheveled. He stumbled toward us, yelling obscenities and flailing his fist. He was me, and I was *him*.

I knew what happened next—a tragic mistake born of my own demons—but even as I moved to stop him—me—it was too late.

Veronica

Car wreck … wrapped around a pole … died upon impact.

James must not have changed my info in his phone after the divorce, because when the call came, the county police treated me with all the tenderness meant for a doting wife. They sounded confused when I didn't cry. I was only surprised this hadn't happened sooner.

James had been the product of the worst kind of childhood: born addicted, raised abusively, and abandoned before he was old enough to know right from wrong. From the moment we had met, he recklessly flaunted his wild side. It was exciting at first and later endearing when I had tamed his instabilities with my love.

We had married quickly, naively ensconced in our all-consuming passion, but soon he started drinking again, talking to himself and succumbing to all his old paranoias. I'd tried to reason with him, to hold us together as long as I could, but, after that night—when he broke my heart and split my skull—I knew it would never be enough to save him from himself.

Transference
Cody Larson

"So … when's the first virgin sacrifice?"

Her breath sent shivers up my spine as her whispered words slithered across my neck. I smirked, pushed the dull blond hair behind my ear, and flashed my eyes at her, hoping my cheeks weren't flushed.

"Not until next week, Jess. Don't worry, you're not on the menu."

She returned the smirk and rolled her eyes theatrically. "Ha-ha, Stevie. You can suck it."

Her eyes flicked to the book I was reading, and she nodded.

"What's that mean there? *Transference?*" she asked, standing and popping her hip to one side.

"Oh, that? I …" The words caught in my throat as I fumbled to close the book and shove it aside. I knew I was blushing then. I just hoped she didn't think it was because of how she was standing or the fact that her perfume was swirling around my nostrils, causing my brain to backfire. I had a sudden irrational fear that she could hear the sound.

Her musical laughter broke the awkward silence, and she play-shoved me. "You nerd. Calm down. You don't have to tell me all your secrets." Her phone beeped, and she snatched it off her hip, her fingers flying as she threw digital words into the ether. She looked up, lip curling again, and flipped her hair over her shoulder. "David's here. I'm outtie. Catch ya on the flip flop, girl!"

Her smile sent a warm knife through my heart, and she kissed the top of my head. She spun on her heel and walked towards the door. Standing in the doorway, she turned and winked at me. "Don't summon too many devils, hun. There's enough skulking around these dorms."

Before I could come up with any kind of witty retort, she was gone.

The silence in the empty room was thunderous. I swallowed hard, hearing my throat click, and I shook my head. I flipped the book open again and leaned forward, the air still crackling, like thousands of tiny little needles dancing on my skin. I took a deep breath, louder and more dramatic than was necessary, and heard her voice in the back of my mind. "Calm down."

If only it were that easy, Jess. You have no idea what you do …

Which is exactly why I was doing what I was doing with this decrepit old book.

I began mouthing the words on the page, memorizing, preparing. I turned the pages with care, drinking in every nuance in every word. For this to work, everything had to be perfect. My eyes danced over the lines—stopping, turning, a swift pirouette, back, forth—until the pages were as much a part of my thoughts as she was. Then I closed my eyes and repeated the same routine, every lift and spin, and smiled.

There. Yes.

Standing up, I rolled my shoulders and arched my back, as if I had actually been dancing. I turned and slid open the top drawer of my dresser. The blade felt cold in my hand. I balanced it on my palm for a brief moment, then with one smooth motion, flipped it up and pierced the tip of my finger. The pain did not surprise me. I had done this before. What came next was always worse.

Without really thinking, I pushed the book to one side of my desk and let my fingers flutter upon the surface. The same tickling buzz that had been in the air seemed to run down my arm and out of my fingertips, burning red marks into the wood. The silence hung thick around me, a sludge which only the hammering of my heart could pierce. Then the murmuring rose.

It started deep in my throat, a voice that was not mine. A voice jagged with age and death. It was repeating the words I had memorized, as it had so many times before.

"Jessica," the voice spoke, splintering the silence.

The screams that followed always shook me, no matter how many times they ate into my thoughts. The cries of a thousand souls, pleading … The tears spilled down my cheeks as I held the blade aloft. The light from the nearby desk lamp, a silly little thing that Jess had bought me, glittered off the metal. With a final blistering mind scream, and with every ounce of strength I had, I plunged the knife deep into my own throat.

The blood shot like a geyser, splattering on the wall, pouring out over my desk, and the black fingers began crawling up into my skin, pulling me away, away …

As everything faded, I heard the ever so faint sound of the door clicking … and an ear shredding shriek …

Floating … spinning …

Hands on my lifeless body …

For the briefest of moments, everything stopped. The air itself seemed to pause. The final few synapses fired off in my brain, and the ancient camera of my mind clicked off one final image. That ridiculous lamp, shadows flung across the wall, scattered sprays of blood.

Then … nothing. Until …

I blinked.

I licked lips that were not my own.

And something felt very wrong.

"No …"

The voice was not right.

With a weight I was not expecting, I lifted my hand in front of my eyes.

Jessica's terrified sob met my ears. "David! Get help! Stevie is …" Her voice cracked.

No. This was not right at all. He was not supposed to be here.

With David's eyes, I scanned the floor.

"David! Please!" Jessica's voice clawed at the remnants of David's conscience, but I ignored it.

There … under the body that not long ago was my own. I crouched, David's body cumbersome, and picked up the blade. Jessica's wide, glistening eyes followed the movements.

"David … what are you doing …?"

Her perfect complexion began to wrinkle in confusion and worry, and the heart beating in the chest that was not my own skipped.

"I'm sorry, Jess."

No. I did not like this voice.

I held the knife in David's hand. Jessica stumbled back and bumped into the desk, rattling the lamp. The light shuddered on the walls, casting shadows at odd angles across the bloodied husk slumped over at her feet. My eyes locked with hers. The fear I saw in them broke David's heart. I had to finish this. Now.

"This was meant to be different, Jess. But it's okay. The incantation will work now. Trust me."

Before Jessica could scream, the blade glinted in the still shuddering light, and I tore open David's throat. The world spun into darkness again. Another ancient camera click, another image burned into another set of eyes I was discarding. For a brief second, our souls became fused, then the black fingers ripped them away, until only I remained.

I blinked Jessica's eyes and wiped David's blood off of Jessica's face.

Yes. Perfect.

And now I will be with you forever, my love.

I opened Jessica's mouth and licked her lips. I blinked her beautiful blue eyes. Reaching out a perfectly manicured hand, I clicked off the desk lamp. The shadows fell over the two dead husks, cast aside like refuse.

"I'm outtie."

I smiled, her voice tasting sweet on my tongue. I glanced over at the mirror hanging on Jessica's side of the small dorm room, flashed her perfect teeth, and ran a hand through her long dark hair. An electric buzz crackled down my spine, raising the tiny hairs on my arms. I popped my hip how she always would, smirked, and walked out the door.

Into our new lives together.

Spiders

Michael J. Ingram

Spiders, heights, and stuff.

My day was going swimmingly. Perhaps it wasn't the best day of my life so far, not even scoring close to being in the top ten, but it wasn't a bad day by any stretch of the imagination. It certainly ranked above average by a long way.

Then I ruined it by waking up.

Pain struck me between my temples and behind my eyes. It throbbed and bounced around inside my skull, like an overweight WWE wrestler rebounding off the ropes of the ring. Eventually the pain connected with the part of my brain that produces words, and the word was *hangover*.

"Ow," I groaned. To make matters worse, someone had used my mouth as an ashtray, and then urinated in it whilst I was asleep. At least that's what it tasted like.

"Coffee?" Lucy, the love of my life (largely because she had just brought me coffee), entered the bedroom with a steaming cup of the wonderful aromatic elixir.

I nodded slowly so as not to critically disable myself, then shifted more upright. I admired my washboard abs as I did so, proud of my firm six-pack. It was just a shame it was covered under a thick layer of pasty, hairy flab.

Lucy clunked the coffee down on the bedside table hard enough to make me wince, then sat on the bed with her back to me. I reached for the cup but couldn't quite make it without whimpering.

Despite my hangover, which was surely terminal, my psyche screamed warning bells at me. I assessed the TTL (Tantrum Threat Level). She had brought me coffee, which was a good thing, but was silent, which was a very bad thing. She had also, rather inconsiderately I thought, not asked me how I was or whether my hangover was indeed brain cancer or something. I determined the TTL was somewhere between 'peeved' and 'miffed.' So, nothing to worry about. I should be able to nibble her neck and make a lewd comment, and then everything would be okay.

"Could you—" I asked, reaching as far as I could towards the cup without passing out.

"I really thought you were going to propose to me last night."

Oh fuck.

Pain lanced though my head as I tried to recall the events of the previous evening. I could vaguely remember a restaurant. My stomach churned as visions of downing Hungarian red wine flooded me, but then I spotted the legs of tiny creatures peeping out from under the pillow next to Lucy. Sweat burst out on my brow, and my already foul-tasting mouth dried up.

Lucy turned and followed my gaze to the offending arachnid. She tutted. This made me reassess the TTL. Usually, she would come to my rescue immediately. I raised the TTL to 'huffy.'

"Lucy could you—" I nodded towards the spider, a very brave thing to do I thought, given my tender condition, but she ignored me. I licked the sweat which was pouring off my upper lip, and it tasted distinctly of Rioja. I swallowed the sudden flood of saliva.

Hungarian Rioja? Surely there are international laws against such things?

"Abigail says—"

Oh yes, Abigail, your man-hating lesbian friend with the nice tits—

"That if you haven't proposed by now, you're not going to, and you're just stringing me along."

I zoned out for a bit as my errant neural networks presented my mind's eye with an image of Lucy exploring her sexuality with Abigail. I was pulled out of the reverie by a sharp punch to my shoulder.

"Are you thinking about a threesome again, you twat?"

"No!" *Too quick and too indignant.* "But if you ever did get curious and wanted someone along in an observatory capacity"—I indicated myself as a volunteer willing to sacrifice his time for the good of others—"I promise I'd be quiet and just sit in the corner."

"Don't be such a fucking dickhead. This isn't funny."

I looked pointedly at the spider again and pleaded with Lucy. "Please sort it out, babe. You know I can't stand spiders."

Lucy sighed, picked it in her hand (*howthefuckcanshedothat?*), and walked to the bathroom. Before she could finish flushing it down the toilet, I had a flashback of necking the last bottle of Hungarian red to myself and my stomach roiled. I ran past her to the bowl and emptied a bottle and a half of the cheap wine, plus a rather nice but partially digested rump steak, onto the unfortunate spider.

Charlotte's Web should have ended like this.

By the time I had recovered and showered, Lucy had left. More warning bells.

Quashing the sense of foreboding and thoughts of the inevitable bollocking that would come later, I got myself ready for work.

Before I left, I closed the bedroom window. Presumably Lucy had opened it to clear the stench of my nocturnal flatulence. For some bloody reason, I had bought an apartment on the sixth floor. It seemed a good idea at the time, but I hadn't realised it would be so fucking *high*.

Still thinking of what Lucy had said, I felt nauseous as I reached for the latch, closing my eyes for the last bit to avoid looking at the long drop.

On the walk to work, I spotted a billboard for the new *Spider-Man* movie.

What are they going to call it this time? *Spider-Man: On the Other Side of Town from Home but Close Enough to Get his Laundry Done?*

I pictured a large phone book the size of a house landing on him.

That'll sort the lycra clad little fucker out. Quip your way out of that one, twat. The thought of that kept me smiling the rest of the way to work.

My first patient was Mrs Miggins, and I was already late by the time I arrived.

My assistant (*Lorna, Laura, Lauren?*) had prepared everything, and I just had to slump in my chair and smile at the patient.

"So, have you made an honest woman of your lovely Lucy yet?" Mrs Miggins asked.

How the fuck do you know about Lucy?

Even after my shower, I think I was sweating pure Rioja, and I was surprised when I wiped my brow that my hand didn't come away red.

"Not quite yet, Mrs M." I smiled. *Think of something witty to say.* "She's far too sensible to get hitched to me."

Mrs Miggins laughed, and I spied two decades of my dental work. Christ, I'm a shit dentist. She looked hideous. Still, maybe these new dentures would make her look better. Or maybe not.

I gave Lorna, or whatever her name was, an accusing stare, and her cheeks flushed. *So you've been gossiping about my private life to the patients have you, you little strumpet?*

Dental scrubs are the most unflattering things to wear. Shapeless and easy to crease, it is near impossible to look sexy in them, yet I noted the pert cheeks of Lorna's arse jiggling nicely as she mixed the impression material. *How many hours have you spent on the step-trainer to get an arse like that, you minx?*

She caught me staring at her, and I looked away, but not before I saw her crooked smile. My brother always said there are two sure things in life: death and a dental nurse. A hypothesis I had yet to see disproven.

"She sounds perfect for you." Mrs Miggins was like a dog with a bone—if only she could chew a bone with the crappy teeth I was about to make her.

Unfortunately, my surgery was on the third floor of a redeveloped Victorian house, with a huge glass wall taking up one side. I always kept clear of this, as I felt giddy whenever I looked at the street below. People say it's not the fear of falling that should scare you but the landing. But they're twats. I'm scared of heights, so what?

"Hmm?" My attention came back into the room, and I took the impression tray from Laura. "I not sure she's right for me Mrs M. I like my women like I like my coffee."

Mrs Miggins smiled. "Oh, dark, strong, and Brazilian?"

"No. Cheap, white, and instant." I said this whilst looking at Lauren, gratified to see her reaction, simultaneously inserting the impression tray to stop Mrs Miggins talking.

I made it through the rest of the morning, half-heartedly enjoying the flirting from my assistant, whom I later discovered was actually called *Sharon*. My survival was helped by me hiding in the stockroom during lunch whilst I dosed myself on a stomach-lining burning amount of ibuprofen and infused myself with half a litre of saline.

Whilst I was in there, I got a call from Lucy.

"Hi." She sounded quiet.

I rattled my brain for a conciliatory yet sympathetic and erudite response. After some thought, I settled for: "Hi."

"Hi."

Well, wasn't this just fucking scintillating? "What's up?"

She breathed down the phone, and I could sense the tears waiting in the wings, like the cast of *Swan Lake*.

"I've been thinking."

Klaxons sounded in my head, and I raised the TTL to 'pissed off.' She was now only one small step below the highest alert level of 'P.A.M.' (Potential Axe Murderer).

"Oh really?" My tone was light and conversational.

"Yeah, you said last year that by this time we would be married."

Did I? Why the fuck would I say such a stupid thing as that?

Then I remembered: it was the promise of dirty sex. *Cool.*

"Babe ..." *Bad start. Think fast.* "You know I'm very fond of you, and we're young, and there's no reason to rush into anything."

"It's been six fucking years, and you're nearly fifty."

I started to formulate one of my pat responses but saw a spider descending from the ceiling beyond the boxes of gauze. My mouth dried up, and I started to sweat yet again. "Babe, I ..." I swallowed, watching the eight-legged freak abseil towards me.

"Don't bother. I've heard it all before. I'm done. We're done. I've had enough of you."

"Babe!" I managed to string it out to three syllables.

She hung up. And that was it.

The spider descended far enough to be within reach. I grabbed it and crushed the life out of it.

I had an epiphany.

I was not scared of spiders or heights. I had a phobia of commitment.

The door to the storeroom opened, and Sharon popped her head in. "You okay? Do you need a coffee?"

I grinned at her square in the face. "You'll do just fine, babe."

Utopia

Kitt Harris

When it happened, I was standing semi-dressed in my boxers and a half-buttoned-up, buttoned-down Oxford business shirt, mentally preparing for the biggest sale of my life. I practised my smile, and under my breath, I ran through my pitch, pausing for effect, smoothing over the half-truths and selling those blatant lies. I came out of the hotel bathroom searching for my cologne, stubbed my toe on the trouser press, wheeled around, and there he was. And there it was, the gun, right in front of me, calmly staring at the spot right between my eyes. Run, scream, shout for help, that often-stifled courageous part of me demanded, but all I could manage was a soft gargle at the back of my throat as my feet anchored into the floor and my legs refused to move. You can do it, that little voice of survival insisted, distract him, throw something, just peg it out of here. Instead, I pissed myself.

What was this, an assassin? He didn't look like one, but then I was basing this off all those years of watching *Bond* and *Bourne* movies and reading about JFK. Perhaps they did wear yellow marigold gloves, a fishing hat complete with hooks and tackle, denim dungarees and green Wellington boots—one of which was worn away at the toes, and I could see a large black nail poking through.

"There must be a mistake," I blurted out.

What could he possibly want from me? A forty-two-year-old divorcée, with no savings and no dignity, a traveling salesman with a bad credit score, high cholesterol, and an ever-expanding waistline?

"Ian Smith."

There was no mistake. That was my name. My eyes flicked to the half-opened cardboard box on the bed, my latest stock of Arelestat, primed and ready to be flogged at the South Bank Wellness Centre Conference later today. A disgruntled client, perhaps? He looked like he needed a good few handfuls of Arelestat stuffed into his gob; the stench of bitter BO rolled off him, his right eye twitched spasmodically, and the dark bags beneath them were bigger than the bluey-whites themselves. Did I remember him? No. But I sold this shit to a lot of desperate people, and desperation reeks all the same, no matter what they actually look like.

But still. He was the one holding the gun, and I was the one caught without my trousers. I closed my eyes, expecting a bang, the impact, pain, blackness. It was going to hurt. There was a prolonged tension-filled silence. Then nothing. I blinked in disbelief. Shouldn't assassinations be quick? Brutal? Effective? I shouldn't be given time to take in the hitman's face—should I? I guess it didn't matter if I was going to die anyway.

"Who are you? What do you want from me? Please, I've got kids, two boys. They need their dad …"

I gabbled on about Henry's straight-A exam results, his captaincy of the school's rugby team and his desire to be a heart surgeon, and then little Oliver, a burgeoning musical prodigy, who at the tender age of eleven was already touring with the London Symphony Orchestra and was a renowned classical solo cellist. I reached for my wallet perched on the desk and flipped it open to the picture I always used when showing clients my perfect nuclear family; two strapping young lads, with broad chins and charming smiles, sat on either side of a beautiful dark-eyed, dark-haired woman, her body covered tightly in a wrap dress that was simultaneously modest and motherly while accentuating the curve of her breasts and hips, alluding to the smoking hot body beneath the cashmere.

"Here, see. And that's my wife, Camilla. She's beautiful, isn't she?"

My actual ex-wife was Hillary, who was about as unsexy, bitter, and disgruntled as her name sounded. The last time I saw her was at the court hearing six months ago where she was granted full custody of my boys (neither called Henry nor Oliver, neither handsome, clever, sporty or musical) following an embarrassing incident involving a fire extinguisher, Vaseline and a prostitute, who—despite what anyone may lead you to believe—*was* over eighteen and *did* consent to erotic firefighter foreplay.

"Don't kill me. My boys need me. My wife needs me. Please, I'm begging you …"

"I come from Utopia," he interrupted.

"Where's that?"

"It's not anywhere; it's everywhere. It's in here." He tapped his forehead with the butt of his gun. "Utopia isn't a place; it's a state of mind. Utopia is your salvation."

Great. A religious nutcase. With a gun.

"What do you want from me?"

"I'm here to save you."

"Then, what's the gun for?"

"This old thing?" He shrugged. "Sometimes people don't want to be saved."

"And what happens to those people?"

"Isn't it obvious? I kill them."

"Why me?"

"You're special, Ian."

"I can assure you, there is absolutely nothing special about me."

Nope. Nada. Zero. Zilch.

"Ian, you have the power to change this world for the better." Abruptly, he broke off mid-sentence. He then turned and craned his head down towards his chest with a concerned look on his face. His ear angled towards the huge pocket on the front of his dungarees, as if listening to someone or something. After a second or two he nodded. "Yes, you're right," he said, speaking softly to the pocket.

I didn't notice it before—not surprising considering the guy was pointing a gun at my head—but peeping out from the denim dungaree pocket was a small Paddington Bear toy, no bigger than my palm, complete with a yellow hat and blue trench coat. The man caught me looking and straightened, hiding the toy once again in his pocket.

"I've said too much," he said, retraining the gun on my head. "It's time to decide, Ian. What's it going to be? Die? Or join me in my cause? The most noble and righteous cause of Utopia. Let me save you."

"You know, I think I could do with saving," I said.

And that was that.

"Excellent choice, Ian!" He slid his gun into his dungarees. "Most people just tell me to go to hell."

He then embraced me with a warm, "Welcome, Brother," politely ignoring the trail of warm wee down my leg and the puddle on the floor. He called himself Thomas, and for the next twelve hours, he never left my side.

"First, you must be ordained," Thomas said. "Let's find you some clothes fitting for a Brother of the Utopian Order."

He searched through my suitcase. "Everything in here reeks ...." he said.

"I have been living out of a suitcase for the past ten weeks."

"Reeks of materialism and entitlement. This won't do." He surveyed the room. "Aha! This is very becoming for a member of the Brotherhood." From the back of the hotel room door, he pulled down the white bathrobe. "And matching slippers too. Take off your clothes and put them on."

"Now?"

It was a subtle movement, but I still clocked his hand move towards where the gun was stowed in his dungarees.

"Now's as good a time as ever," I said and hastily dropped my piss-soaked boxers.

Cloaked in nothing but anxiety and the hotel dressing gown, I made to follow Thomas as he left the room.

"Bring those," he said, gesturing to the Arelestat. "All of it."

"Why?"

"When you are ordained, everything will become clear."

I highly doubted it but scooped up the little pillboxes from the bed and shoved them back inside the brown cardboard box and followed him out the door.

Every head turned in my direction. It was worse than that night in Magaluf where on a mate's stag do, I paraded down the street in nothing but a thong and feather boa, covered in edible body chocolate proudly demonstrating my breakdancing ability—of which I had none—ending up with grazed knees, grazed shins, grazed palms, and a gashed forehead from the worm gone wrong.

But then, that was Maga. This was London, bang in the middle of the morning commute. And yes, while there are some questionably outrageous fashion choices going down on the hip edgy scene, there is nothing hip nor edgy about two fully grown men strutting down the streets, one looking like an overgrown farmer in midst of washing dishes and the other shuffling like a pensioner in slippers two sizes too big and occasionally flashing from beneath a hotel robe.

After about an hour of fast walking, the back of my dressing gown was drenched in sweat, and my arms killed from cradling the box of Arelestat to my chest. We emerged onto an empty street so dilapidated it could have been the setting for a nineteenth-century slum epic; it stank of misery and stale kebabs, week-old rubbish lined the alleyway, and there was actual human shit on the pavement. It was the kind of place you wouldn't want to walk through alone at night, not because you were going to get stabbed—although, you might—but because the rats were likely rabid and the size of small dogs. Thomas led me down some steps overlooking the Over Ground; he clambered through a carefully cut hole in the wire mesh fencing, ignoring both the TRESPASSERS WILL BE PROSECUTED and DANGER OF DEATH signs, and eagerly gestured for me to follow him.

I hesitated. Out came the gun.

"Hurry or someone will see you," he said, once again pointing the thing in my direction.

I didn't have a choice. Lumbered with the cardboard box, I fought my way through the fencing and stumbled down the steep banks, the barrel steadily trained on my skull the entire time. We walked next to the thick wires and rails for about a hundred yards before coming to a disused signalling box covered with graffiti, a rotting wooden shack on legs quaking above the tracks. Thomas unlocked the padlock and removed the heavy chains from the door, and we went inside.

"Welcome to the Chapel of the Utopian Order," he said, locking the padlock behind me and dropping the key back into his dungaree pocket.

It was damp, draughty, and the fabric of my slippers kept snagging on the exposed floorboards. There was a nest of sleeping bags and threadbare blankets in one corner, and just next to it, an open Macbook Pro, a little camping stove surrounded by empty packs of super noodles, and at least fifty unopened jars of marmalade in a little mound. The walls were lined with shelves, all of which were packed with varying sizes of Paddington Bear cuddly toys. A thousand beady eyes stared down at me. All of them seemed to be watching me.

"Meet your Brothers," Thomas said. He approached the far end of the shack where beneath a smashed windowpane he'd assembled a makeshift altar out of a shopping trolley, tinsel, and a huge effigy of Paddington that sat, at least four feet tall and overly stuffed, propped on the trolley's handlebars. He knelt and clasped his raised hands in front of it and began talking in tongues to the toy.

What did I do now?

I dumped the box on the floor, my arms aching and deadened from the marathon to get here, and began scoping up the pace, looking for some means of escape. There were none. The door was locked, and I didn't fancy jumping out a broken window onto the tracks below—if I didn't die in the fall, I'd be electrocuted, or just end up in a crumpled heap with two broken legs, agonisingly waiting for the next train to come along and put me out of my misery.

"When I first saw you, I just knew it," Thomas said. "It was several months ago now. You were thinner. I listened to you preach, and I knew, right there and then, that you had the answers." He pointed the gun at me again. "Kneel here." He indicated the spot next to him by the shopping trolley.

I knelt. He put a blindfold over my head; my vision plunged into darkness. I felt him open up the lapels of the dressing gown. Moments later, something cold and sticky was smeared across my chest, pulling against my thick carpet of chest hair. Hillary always badgered me to shave it off. Two lines overlapped in a cross, one that went between my nipples and one that stretched from my chin down to my belly button. It smelt sweet, tangy—was it, it couldn't be, marmalade?

"There's so much wrong with this world," he said. "I look around, I see misery, I see anxiety, I see depression, I see people so lost they don't realise what they have. But you know this already, don't you? That's why you are working to save it."

There was some rustling, and my blindfold was removed. Stacked in a disorganised pyramid were dozens of boxes just like the one I carried here, the printed Arelestat branding clear and unmistakable. That was hundreds, if not thousands of packs, which meant there were thousands and thousands of individual pills.

"You bought all of these?"

"I had to be ready."

But it doesn't even work! I wanted to blurt out, but even if I did, it wouldn't make a difference, not when he believed it did.

"This is the cure," Thomas said.

Cause of constipation more like. Nausea. Dizziness, maybe. Probably. Addiction, absolutely.

"And we are going to make sure everyone tastes it."

First, we waited, and then several hours later, we headed back to Central London, me still in my hotel robe and Thomas in his eclectic attire, only now supporting a large Paddington Bear backpack and an even larger suitcase that was missing a wheel, stuffed with Arelestat pills, that wiggled erratically behind him. We headed into the finance district and down into the narrow tube station. The stairs bristled with angry commuters, wireless headphones whirred, the bleep of contactless and oyster cards and the soft mechanical putt-putt of the gantries opening and closing. A busy hour on a busy day, just like any other, everybody was in such a rush that, apart from the occasional shoulder bump and glare of disdainful annoyance, we were ignored. The marmalade was beginning to dry, irritating my skin as clumps of chest hair stuck and tugged on the inside of the hotel robe. Perspiration collected on my brow, only this time it wasn't from the walking or the chafing towel material around my groin. It was the dubious blue and red wires that ominously poked out behind Paddington's left ear and the soft sound of ticking emanating from his chest.

With his back to the entrance, Thomas stopped and, with closed eyes, inhaled deeply. "Now's the time," he said. "Open the suitcase, Ian."

I was about to refuse when the handgun was on me once more.

"Do it now."

Somewhere a woman screamed. I knelt and tugged open the zipper. The Arelestat packets pooled out onto the dirty concrete floor.

Thomas raised his hands above his head, as if worshipping the skies, and raised his voice. "Children, your salvation is here."

It was like the Red Sea parting. Thomas, a human magnet, repelling everybody around him. The crowd receded as far as possible, which wasn't far as they were trapped by the sloping walls, low-curved ceiling, and the sheer volume of commuters. Some struggled, scrabbling to get away but finding their paths blocked by bodies not yet aware of the scene unfolding before them. A semi-circle formed around us, and the onlookers stood frozen, unsure if they should move as the barrel switched from one to another in a smooth steady arch.

"That's it, stay right where you are. If everyone does as I say, there's no need for anyone to get hurt. Take a pill from my Brother here and save yourselves. Embrace Utopia—this pill is the solution to all your problems, happiness, love, contentment, satisfaction, confidence. Take it and spare yourselves from this reality."

Nobody moved.

"I'm trying to help you. Why doesn't anybody want my help?" He turned the gun on me. "Ian, make them take it."

I scooped my hands into the opened suitcase. It was like grasping at sand; the pill packets spilled through my fingers as I tossed handful after handful towards the crowd.

"If everyone takes it, you will all be saved. If you don't …"

Thomas casually shrugged the Paddington backpack off his shoulder—that was enough. It doesn't take a rocket scientist to know a suspicious package when you see one. The panic was palpable. The first, a tall man in a matching silk suit and brown leather laptop case, pocketed his vape and stooped down to pick up the box by his polished un-scuffed brogues. Then another, in a grey Nike tracksuit and a string bag weighted with White Lightning, and another, in double denim and mismatched shoes, rainbow hair and a rolled cigarette tucked behind her ear. Others quickly followed, and the packets were being snatched from person to person, desperately clawed out of hands squabbling over the blister packs. I watched, unable to believe what I was seeing; people began guzzling down the white circles, as if they were merely palmer violets, chomping them until the powder frothed at their mouths and caught in their throats.

Suddenly there was a great big walloping impact in the centre of my back, and I was flung forwards, wind pasting my ears before I blacked out face down on the cold concrete, my cheek pressed into a mix of trodden gum, grit, and a film of dusty filth, the acrid smell of urine wafting up my nostrils. I was shot by a baton gun.

When I came to, I was arrested on terrorism charges, then taken to a special police investigation centre. Thomas and I were separated. Thank God, I said to the custody sergeants, you've saved me. They authorised my detention, and then called the superintendent. I saw him, nervously tugging at the neck of his white shirt where his tie choked his Adam's apple. He reached into his jacket pocket and whip out a small white branded box, popped the little round tablets quickly into his mouth, and dry swallowed. I was interviewed, twice, by seasoned detectives, before being released without charge. I mean, who could blame me? Held hostage by a crazy guy in dungarees with a gun?

I never saw Thomas after that, except for on the news when the image cut from a Paddington Bear backpack packed full of marmalade, to his marigold-gloved hands waving at the press as he made a beeline for the reporters' microphones while his solicitor did all she could to bundled him into the courtrooms. They pleaded insanity, and the case was acquitted. The last I knew of him, he was sent to a secure hospital facility somewhere far away.

"Now, you may not want to believe me," I said to the audience gathered in front of me, eyes glazed in raptor, as they stared up at the podium at the London South Bank Well-Being Conference. In the front row, I noticed a woman in her early forties, taut physique, tanned skin, the yoga teacher type—or guru, or whatever the hell they went by these days—who I would definitely be speaking to later.

I paused, thinking of all the ways her body would bend upstairs in my hotel room, and the audience drew closer, hanging off my every word.

"But beneath it all, Thomas wanted what we all wanted—happiness, health, peace—and despite everything he knew this little pill, Arelestat, was the solution. He just went about it the wrong way."

Right on cue, there was a murmur of laughter. There always was. The yoga teacher, hesitantly, smiled along. When

I knew she knew I was watching her, I flashed my most rehearsed, most confident, most charming smile and watched the colour rise in her cheeks. My evening was cemented.

The next morning, I was standing semi-dressed in my boxers and a half-buttoned-up, buttoned-down Oxford shirt, mentally preparing for the biggest sale of my life. Under my breath, I reeled off the patter—it flowed effortlessly, the pauses so natural, the lies so compelling—and practised my smile, confident, captivating, believable, as always. I came out of the hotel bathroom in search of my cologne and stubbed my toe on the trouser press; what was it with these second-rate hotel rooms? Couldn't they find a better place for it? The yoga teacher was still asleep. In the grey light of day, the starched sheets appeared stained and yellow. She was just like the rest, reluctant at first, but so caught up in the peddling and purveying that all it took was one single mention of a free month's supply and she practically flew up the stairs, through the door, and into my bed. Of course, there was no free Arelestat, but she didn't need to know that.

After I pulled on my trousers, I checked my sales figures through the cracked screen on my phone—above average, enough to pay off the latest monthly debt instalment and still have enough for a couple of lines of blow. There was a message from Hillary, asking when she was going to receive the CSA payments from the last three months. The fucker. I deleted it.

Feeling that all-too-familiar tightness in my chest, the same as whenever I thought about the boys, I reached out for that comforting little box that I kept for occasions just like these. I could hear them rattling inside their plastic blister packs, and with a chewed, dirt-laced fingernail, I popped the foil and tipped them straight down my throat. This was happiness all right. Crazy, crazy happiness.

www.ingramcontent.com/pod-product-compliance
Lightning Source LLC
Chambersburg PA
CBHW020747310726

48969CB00002B/461